THE ADVENTURES OF
DANIEL BOOM
A.K.A LOUD BOY

GAME ON!

WRITTEN BY D. J. STEINBERG

ILLUSTRATED BY BRIAN SMITH

GROSSET & DUNLAP

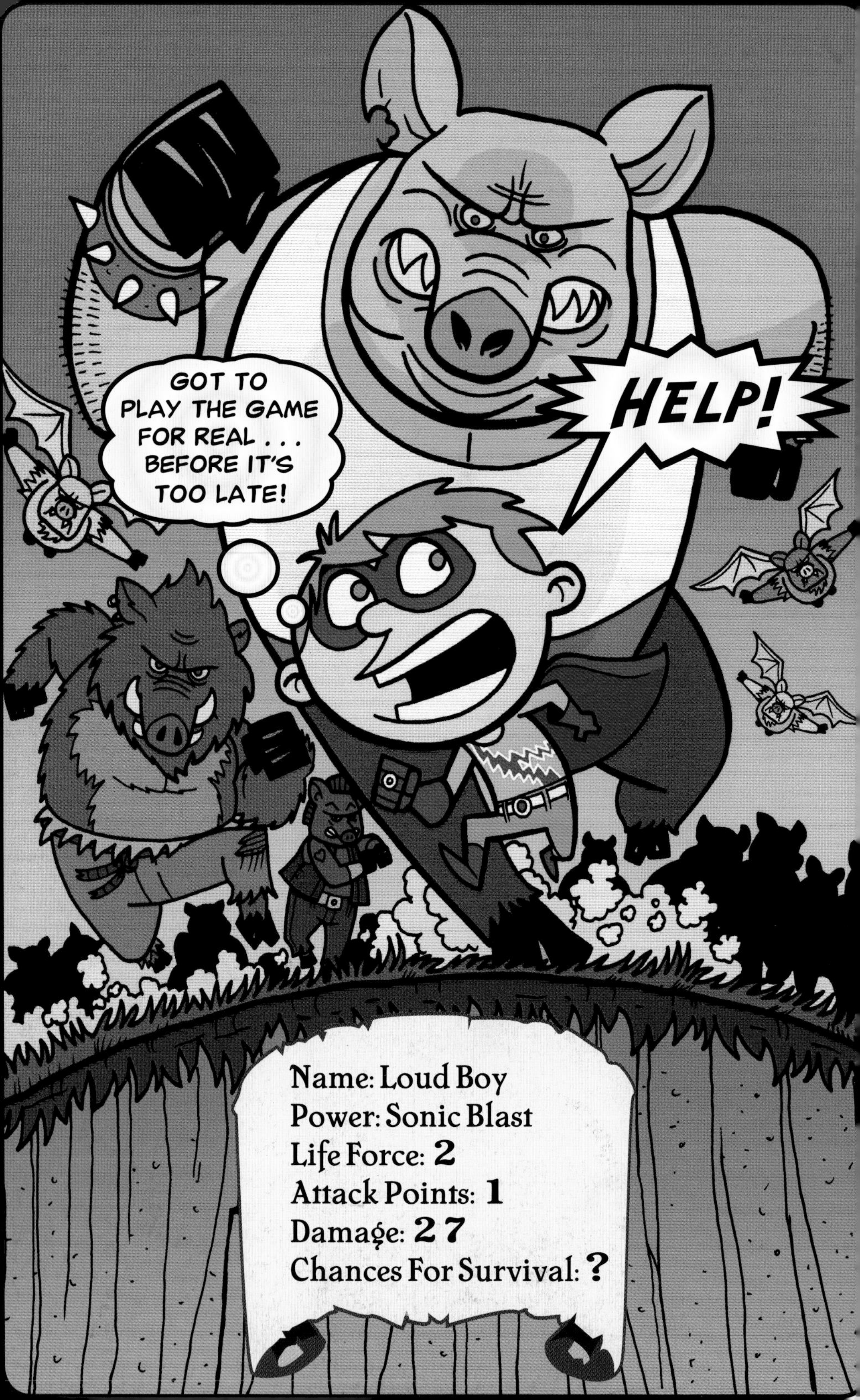
GOT TO PLAY THE GAME FOR REAL . . . BEFORE IT'S TOO LATE!
HELP!
Name: Loud Boy
Power: Sonic Blast
Life Force: 2
Attack Points: 1
Damage: 27
Chances For Survival: ?

WAIT! Is that—could it be . . .

our friend *LOUD BOY*?

Sucked into his favorite game?

Dear reader, you may not want to watch

this. For when this game is over, our

young hero will be trapped forever in

C Y B E R S P A C E .

Play on if you dare.

But don't say I didn't warn you . . .

Not that long ago, five ordinary kids discovered that they had some pretty extraordinary abilities.

DANIEL BOOM

DANIEL BOOM discovered his Decibel Power as LOUD BOY . . .

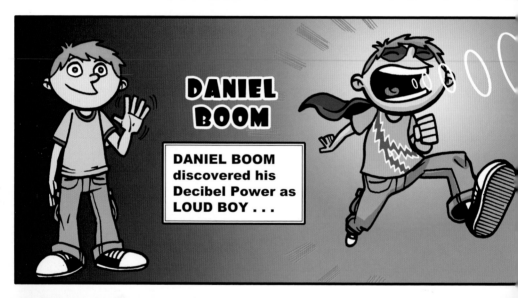

. . . his sister JEANNIE S. BOOM discovered her Know-It-All Power as CHATTERBOX . . .

JEANNIE S. BOOM

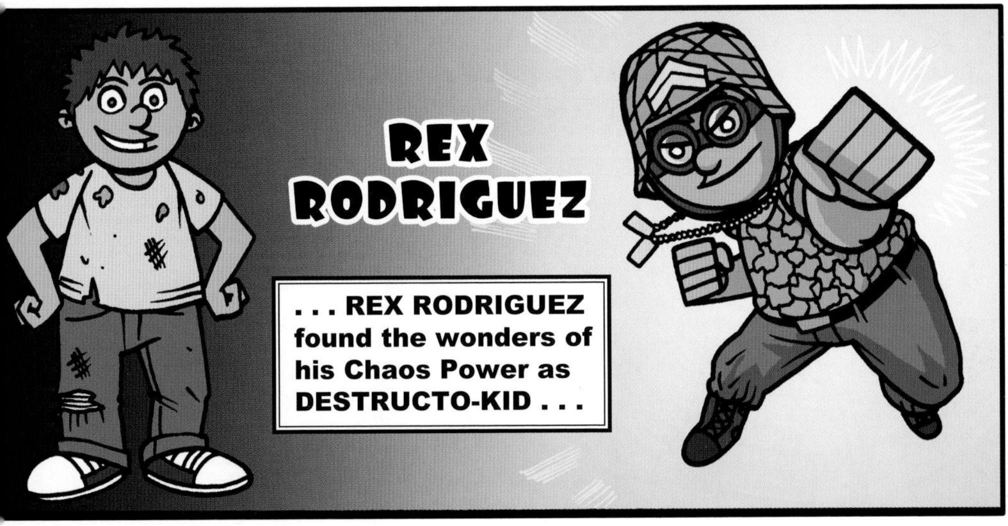
REX RODRIGUEZ
. . . REX RODRIGUEZ found the wonders of his Chaos Power as DESTRUCTO-KID . . .

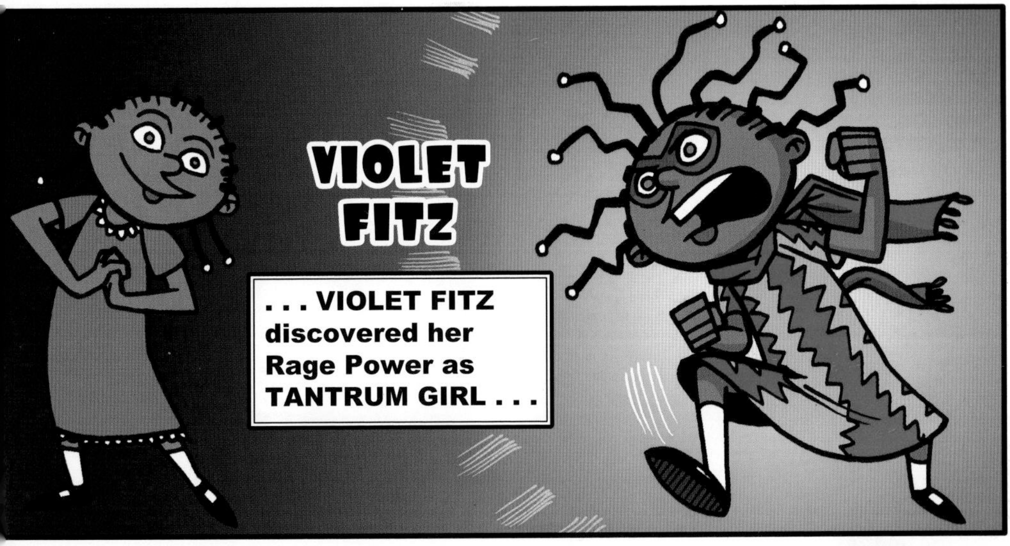
VIOLET FITZ
. . . VIOLET FITZ discovered her Rage Power as TANTRUM GIRL . . .

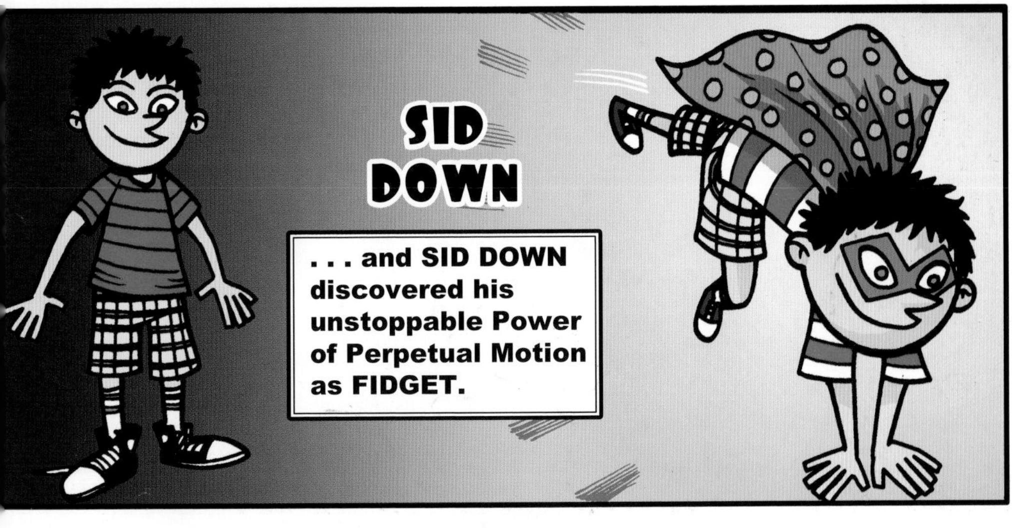
SID DOWN
. . . and SID DOWN discovered his unstoppable Power of Perpetual Motion as FIDGET.

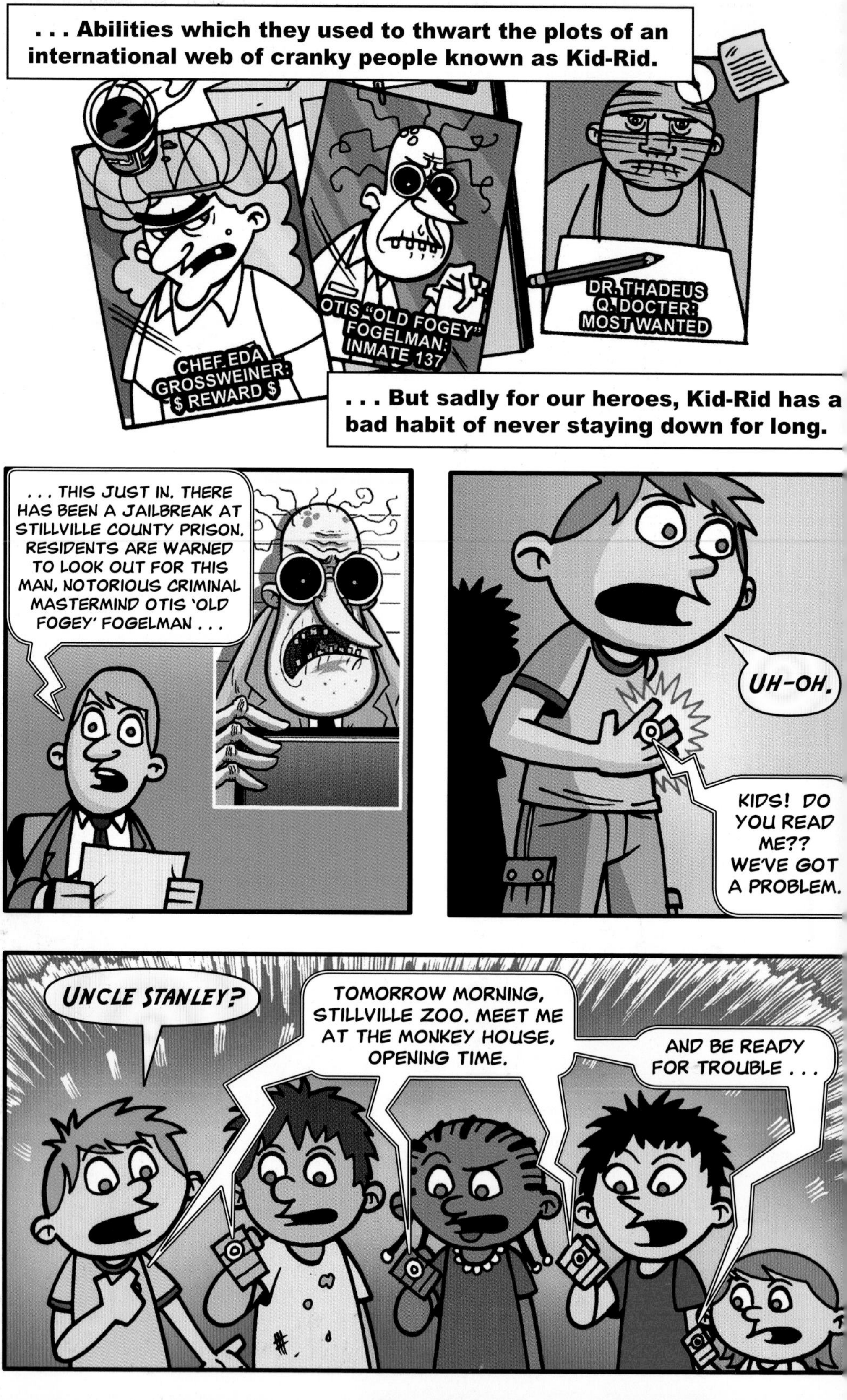

. . . Abilities which they used to thwart the plots of an international web of cranky people known as Kid-Rid.
CHEF EDA GROSSWEINER: $ REWARD $
OTIS "OLD FOGEY" FOGELMAN: INMATE 137
DR. THADEUS Q. DOCTER: MOST WANTED
. . . But sadly for our heroes, Kid-Rid has a bad habit of never staying down for long.
. . . THIS JUST IN. THERE HAS BEEN A JAILBREAK AT STILLVILLE COUNTY PRISON. RESIDENTS ARE WARNED TO LOOK OUT FOR THIS MAN, NOTORIOUS CRIMINAL MASTERMIND OTIS 'OLD FOGEY' FOGELMAN . . .
UH-OH.
KIDS! DO YOU READ ME?? WE'VE GOT A PROBLEM.
UNCLE STANLEY?
TOMORROW MORNING, STILLVILLE ZOO. MEET ME AT THE MONKEY HOUSE, OPENING TIME.
AND BE READY FOR TROUBLE . . .

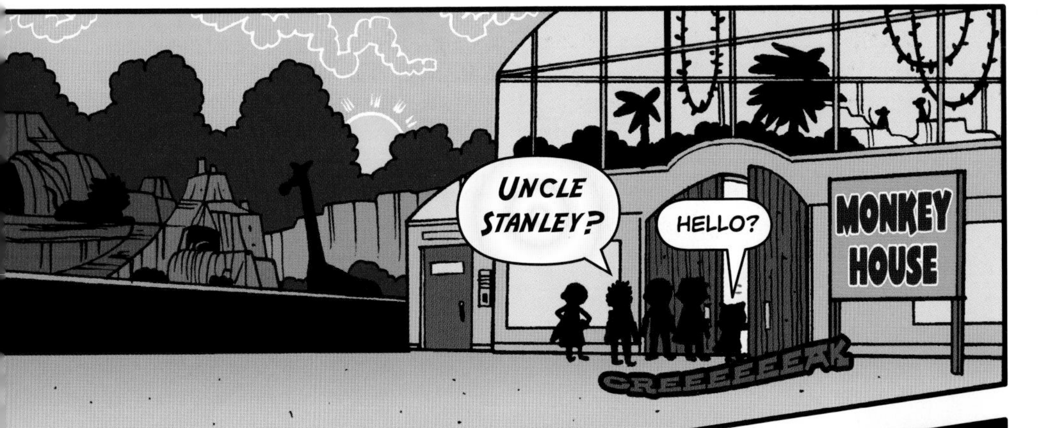
UNCLE STANLEY?
HELLO?
MONKEY HOUSE
CREEEEEEEAK

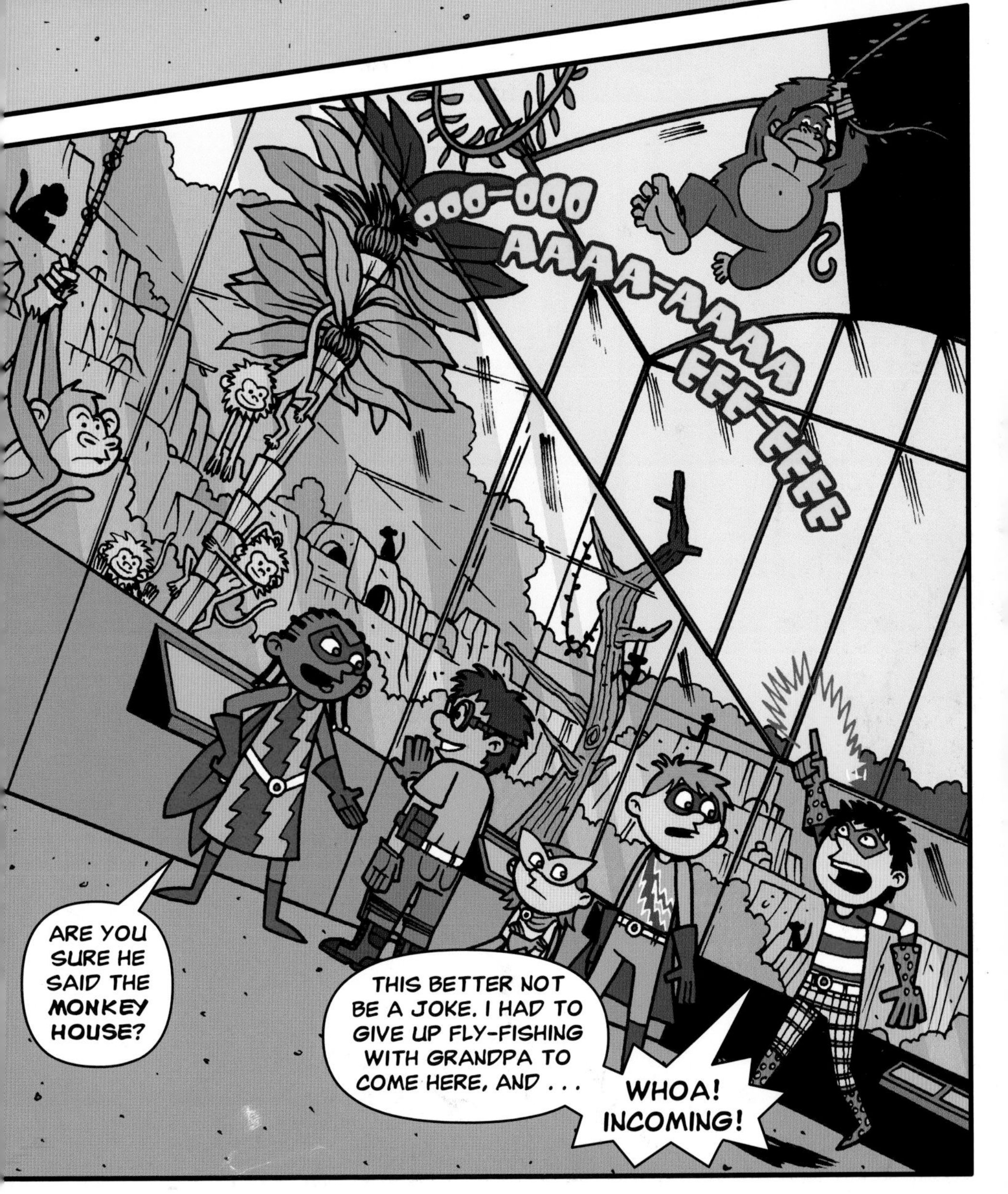
OOO-OOO AAAAA-AAAAA EEE-EEEE
ARE YOU SURE HE SAID THE MONKEY HOUSE?
THIS BETTER NOT BE A JOKE. I HAD TO GIVE UP FLY-FISHING WITH GRANDPA TO COME HERE, AND . . .
WHOA! INCOMING!

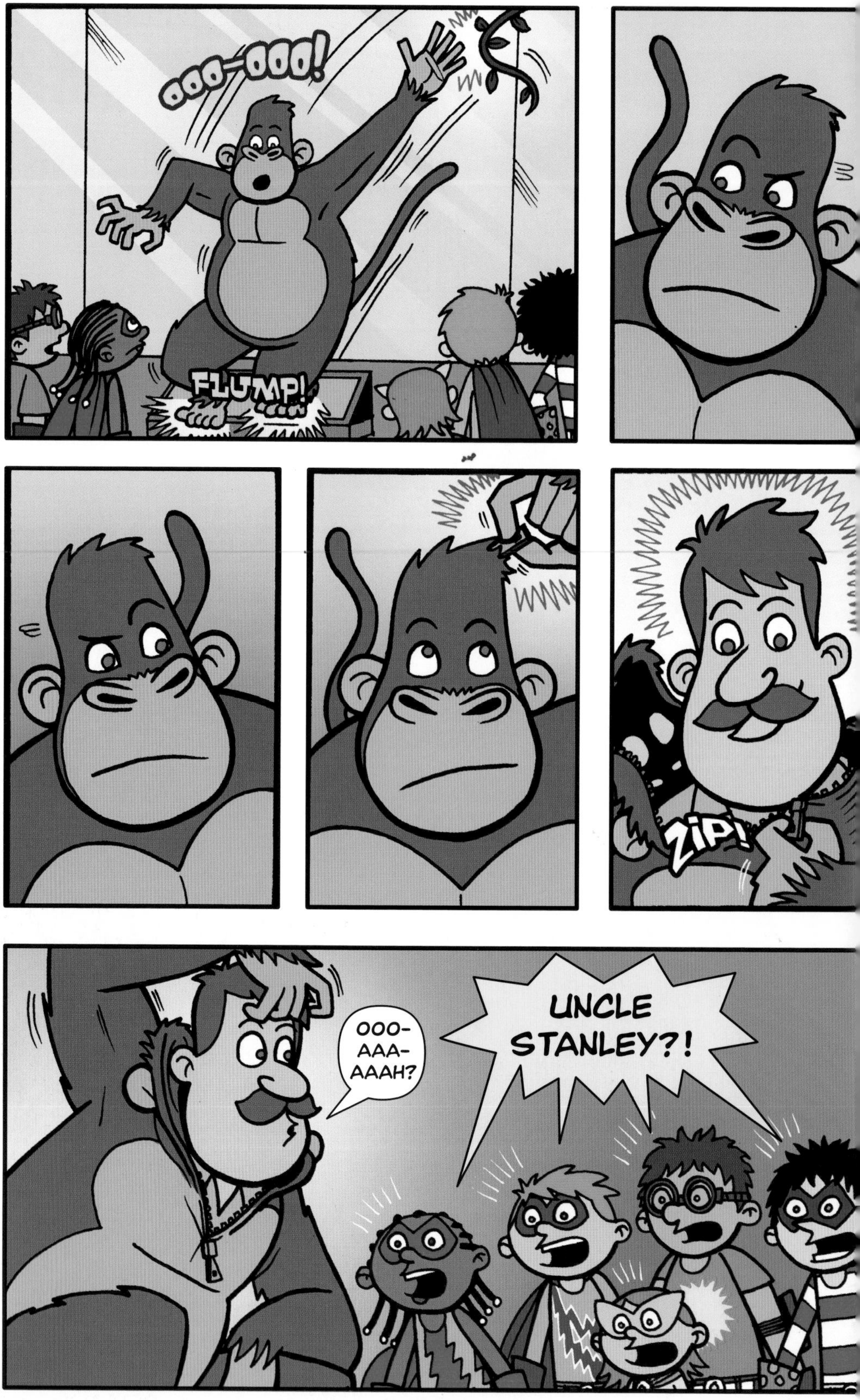
OOO-OOO!
FLUMP!
ZIP!
OOO-AAA-AAAH?
UNCLE STANLEY?!

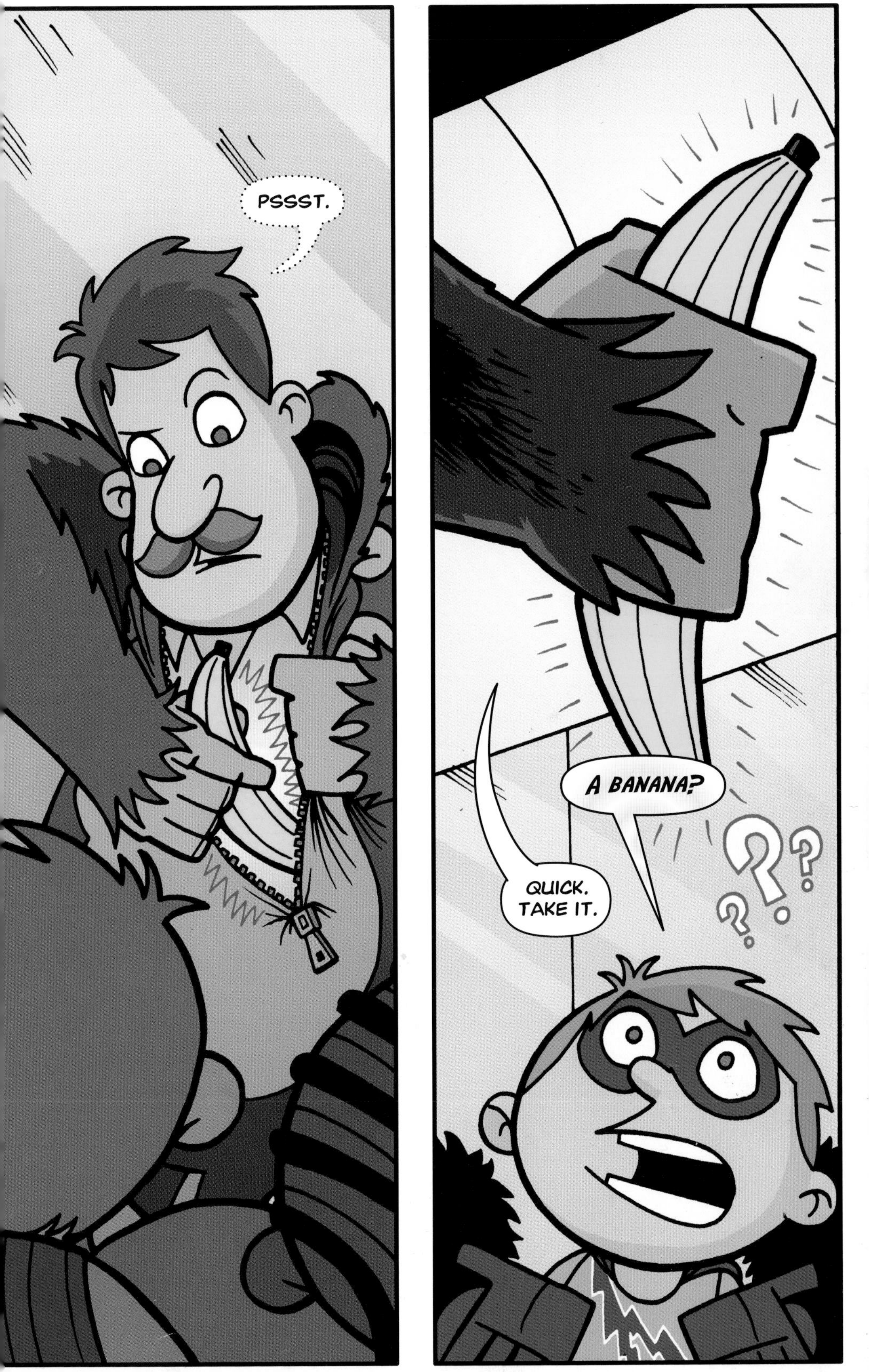
PSSST.
A BANANA?
QUICK. TAKE IT.

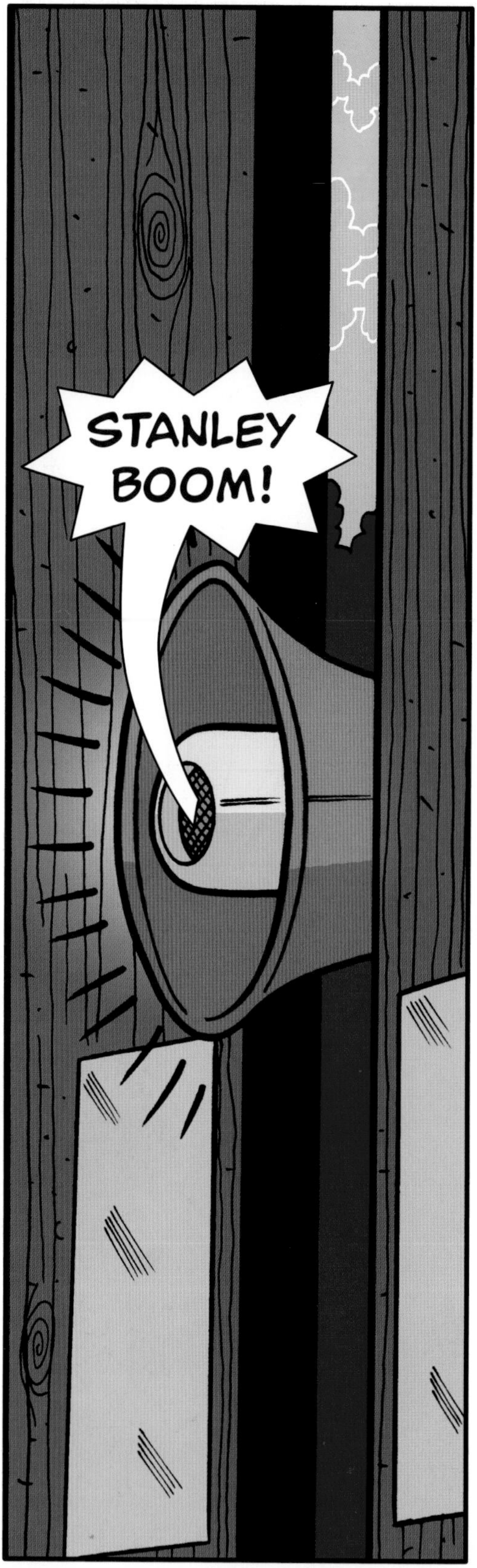
STANLEY BOOM!

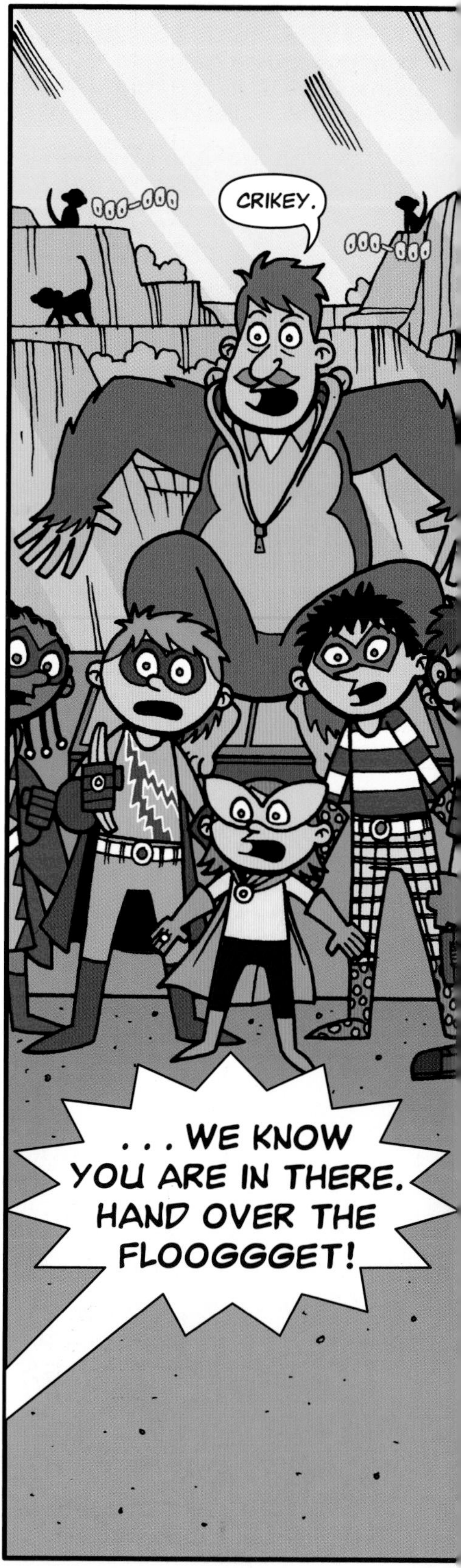
CRIKEY.
. . . WE KNOW YOU ARE IN THERE. HAND OVER THE FLOOGGGET!

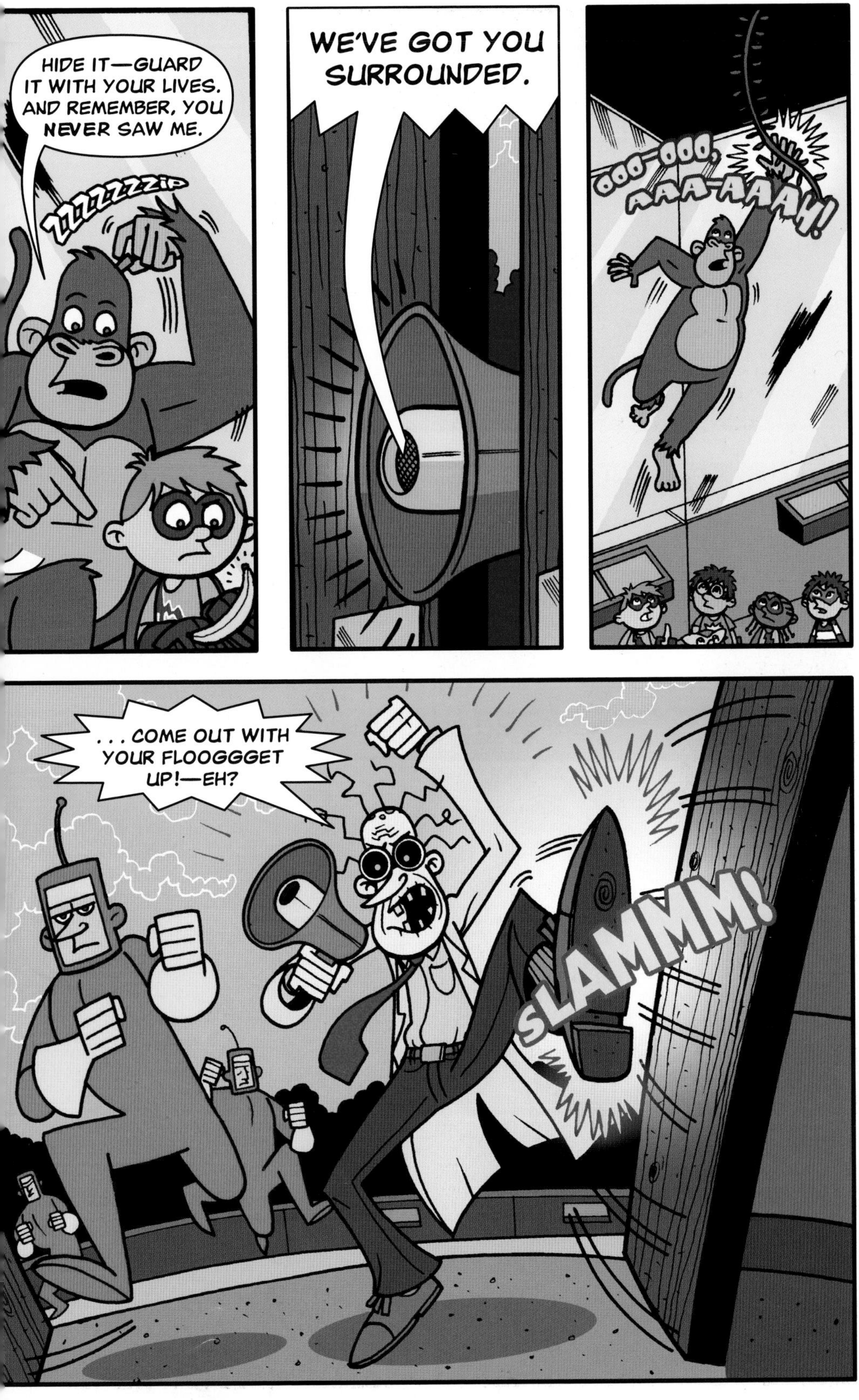
HIDE IT—GUARD IT WITH YOUR LIVES. AND REMEMBER, YOU NEVER SAW ME.
ZZZZZZZZIP
WE'VE GOT YOU SURROUNDED.
OOO-OOO, AAA-AAAAH!
. . . COME OUT WITH YOUR FLOOGGGET UP!—EH?
SLAMMM!

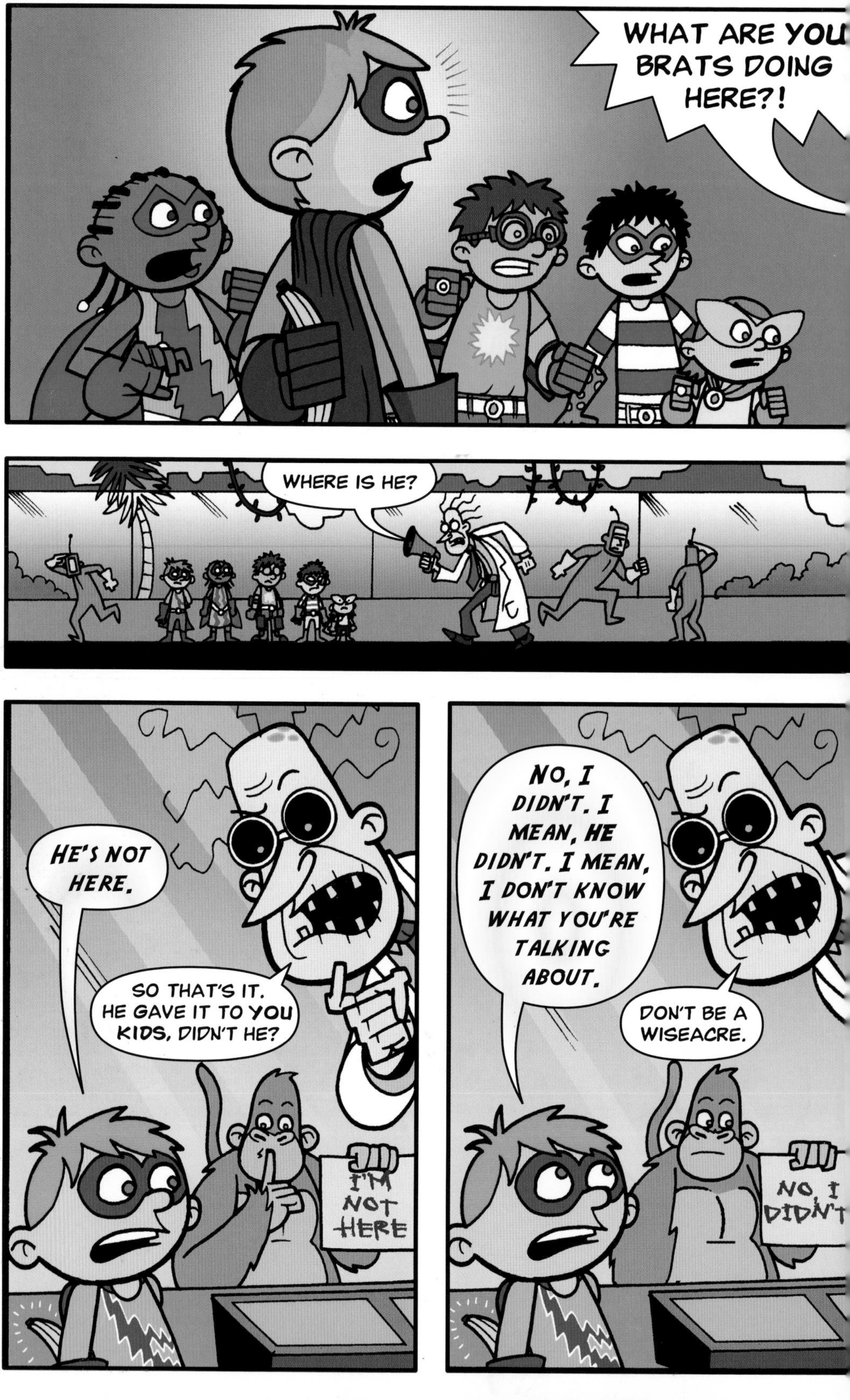
WHAT ARE YOU BRATS DOING HERE?!
WHERE IS HE?
HE'S NOT HERE.
SO THAT'S IT. HE GAVE IT TO YOU KIDS, DIDN'T HE?
I'M NOT HERE
NO, I DIDN'T. I MEAN, HE DIDN'T. I MEAN, I DON'T KNOW WHAT YOU'RE TALKING ABOUT.
DON'T BE A WISEACRE.
NO, I DIDN'T

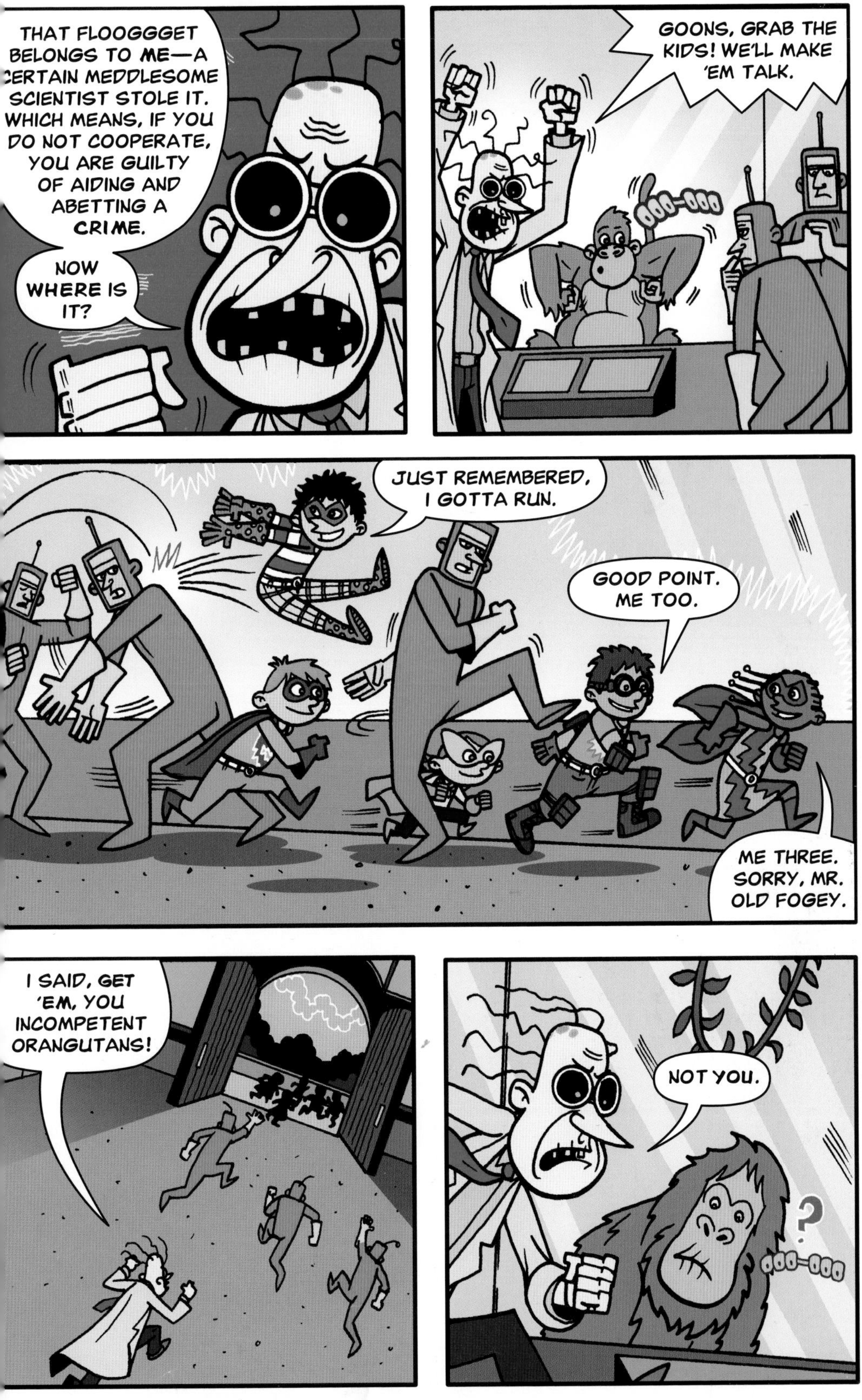
THAT FLOOGGGET BELONGS TO ME—A CERTAIN MEDDLESOME SCIENTIST STOLE IT. WHICH MEANS, IF YOU DO NOT COOPERATE, YOU ARE GUILTY OF AIDING AND ABETTING A CRIME.
NOW WHERE IS IT?
GOONS, GRAB THE KIDS! WE'LL MAKE 'EM TALK.
OOO-OOO
JUST REMEMBERED, I GOTTA RUN.
GOOD POINT. ME TOO.
ME THREE. SORRY, MR. OLD FOGEY.
I SAID, GET 'EM, YOU INCOMPETENT ORANGUTANS!
NOT YOU.
?
OOO-OOO

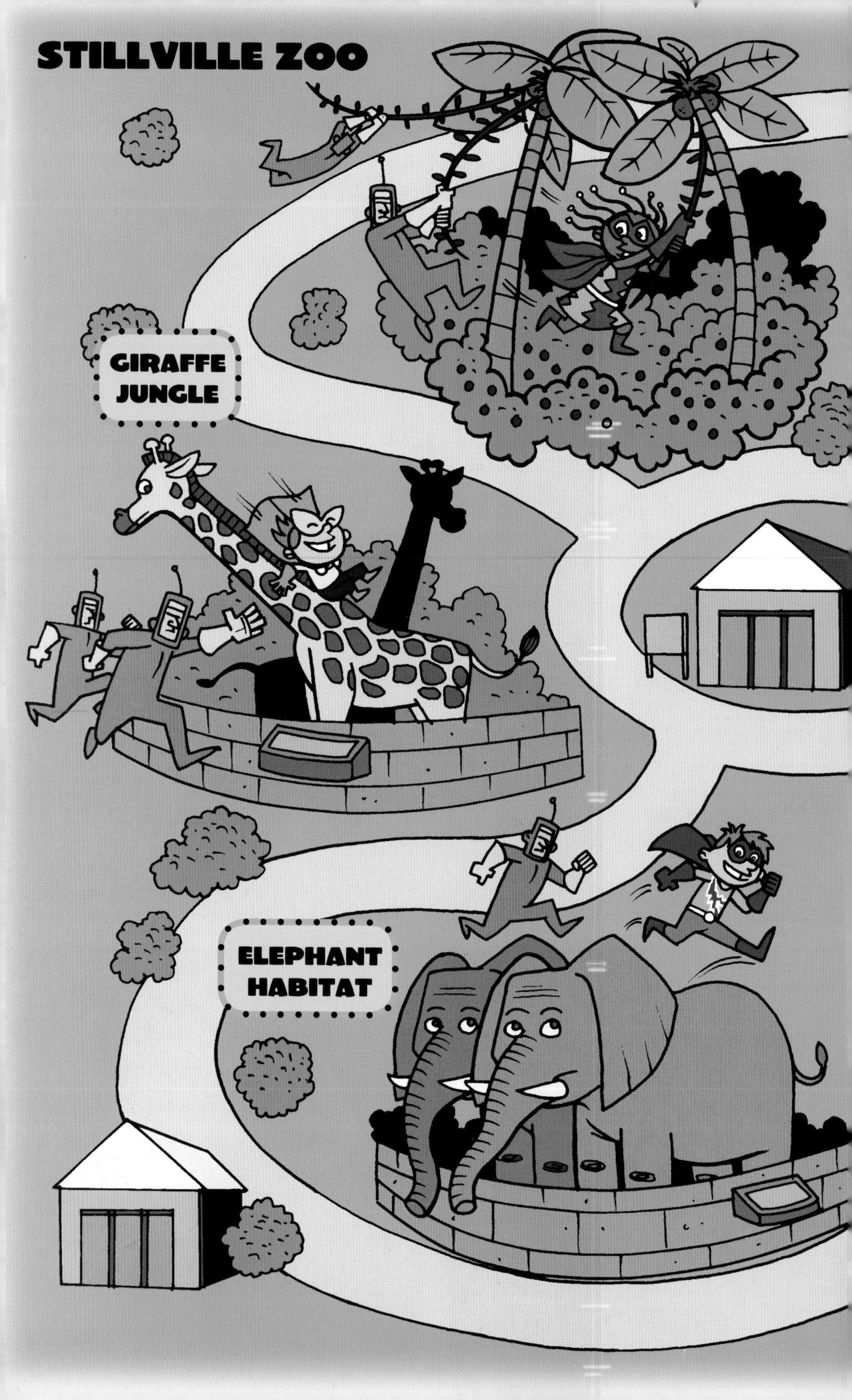
STILLVILLE ZOO
GIRAFFE JUNGLE
ELEPHANT HABITAT

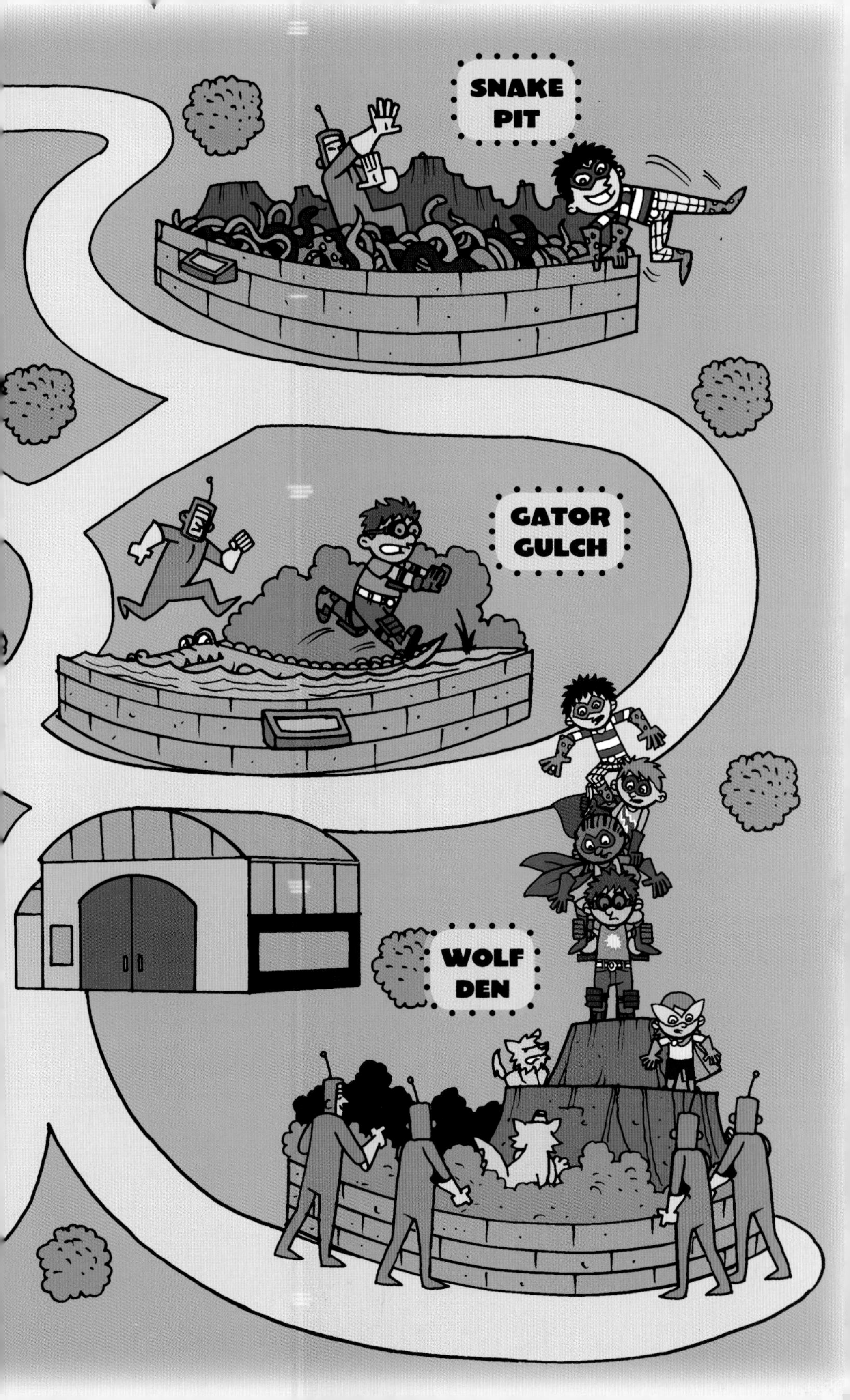
SNAKE PIT
GATOR GULCH
WOLF DEN

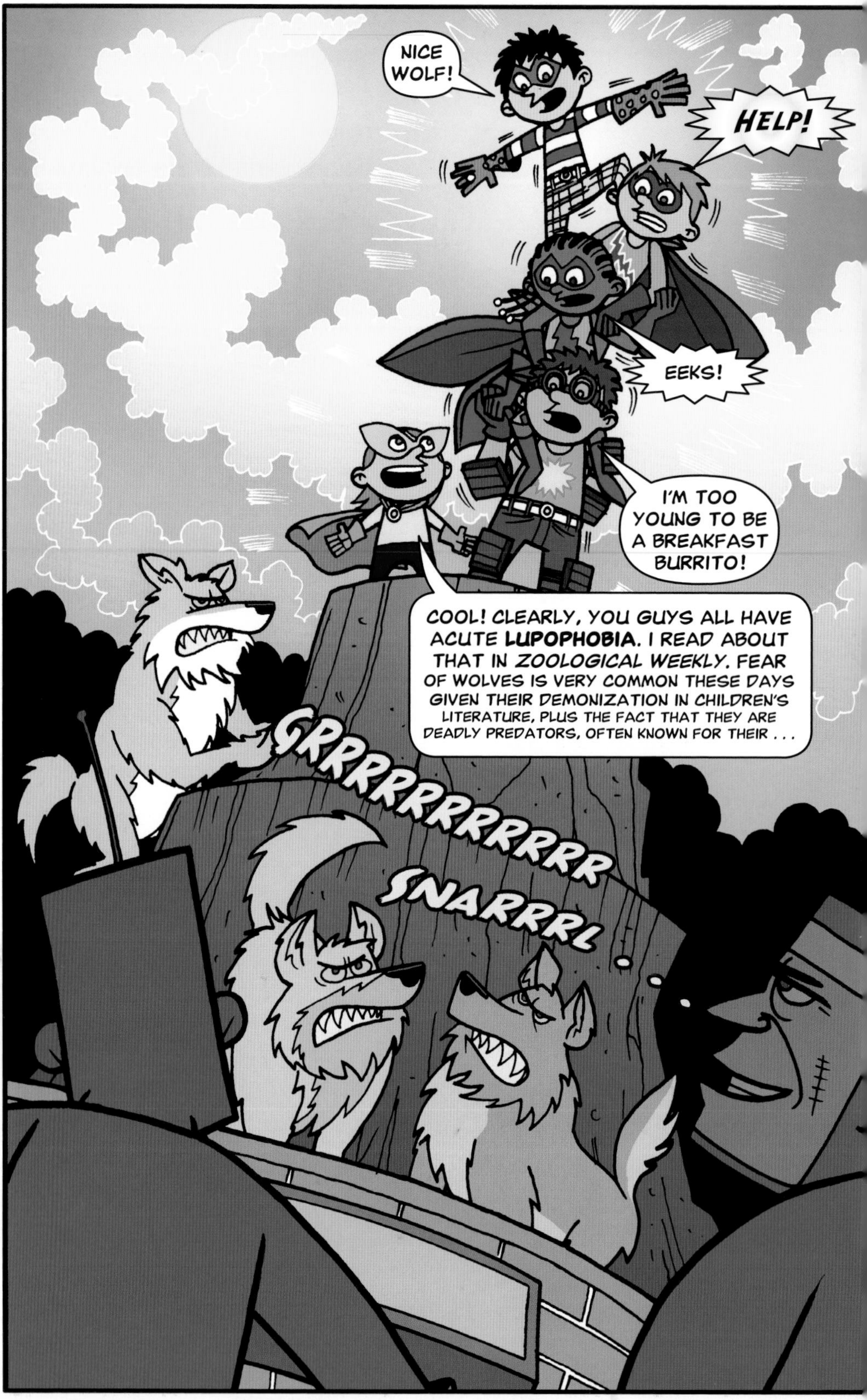
NICE WOLF!
HELP!
EEKS!
I'M TOO YOUNG TO BE A BREAKFAST BURRITO!
COOL! CLEARLY, YOU GUYS ALL HAVE ACUTE **LUPOPHOBIA**. I READ ABOUT THAT IN *ZOOLOGICAL WEEKLY*. FEAR OF WOLVES IS VERY COMMON THESE DAYS GIVEN THEIR DEMONIZATION IN CHILDREN'S LITERATURE, PLUS THE FACT THAT THEY ARE DEADLY PREDATORS, OFTEN KNOWN FOR THEIR . . .
GRRRRRRRRRRRRR
SNARRRL

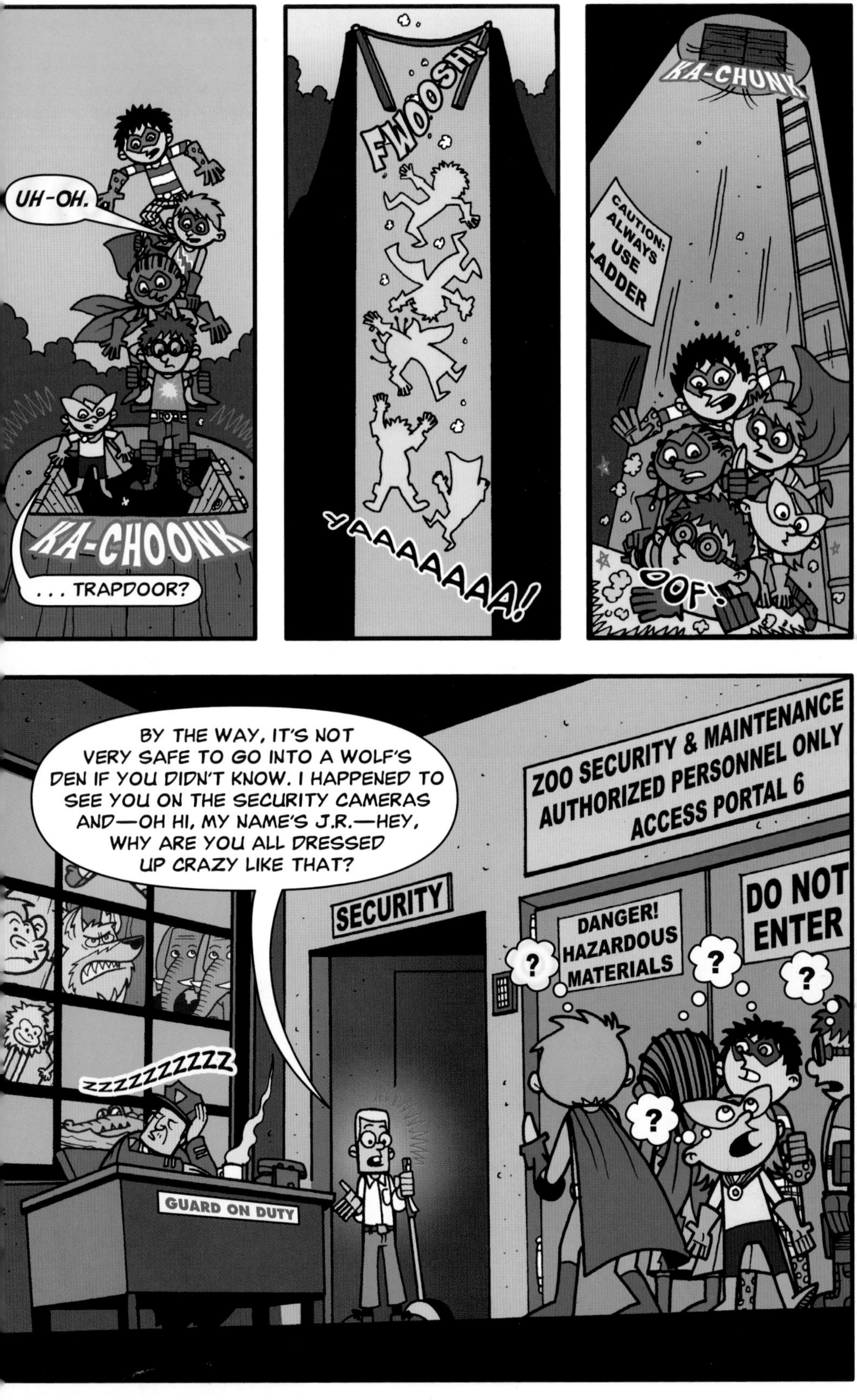
UH-OH.
KA-CHOONK
. . . TRAPDOOR?
FWOOSH!
YAAAAAAAA!
KA-CHUNK
CAUTION: ALWAYS USE LADDER
OOF!
ZOO SECURITY & MAINTENANCE
AUTHORIZED PERSONNEL ONLY
ACCESS PORTAL 6
BY THE WAY, IT'S NOT VERY SAFE TO GO INTO A WOLF'S DEN IF YOU DIDN'T KNOW. I HAPPENED TO SEE YOU ON THE SECURITY CAMERAS AND—OH HI, MY NAME'S J.R.—HEY, WHY ARE YOU ALL DRESSED UP CRAZY LIKE THAT?
SECURITY
DANGER! HAZARDOUS MATERIALS
DO NOT ENTER
ZZZZZZZZZZ
GUARD ON DUTY
?
?
?
?

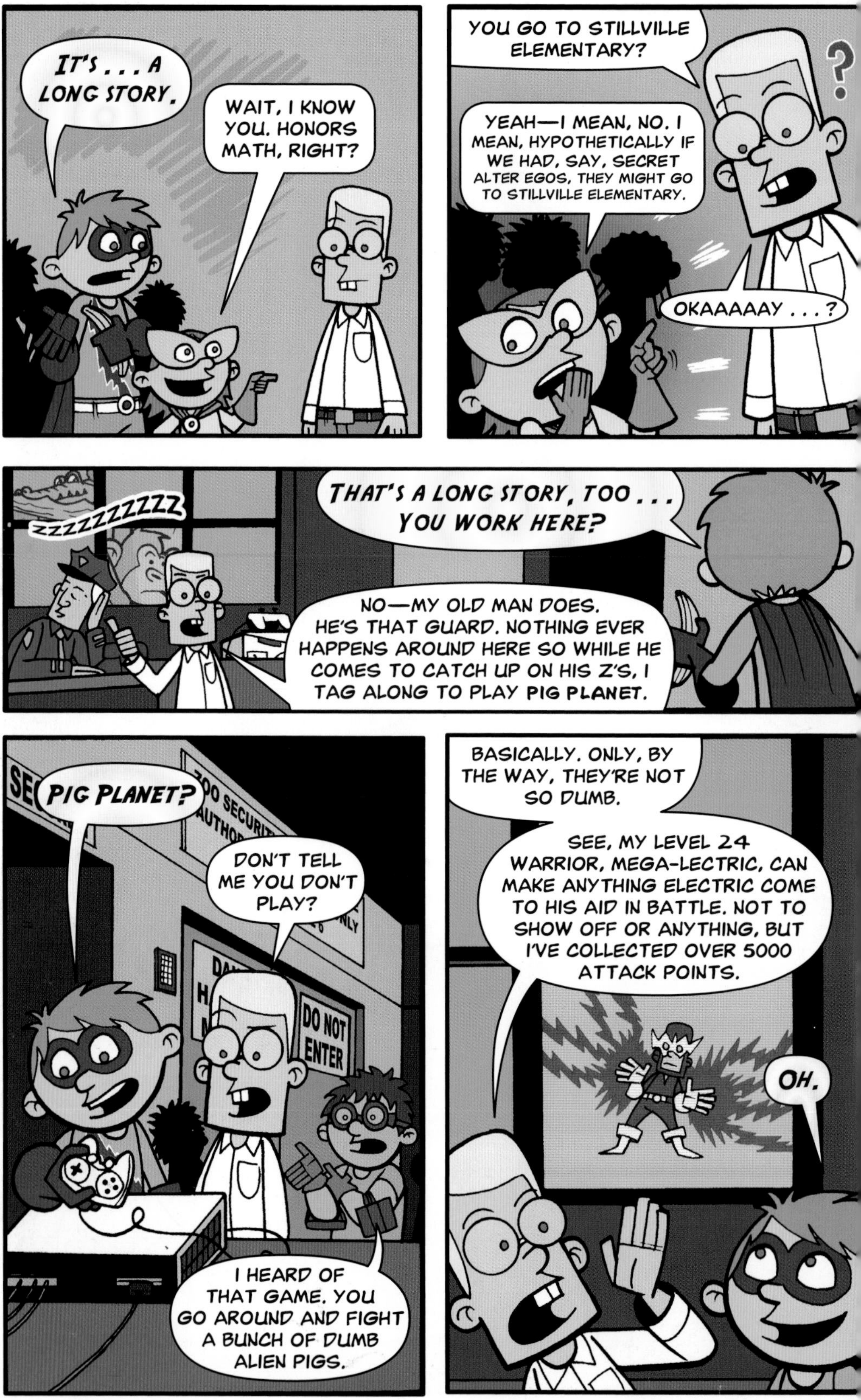
IT'S . . . A LONG STORY.
WAIT, I KNOW YOU. HONORS MATH, RIGHT?
YOU GO TO STILLVILLE ELEMENTARY?
YEAH—I MEAN, NO. I MEAN, HYPOTHETICALLY IF WE HAD, SAY, SECRET ALTER EGOS, THEY MIGHT GO TO STILLVILLE ELEMENTARY.
OKAAAAAY . . . ?
ZZZZZZZZZZZ
THAT'S A LONG STORY, TOO . . . YOU WORK HERE?
NO—MY OLD MAN DOES. HE'S THAT GUARD. NOTHING EVER HAPPENS AROUND HERE SO WHILE HE COMES TO CATCH UP ON HIS Z'S, I TAG ALONG TO PLAY PIG PLANET.
PIG PLANET?
DON'T TELL ME YOU DON'T PLAY?
DO NOT ENTER
I HEARD OF THAT GAME. YOU GO AROUND AND FIGHT A BUNCH OF DUMB ALIEN PIGS.
BASICALLY. ONLY, BY THE WAY, THEY'RE NOT SO DUMB.
SEE, MY LEVEL 24 WARRIOR, MEGA-LECTRIC, CAN MAKE ANYTHING ELECTRIC COME TO HIS AID IN BATTLE. NOT TO SHOW OFF OR ANYTHING, BUT I'VE COLLECTED OVER 5000 ATTACK POINTS.
OH.

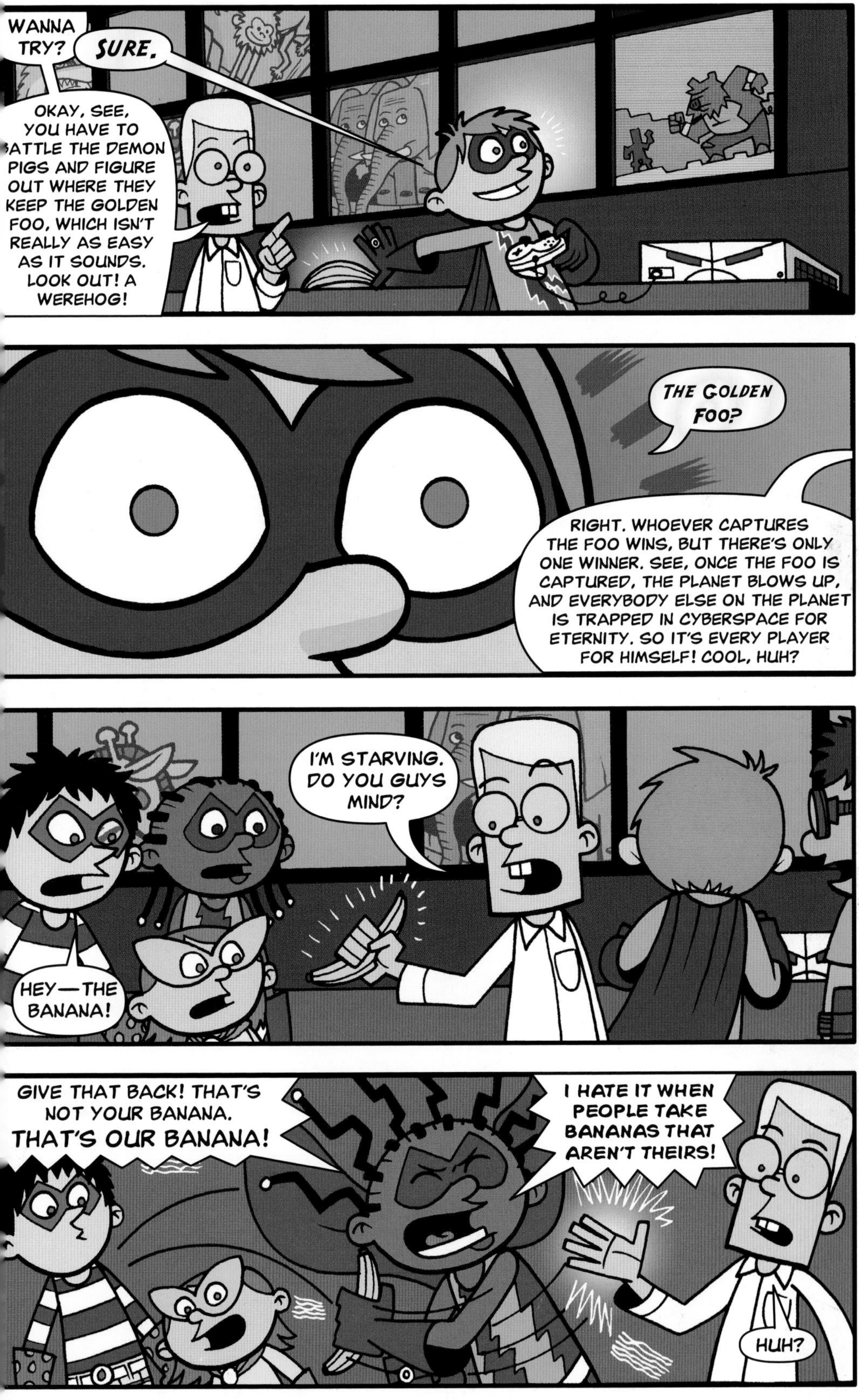

WANNA TRY?
SURE.
OKAY, SEE, YOU HAVE TO ATTLE THE DEMON PIGS AND FIGURE OUT WHERE THEY KEEP THE GOLDEN FOO, WHICH ISN'T REALLY AS EASY AS IT SOUNDS. LOOK OUT! A WEREHOG!
THE GOLDEN FOO?
RIGHT. WHOEVER CAPTURES THE FOO WINS, BUT THERE'S ONLY ONE WINNER. SEE, ONCE THE FOO IS CAPTURED, THE PLANET BLOWS UP, AND EVERYBODY ELSE ON THE PLANET IS TRAPPED IN CYBERSPACE FOR ETERNITY. SO IT'S EVERY PLAYER FOR HIMSELF! COOL, HUH?
I'M STARVING. DO YOU GUYS MIND?
HEY—THE BANANA!
GIVE THAT BACK! THAT'S NOT YOUR BANANA. THAT'S OUR BANANA!
I HATE IT WHEN PEOPLE TAKE BANANAS THAT AREN'T THEIRS!
HUH?

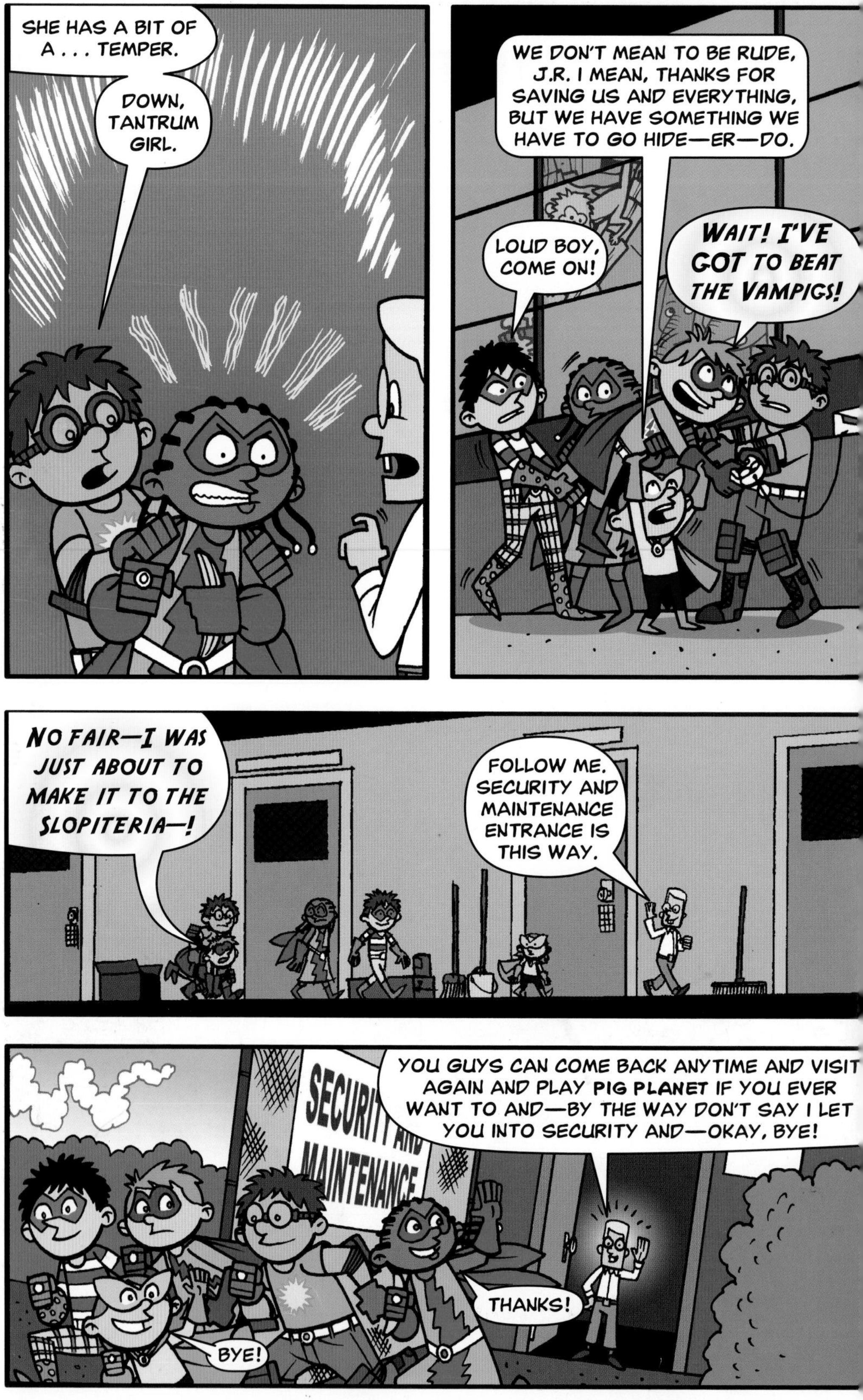
SHE HAS A BIT OF A . . . TEMPER.
DOWN, TANTRUM GIRL.
WE DON'T MEAN TO BE RUDE, J.R. I MEAN, THANKS FOR SAVING US AND EVERYTHING, BUT WE HAVE SOMETHING WE HAVE TO GO HIDE—ER—DO.
LOUD BOY, COME ON!
WAIT! I'VE GOT TO BEAT THE VAMPIGS!
NO FAIR—I WAS JUST ABOUT TO MAKE IT TO THE SLOPITERIA—!
FOLLOW ME. SECURITY AND MAINTENANCE ENTRANCE IS THIS WAY.
SECURITY AND MAINTENANCE
YOU GUYS CAN COME BACK ANYTIME AND VISIT AGAIN AND PLAY PIG PLANET IF YOU EVER WANT TO AND—BY THE WAY DON'T SAY I LET YOU INTO SECURITY AND—OKAY, BYE!
THANKS!
BYE!

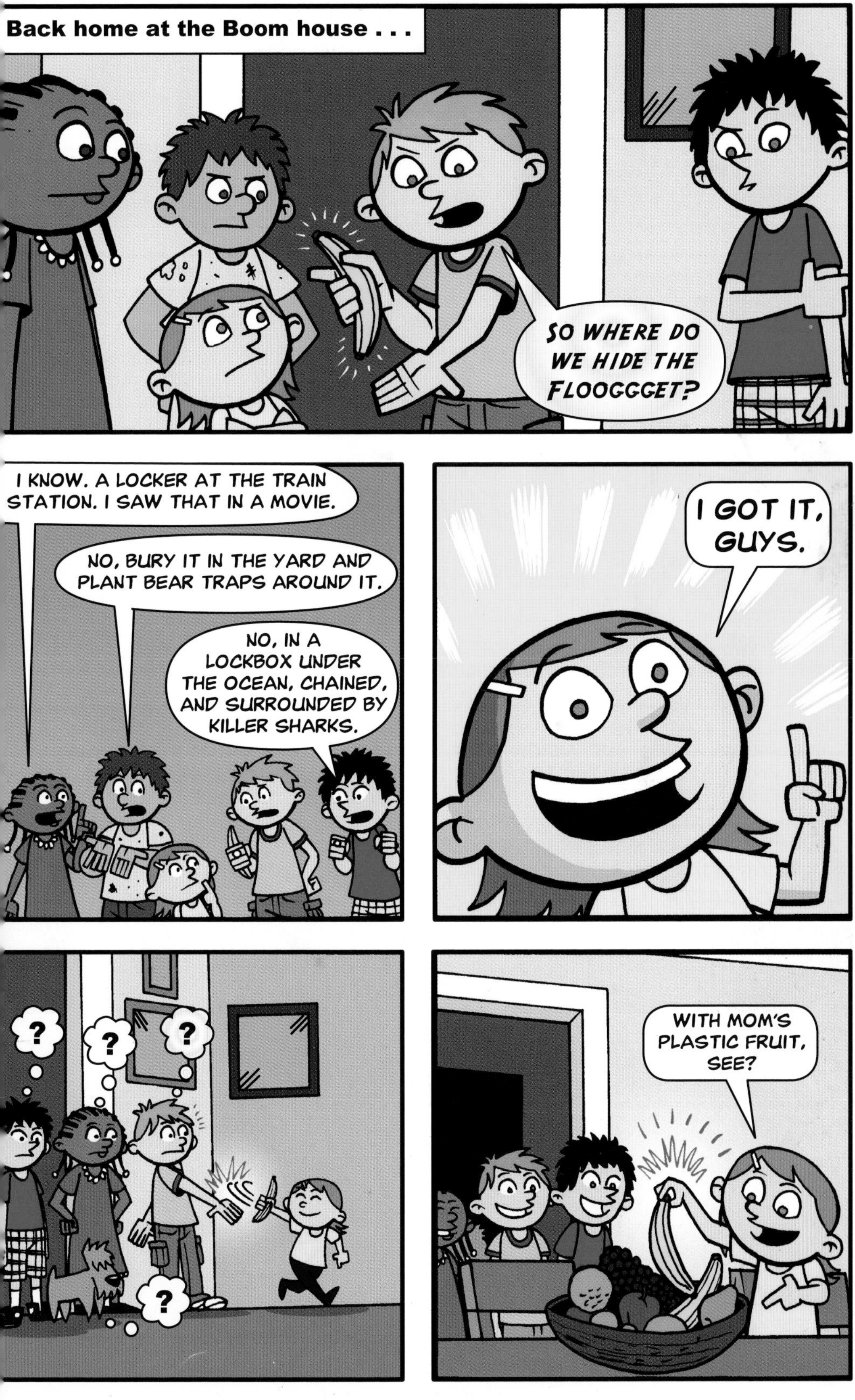
Back home at the Boom house . . .
SO WHERE DO WE HIDE THE FLOOGGGET?
I KNOW. A LOCKER AT THE TRAIN STATION. I SAW THAT IN A MOVIE.
NO, BURY IT IN THE YARD AND PLANT BEAR TRAPS AROUND IT.
NO, IN A LOCKBOX UNDER THE OCEAN, CHAINED, AND SURROUNDED BY KILLER SHARKS.
I GOT IT, GUYS.
?
?
?
?
WITH MOM'S PLASTIC FRUIT, SEE?

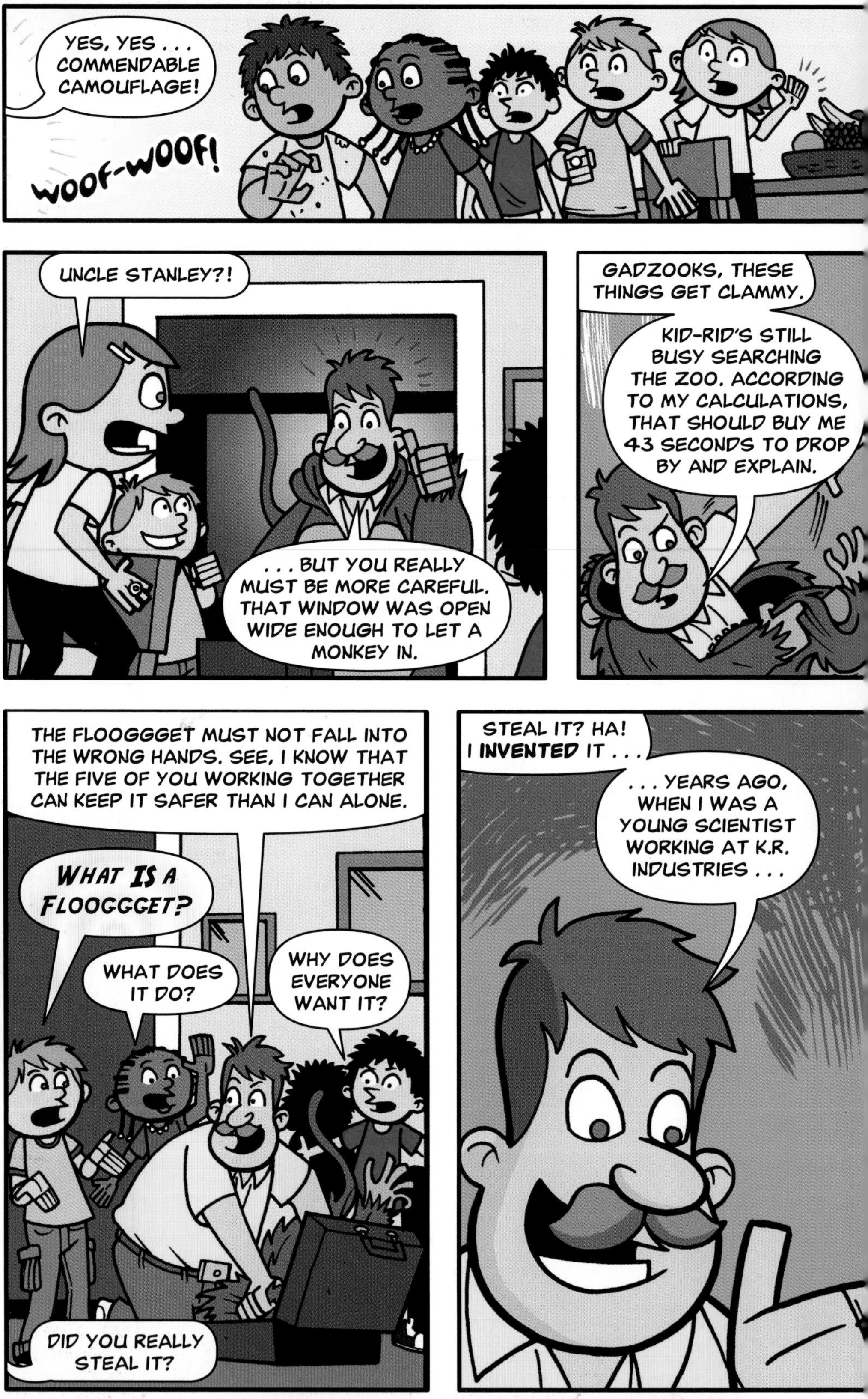
YES, YES . . . COMMENDABLE CAMOUFLAGE!
WOOF-WOOF!
UNCLE STANLEY?!
. . . BUT YOU REALLY MUST BE MORE CAREFUL. THAT WINDOW WAS OPEN WIDE ENOUGH TO LET A MONKEY IN.
GADZOOKS, THESE THINGS GET CLAMMY.
KID-RID'S STILL BUSY SEARCHING THE ZOO. ACCORDING TO MY CALCULATIONS, THAT SHOULD BUY ME 43 SECONDS TO DROP BY AND EXPLAIN.
THE FLOOGGGET MUST NOT FALL INTO THE WRONG HANDS. SEE, I KNOW THAT THE FIVE OF YOU WORKING TOGETHER CAN KEEP IT SAFER THAN I CAN ALONE.
WHAT IS A FLOOGGGET?
WHAT DOES IT DO?
WHY DOES EVERYONE WANT IT?
DID YOU REALLY STEAL IT?
STEAL IT? HA! I INVENTED IT . . .
. . . YEARS AGO, WHEN I WAS A YOUNG SCIENTIST WORKING AT K.R. INDUSTRIES . . .

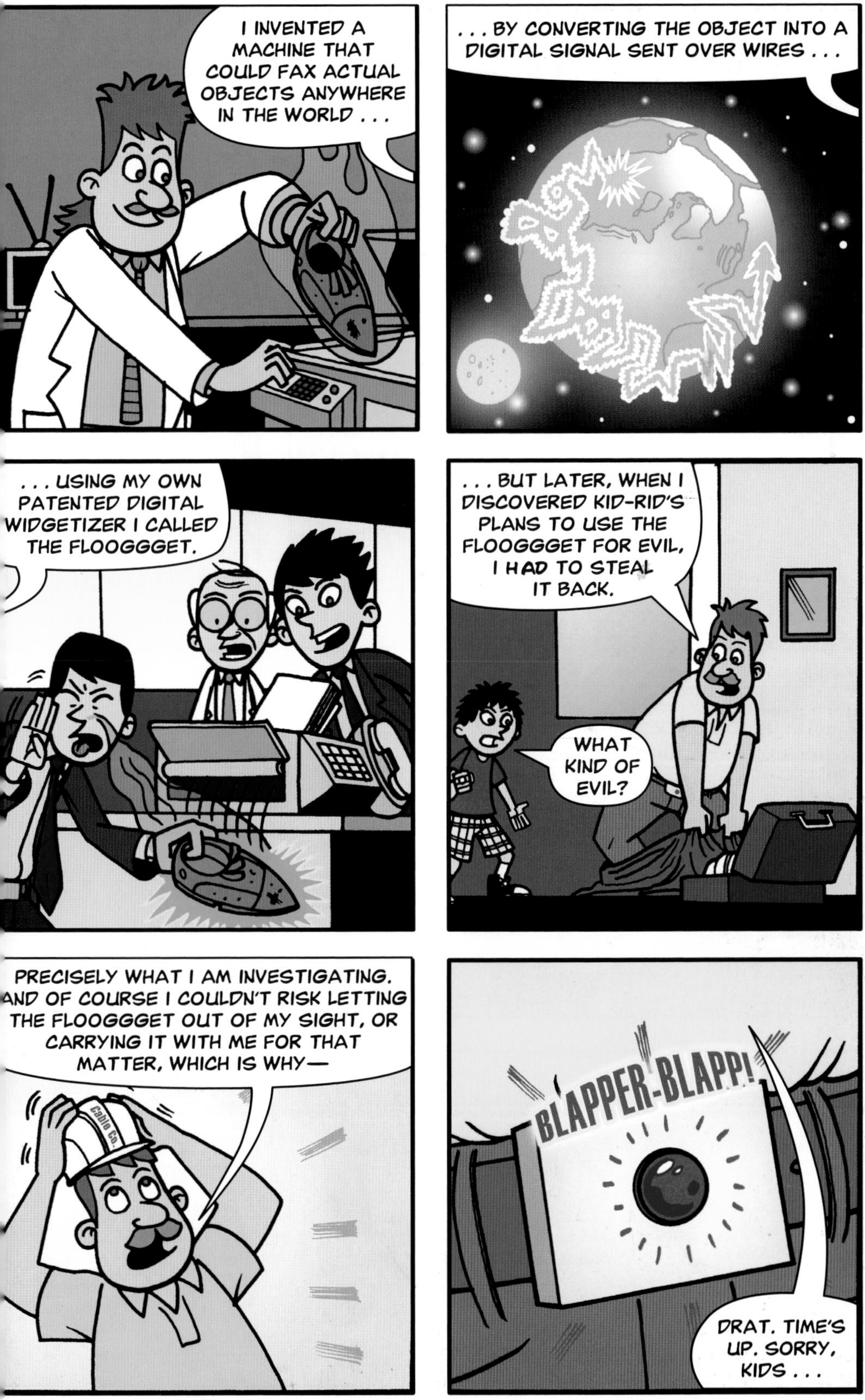
I INVENTED A MACHINE THAT COULD FAX ACTUAL OBJECTS ANYWHERE IN THE WORLD . . .
. . . BY CONVERTING THE OBJECT INTO A DIGITAL SIGNAL SENT OVER WIRES . . .
. . . USING MY OWN PATENTED DIGITAL WIDGETIZER I CALLED THE FLOOGGGET.
. . . BUT LATER, WHEN I DISCOVERED KID-RID'S PLANS TO USE THE FLOOGGGET FOR EVIL, I HAD TO STEAL IT BACK.
WHAT KIND OF EVIL?
PRECISELY WHAT I AM INVESTIGATING. AND OF COURSE I COULDN'T RISK LETTING THE FLOOGGGET OUT OF MY SIGHT, OR CARRYING IT WITH ME FOR THAT MATTER, WHICH IS WHY—
Cable Co.
BLAPPER-BLAPP!
DRAT. TIME'S UP. SORRY, KIDS . . .

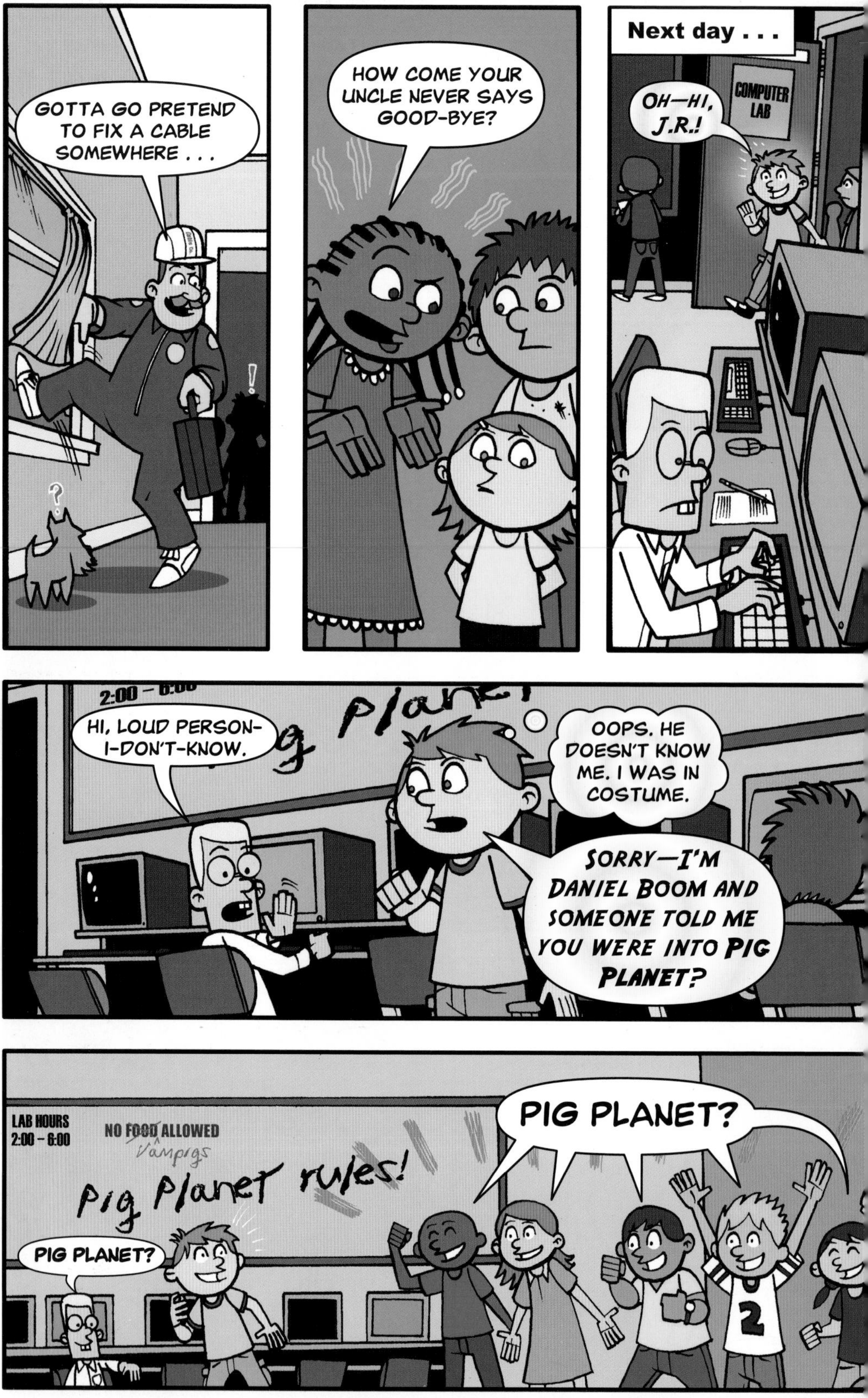
GOTTA GO PRETEND TO FIX A CABLE SOMEWHERE . . .
HOW COME YOUR UNCLE NEVER SAYS GOOD-BYE?
Next day . . .
COMPUTER LAB
OH—HI, J.R.!
HI, LOUD PERSON-I-DON'T-KNOW.
OOPS. HE DOESN'T KNOW ME. I WAS IN COSTUME.
SORRY—I'M DANIEL BOOM AND SOMEONE TOLD ME YOU WERE INTO PIG PLANET?
LAB HOURS 2:00 – 6:00
NO ~~FOOD~~ Vampigs ALLOWED
Pig Planet rules!
PIG PLANET?
PIG PLANET?

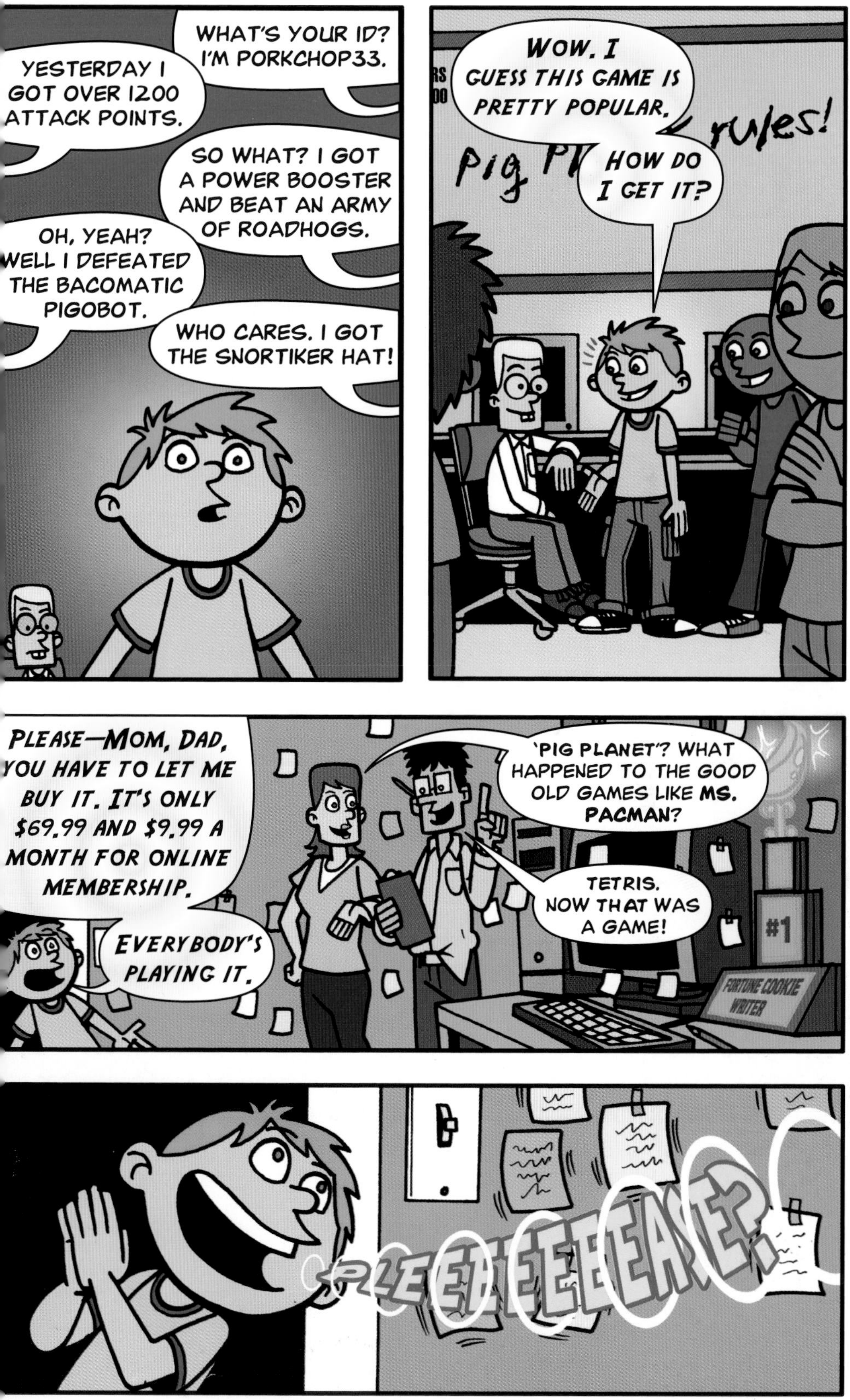
WHAT'S YOUR ID? I'M PORKCHOP33.
YESTERDAY I GOT OVER 1200 ATTACK POINTS.
SO WHAT? I GOT A POWER BOOSTER AND BEAT AN ARMY OF ROADHOGS.
OH, YEAH? WELL I DEFEATED THE BACOMATIC PIGOBOT.
WHO CARES. I GOT THE SNORTIKER HAT!
WOW. I GUESS THIS GAME IS PRETTY POPULAR.
HOW DO I GET IT?
PLEASE—MOM, DAD, YOU HAVE TO LET ME BUY IT. IT'S ONLY $69.99 AND $9.99 A MONTH FOR ONLINE MEMBERSHIP.
EVERYBODY'S PLAYING IT.
'PIG PLANET'? WHAT HAPPENED TO THE GOOD OLD GAMES LIKE MS. PACMAN?
TETRIS. NOW THAT WAS A GAME!
#1
FORTUNE COOKIE WRITER
PLEEEEEEEASE?

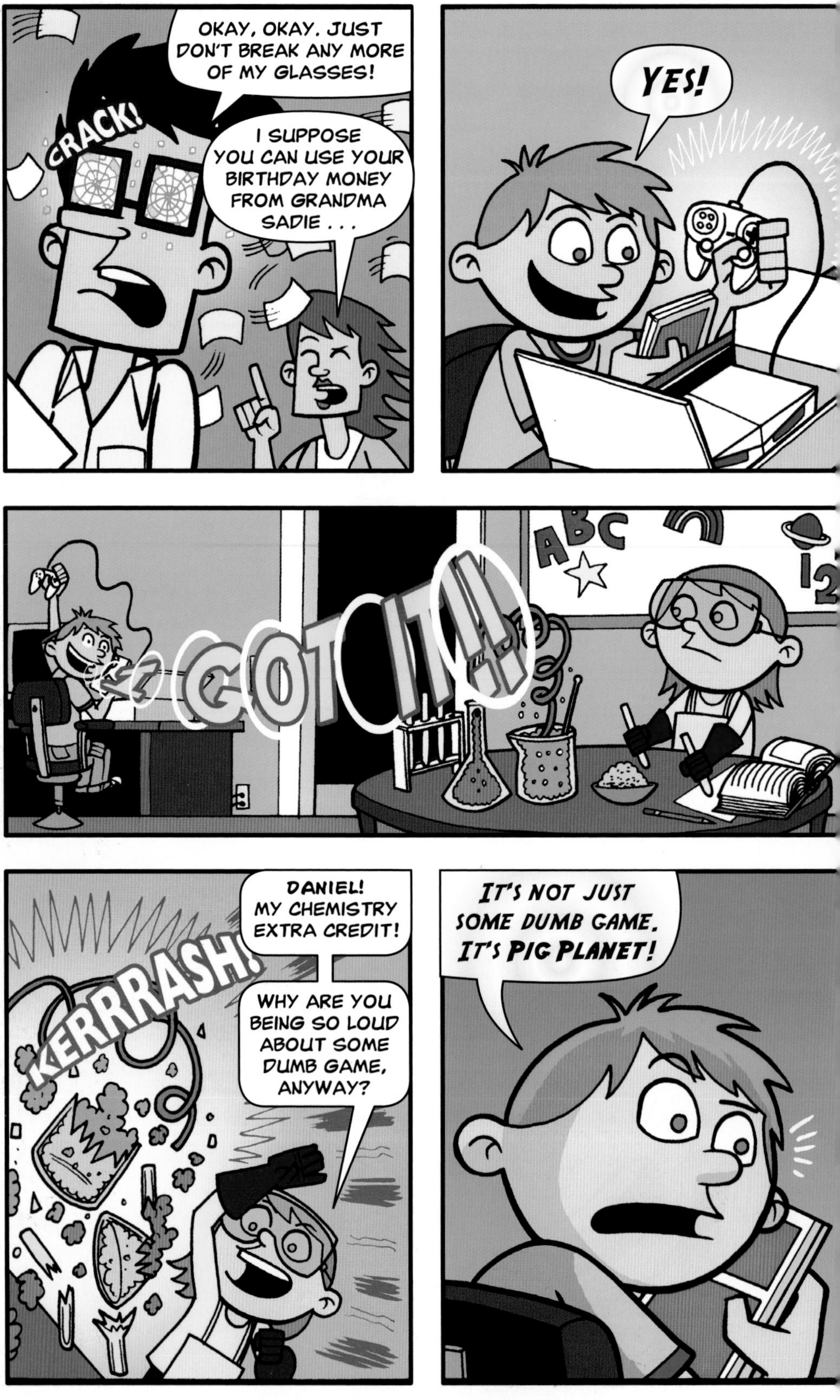
OKAY, OKAY. JUST DON'T BREAK ANY MORE OF MY GLASSES!
CRACK!
I SUPPOSE YOU CAN USE YOUR BIRTHDAY MONEY FROM GRANDMA SADIE . . .
YES!
ABC
12
GOT IT!!
DANIEL! MY CHEMISTRY EXTRA CREDIT!
KERRRASH!
WHY ARE YOU BEING SO LOUD ABOUT SOME DUMB GAME, ANYWAY?
IT'S NOT JUST SOME DUMB GAME. IT'S PIG PLANET!

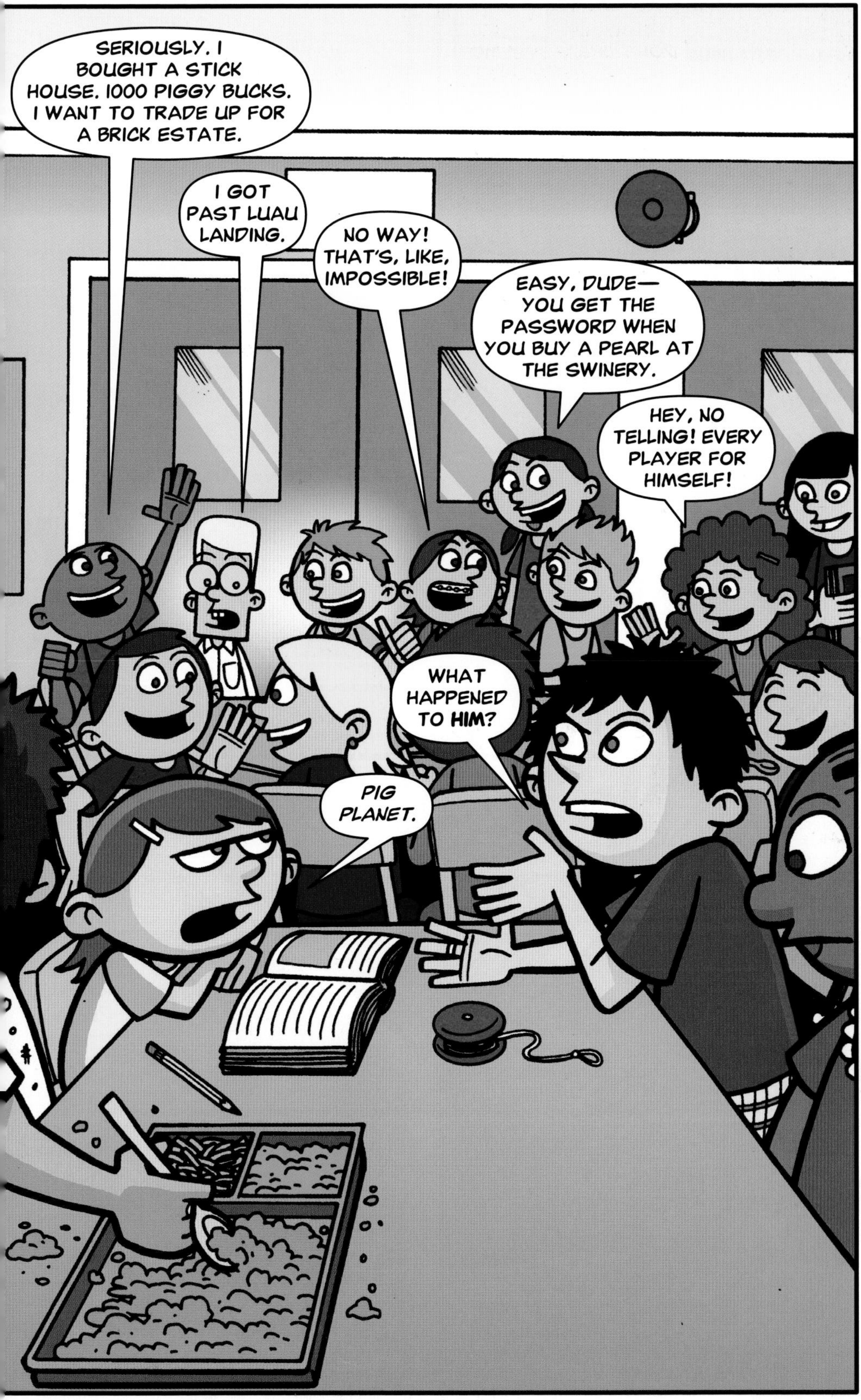
SERIOUSLY. I BOUGHT A STICK HOUSE. 1000 PIGGY BUCKS. I WANT TO TRADE UP FOR A BRICK ESTATE.
I GOT PAST LUAU LANDING.
NO WAY! THAT'S, LIKE, IMPOSSIBLE!
EASY, DUDE— YOU GET THE PASSWORD WHEN YOU BUY A PEARL AT THE SWINERY.
HEY, NO TELLING! EVERY PLAYER FOR HIMSELF!
WHAT HAPPENED TO HIM?
PIG PLANET.

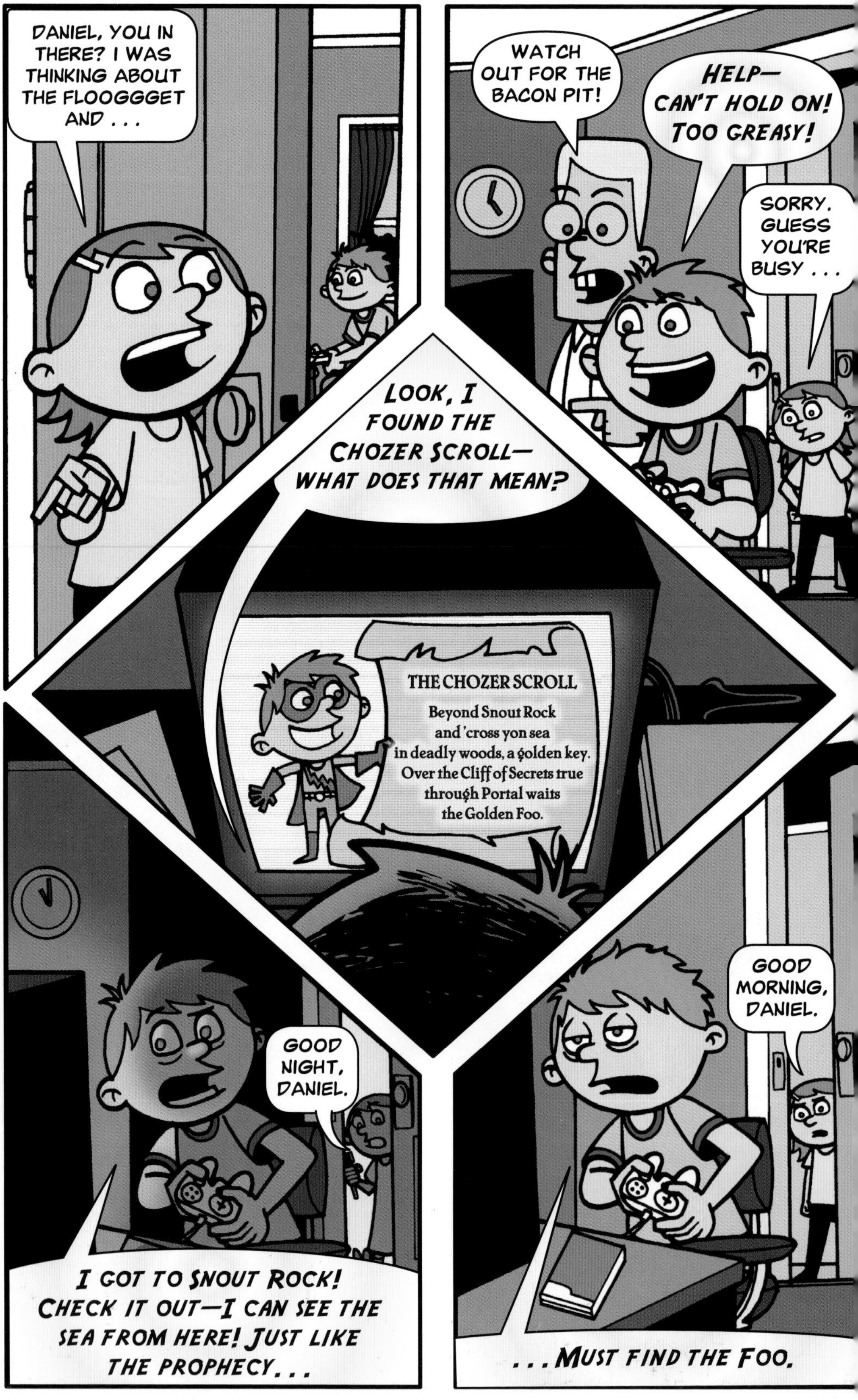
DANIEL, YOU IN THERE? I WAS THINKING ABOUT THE FLOOGGGET AND . . .
WATCH OUT FOR THE BACON PIT!
HELP— CAN'T HOLD ON! TOO GREASY!
SORRY. GUESS YOU'RE BUSY . . .
LOOK, I FOUND THE CHOZER SCROLL— WHAT DOES THAT MEAN?
THE CHOZER SCROLL
Beyond Snout Rock
and 'cross yon sea
in deadly woods, a golden key.
Over the Cliff of Secrets true
through Portal waits
the Golden Foo.
GOOD NIGHT, DANIEL.
I GOT TO SNOUT ROCK! CHECK IT OUT—I CAN SEE THE SEA FROM HERE! JUST LIKE THE PROPHECY. . .
GOOD MORNING, DANIEL.
. . . MUST FIND THE FOO.

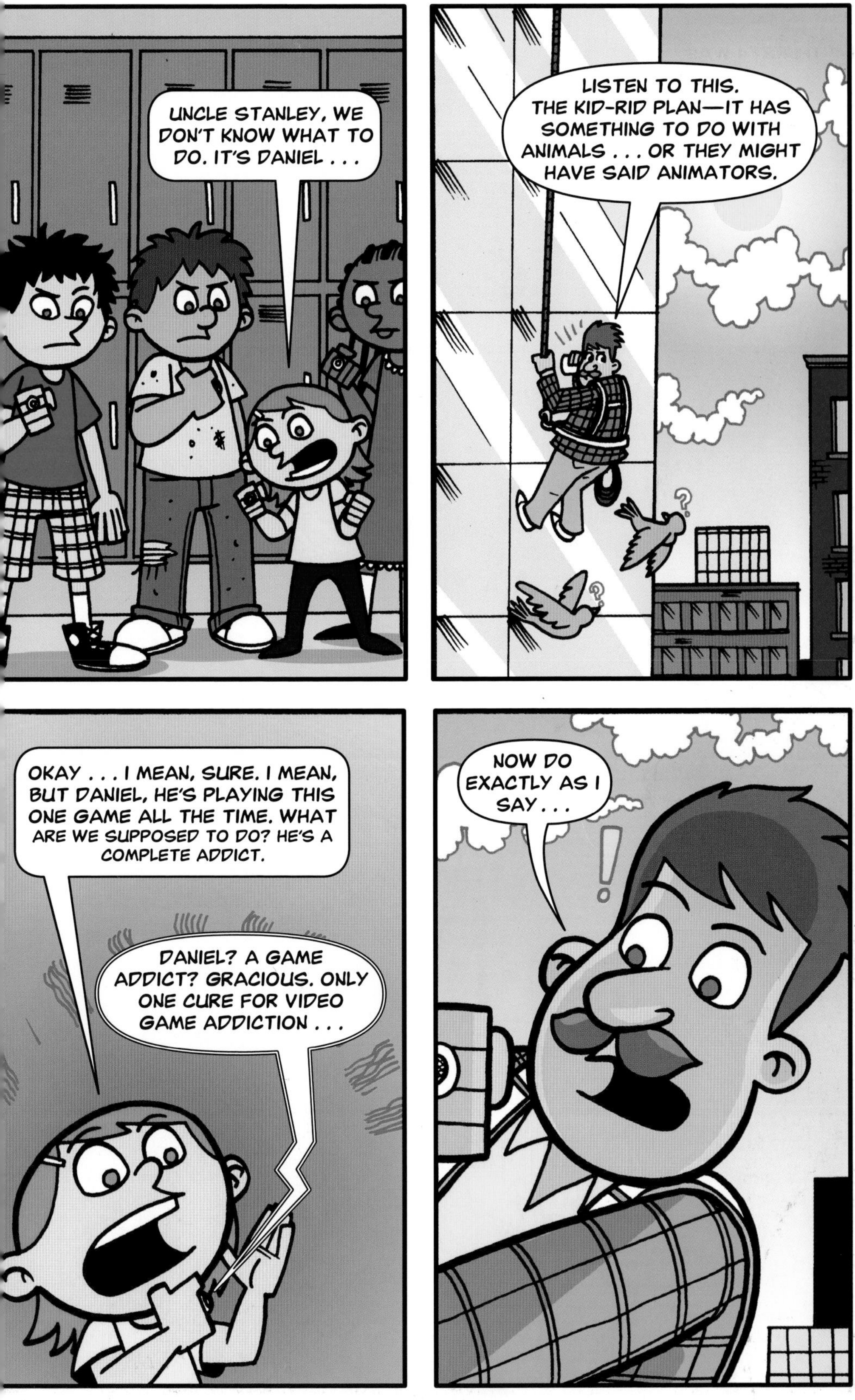
UNCLE STANLEY, WE DON'T KNOW WHAT TO DO. IT'S DANIEL . . .
LISTEN TO THIS. THE KID-RID PLAN—IT HAS SOMETHING TO DO WITH ANIMALS . . . OR THEY MIGHT HAVE SAID ANIMATORS.
OKAY . . . I MEAN, SURE. I MEAN, BUT DANIEL, HE'S PLAYING THIS ONE GAME ALL THE TIME. WHAT ARE WE SUPPOSED TO DO? HE'S A COMPLETE ADDICT.
DANIEL? A GAME ADDICT? GRACIOUS. ONLY ONE CURE FOR VIDEO GAME ADDICTION . . .
NOW DO EXACTLY AS I SAY . . .

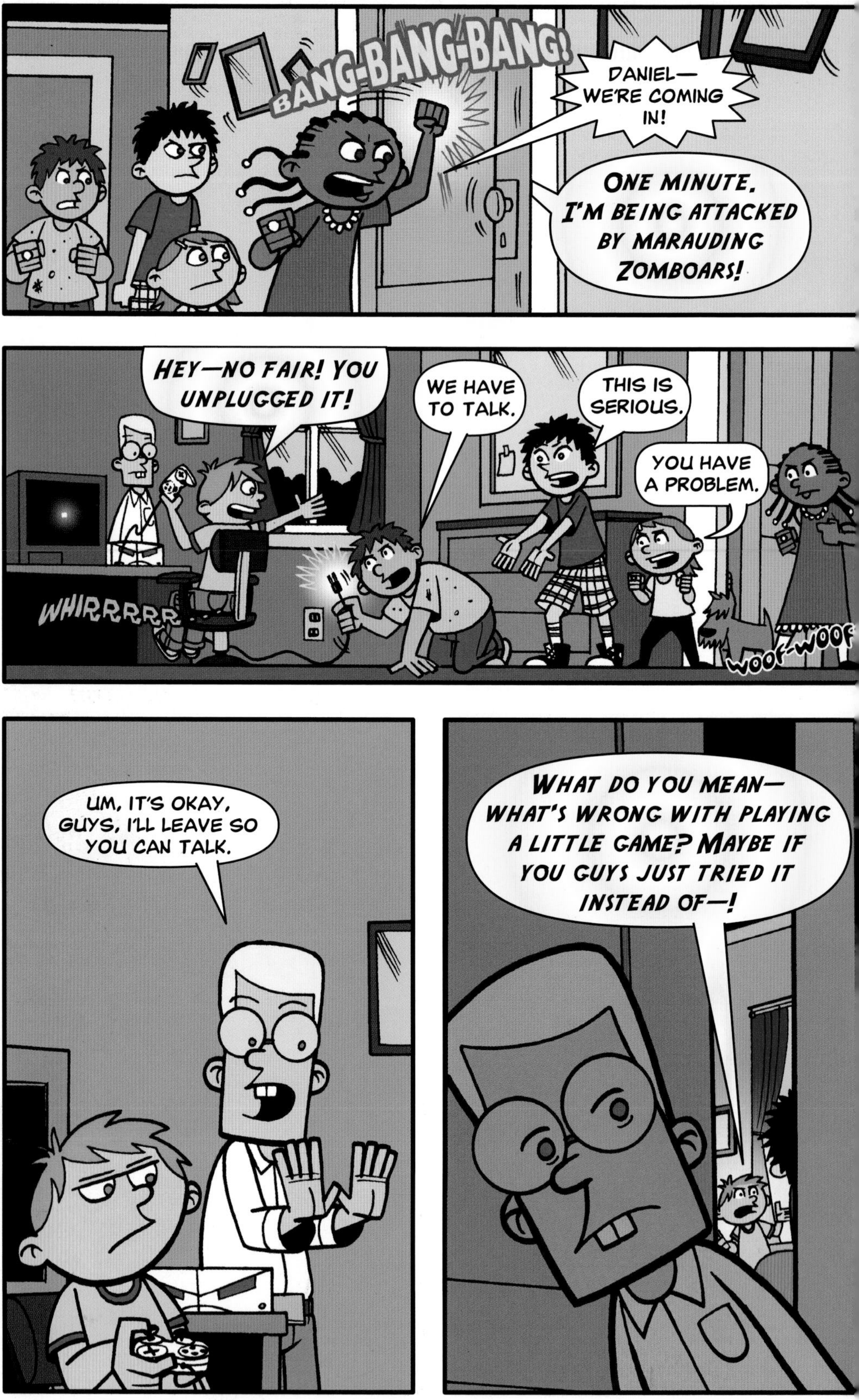
BANG-BANG-BANG!
DANIEL— WE'RE COMING IN!
ONE MINUTE. I'M BEING ATTACKED BY MARAUDING ZOMBOARS!
HEY—NO FAIR! YOU UNPLUGGED IT!
WHIRRRRR
WE HAVE TO TALK.
THIS IS SERIOUS.
YOU HAVE A PROBLEM.
WOOF-WOOF
UM, IT'S OKAY, GUYS, I'LL LEAVE SO YOU CAN TALK.
WHAT DO YOU MEAN— WHAT'S WRONG WITH PLAYING A LITTLE GAME? MAYBE IF YOU GUYS JUST TRIED IT INSTEAD OF—!

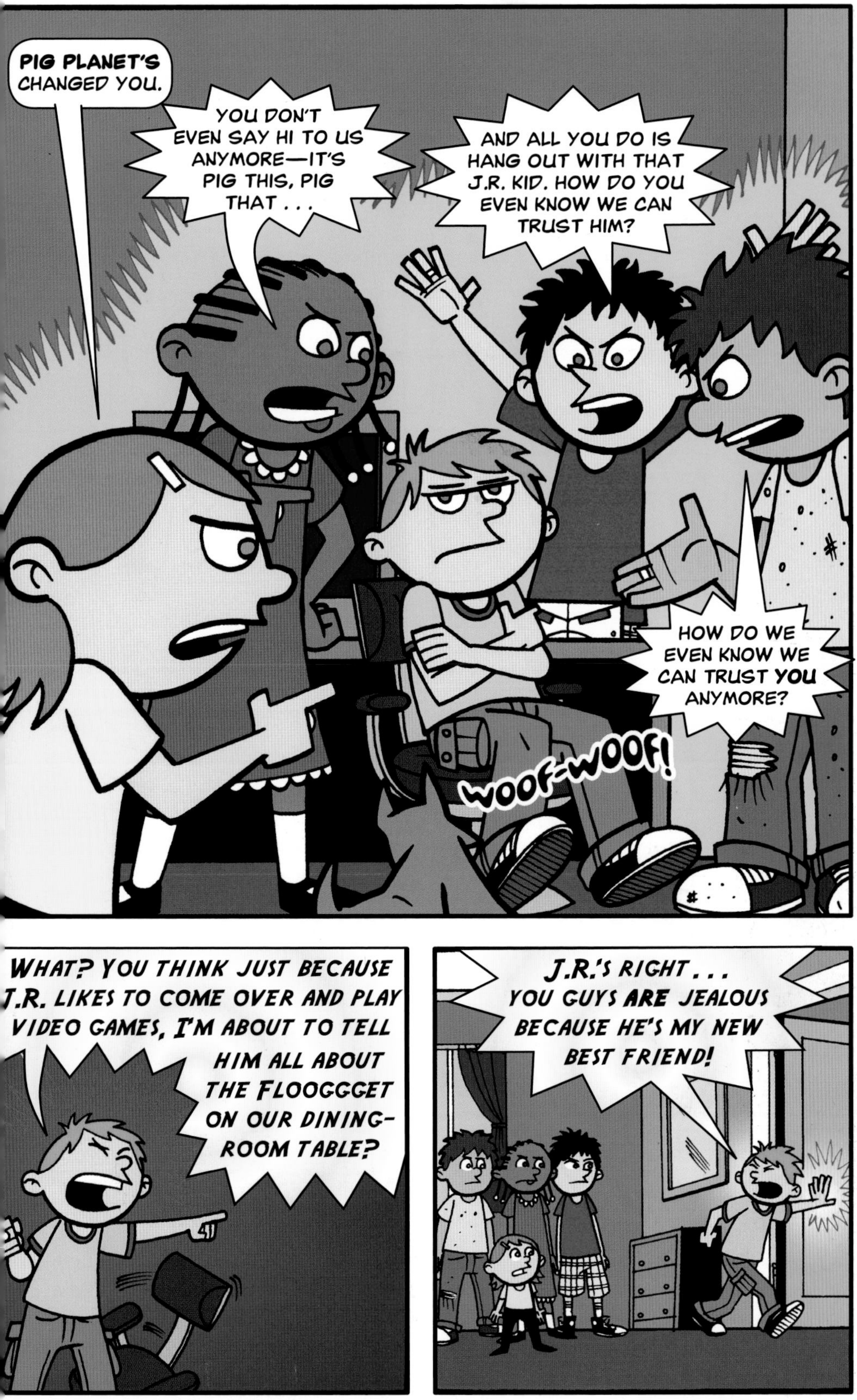
PIG PLANET'S CHANGED YOU.
YOU DON'T EVEN SAY HI TO US ANYMORE—IT'S PIG THIS, PIG THAT . . .
AND ALL YOU DO IS HANG OUT WITH THAT J.R. KID. HOW DO YOU EVEN KNOW WE CAN TRUST HIM?
HOW DO WE EVEN KNOW WE CAN TRUST YOU ANYMORE?
WOOF-WOOF!
WHAT? YOU THINK JUST BECAUSE J.R. LIKES TO COME OVER AND PLAY VIDEO GAMES, I'M ABOUT TO TELL HIM ALL ABOUT THE FLOOGGGET ON OUR DINING-ROOM TABLE?
J.R.'S RIGHT . . . YOU GUYS ARE JEALOUS BECAUSE HE'S MY NEW BEST FRIEND!

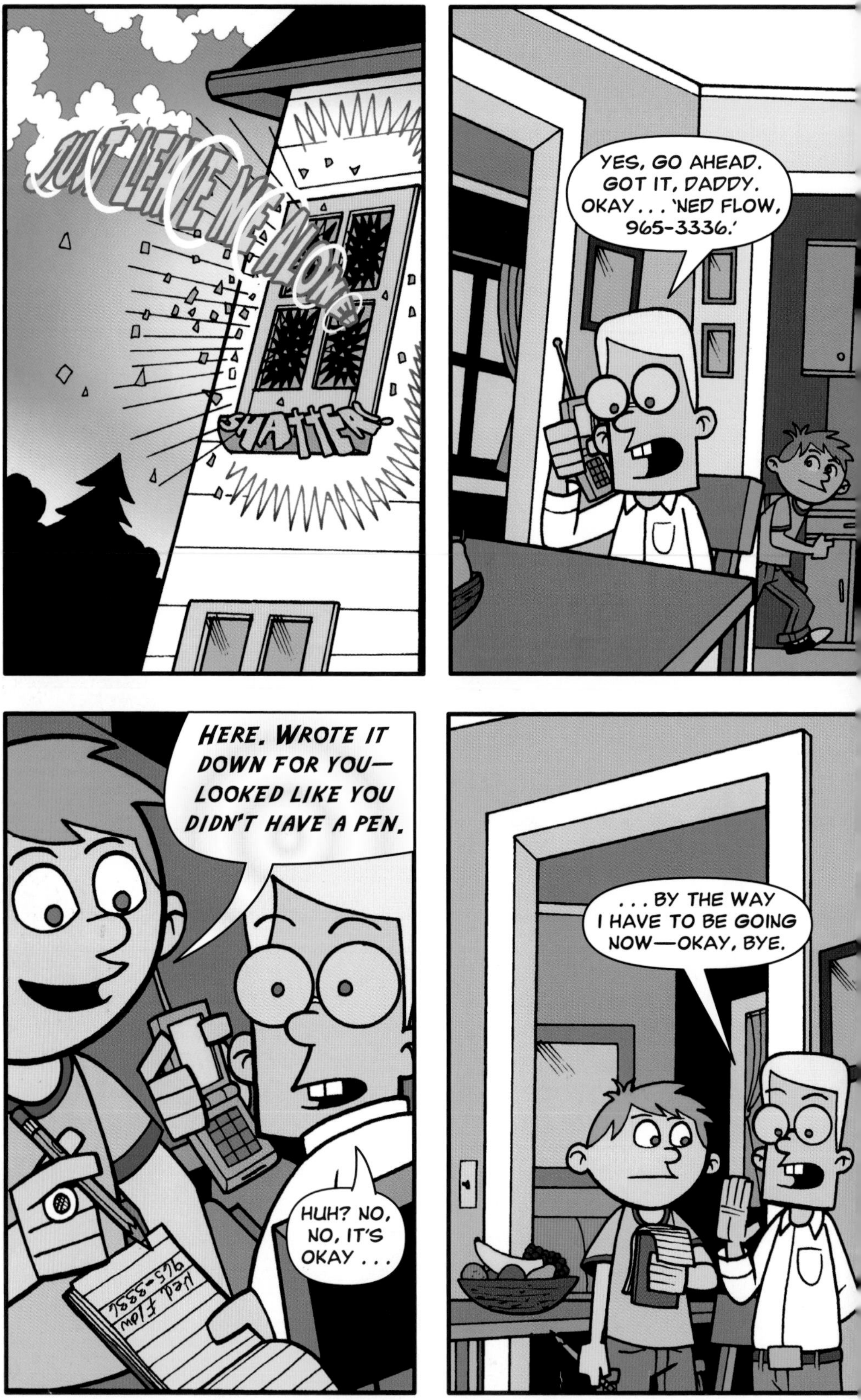
JUST LEAVE ME ALONE!
SHATTER!
YES, GO AHEAD. GOT IT, DADDY. OKAY . . . 'NED FLOW, 965-3336.'
HERE. WROTE IT DOWN FOR YOU— LOOKED LIKE YOU DIDN'T HAVE A PEN.
HUH? NO, NO, IT'S OKAY . . .
. . . BY THE WAY I HAVE TO BE GOING NOW—OKAY, BYE.

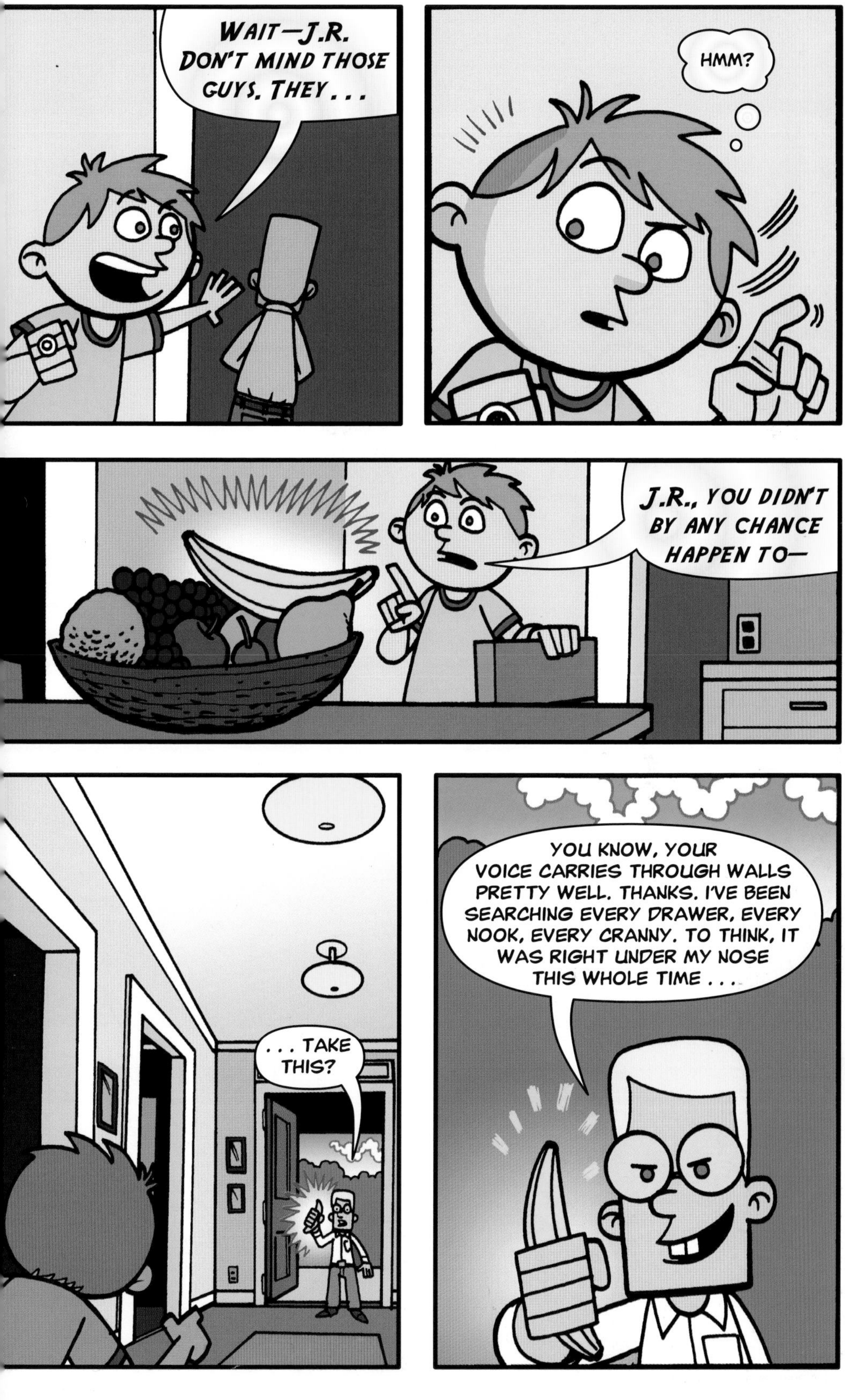
WAIT—J.R. DON'T MIND THOSE GUYS. THEY . . .
HMM?
J.R., YOU DIDN'T BY ANY CHANCE HAPPEN TO—
. . . TAKE THIS?
YOU KNOW, YOUR VOICE CARRIES THROUGH WALLS PRETTY WELL. THANKS. I'VE BEEN SEARCHING EVERY DRAWER, EVERY NOOK, EVERY CRANNY. TO THINK, IT WAS RIGHT UNDER MY NOSE THIS WHOLE TIME . . .

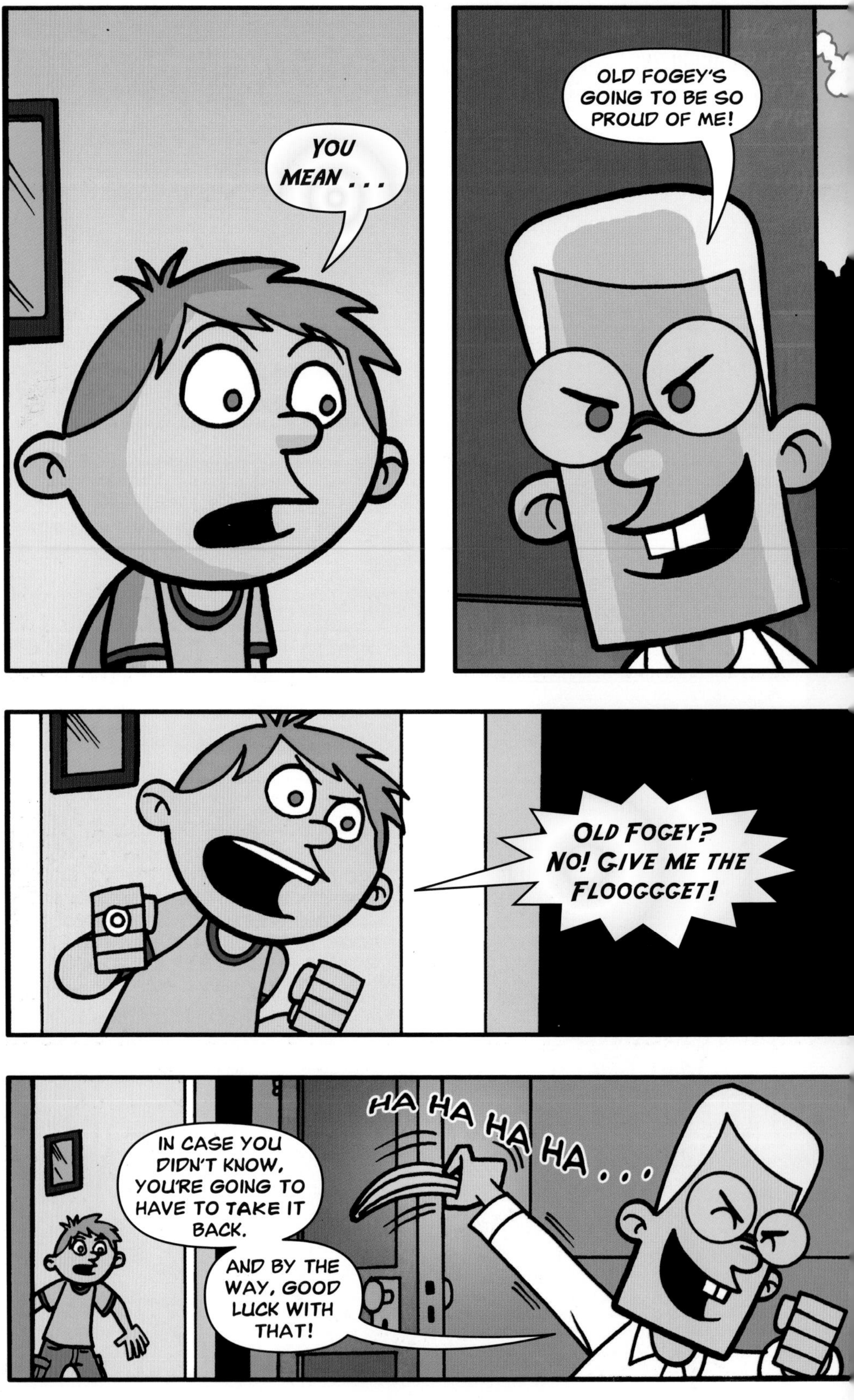
YOU MEAN . . .
OLD FOGEY'S GOING TO BE SO PROUD OF ME!
OLD FOGEY? NO! GIVE ME THE FLOOGGGET!
IN CASE YOU DIDN'T KNOW, YOU'RE GOING TO HAVE TO TAKE IT BACK.
AND BY THE WAY, GOOD LUCK WITH THAT!
HA HA HA HA . . .

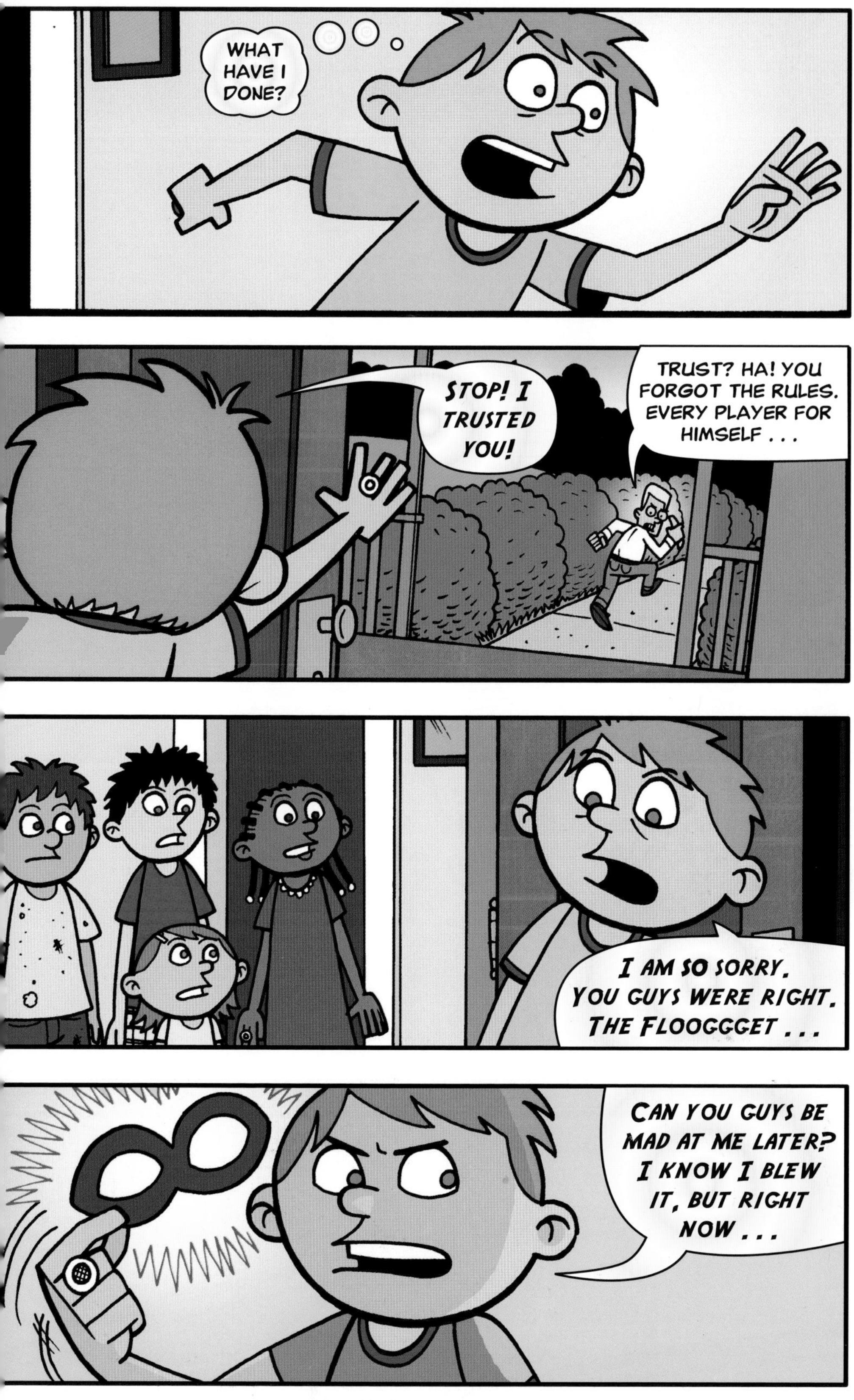
WHAT HAVE I DONE?
STOP! I TRUSTED YOU!
TRUST? HA! YOU FORGOT THE RULES. EVERY PLAYER FOR HIMSELF . . .
I AM SO SORRY. YOU GUYS WERE RIGHT. THE FLOOGGGET . . .
CAN YOU GUYS BE MAD AT ME LATER? I KNOW I BLEW IT, BUT RIGHT NOW . . .

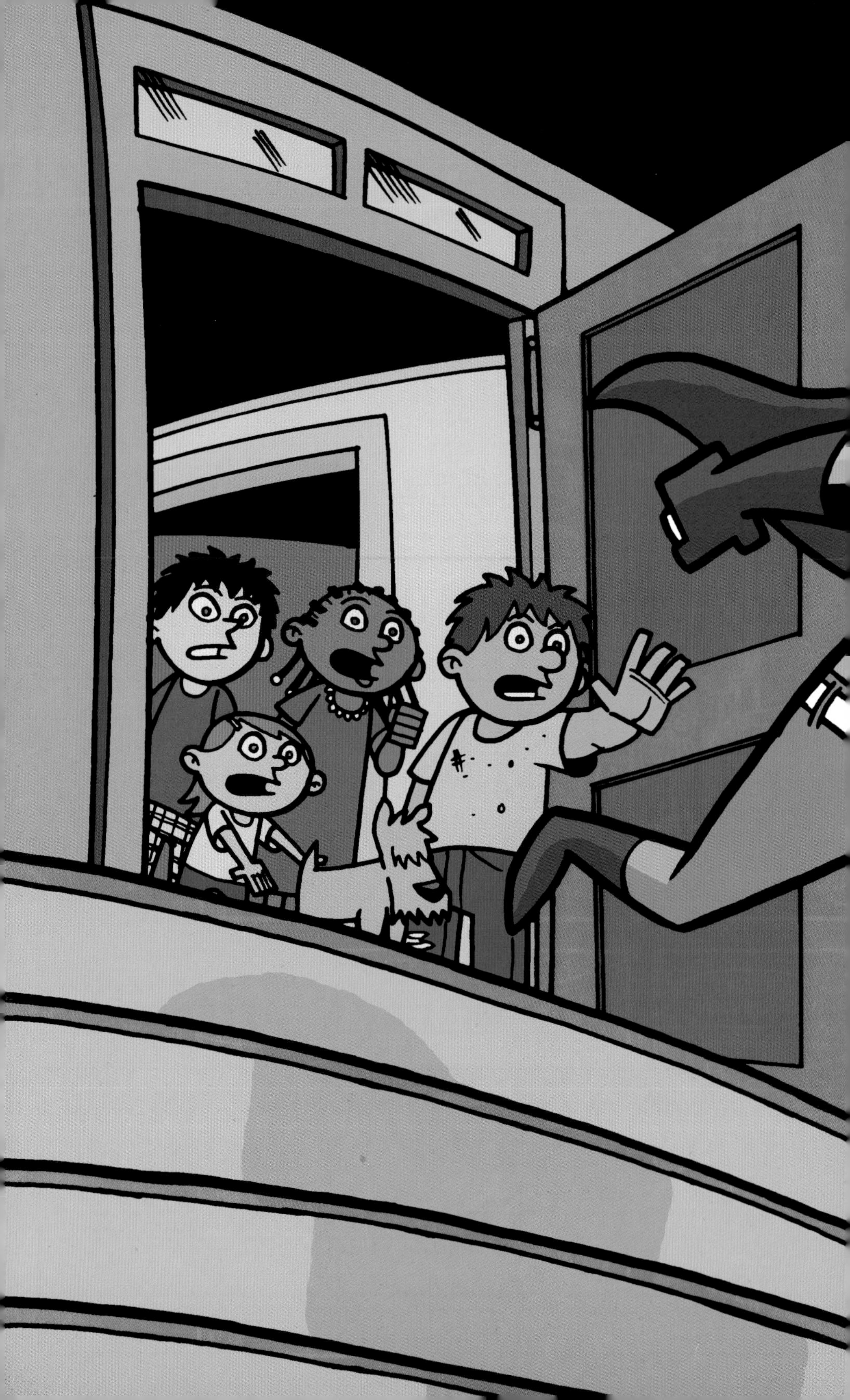

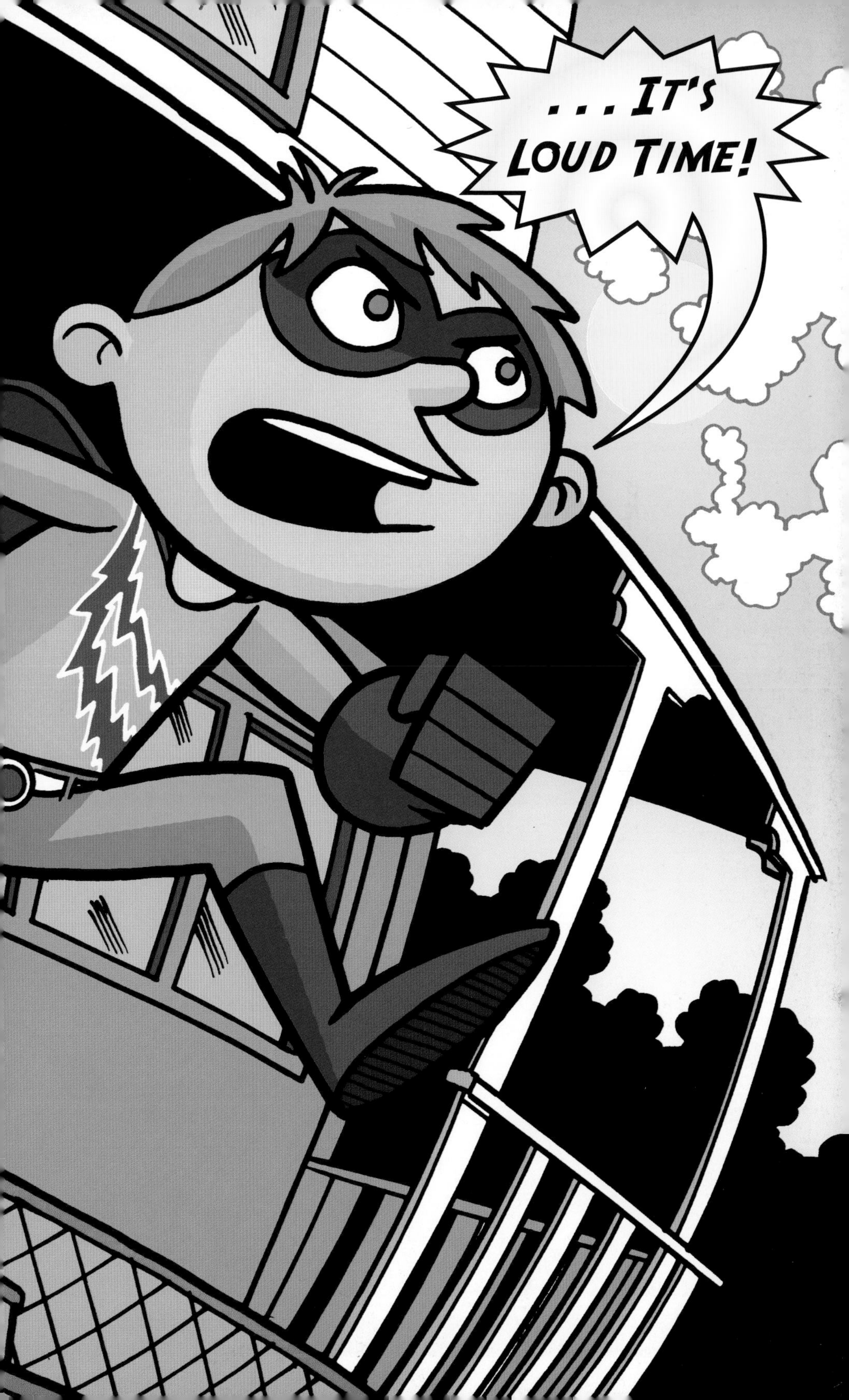
. . . IT'S LOUD TIME!

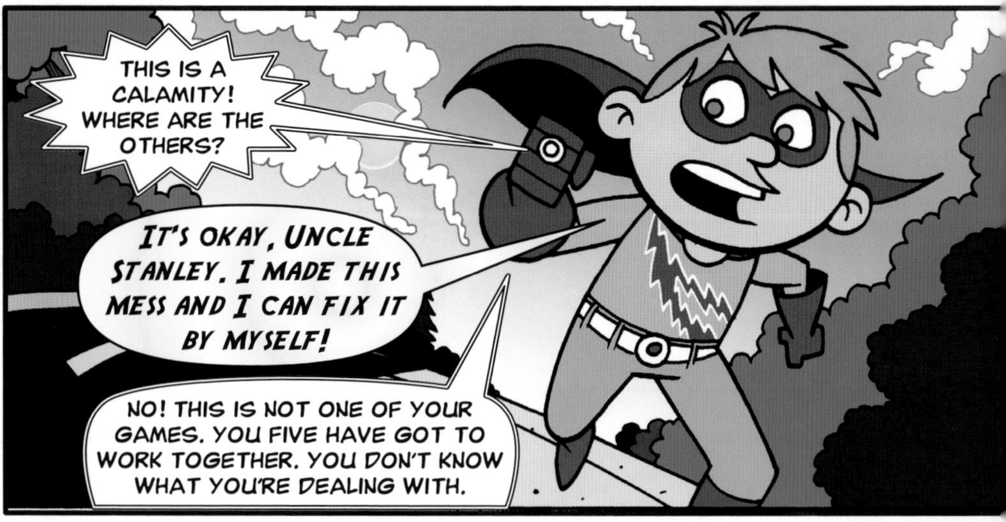
THIS IS A CALAMITY! WHERE ARE THE OTHERS?
IT'S OKAY, UNCLE STANLEY. I MADE THIS MESS AND I CAN FIX IT BY MYSELF!
NO! THIS IS NOT ONE OF YOUR GAMES. YOU FIVE HAVE GOT TO WORK TOGETHER. YOU DON'T KNOW WHAT YOU'RE DEALING WITH.

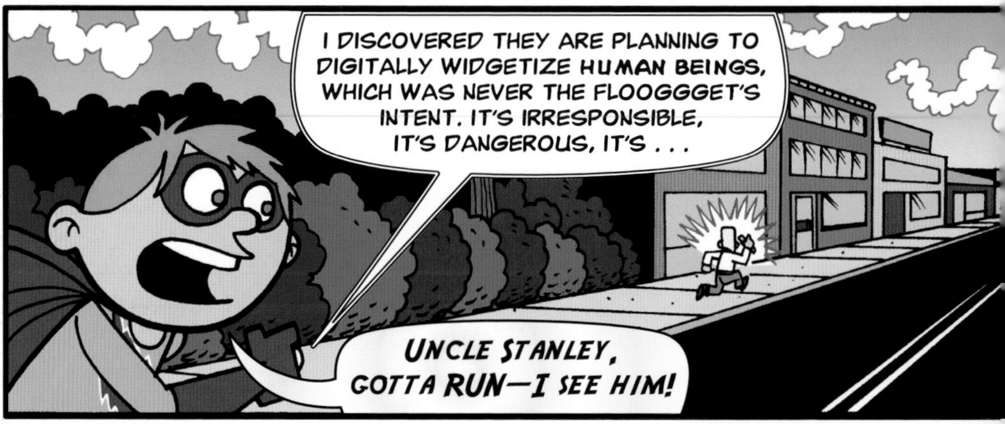
I DISCOVERED THEY ARE PLANNING TO DIGITALLY WIDGETIZE HUMAN BEINGS, WHICH WAS NEVER THE FLOOGGGET'S INTENT. IT'S IRRESPONSIBLE, IT'S DANGEROUS, IT'S . . .
UNCLE STANLEY, GOTTA RUN—I SEE HIM!

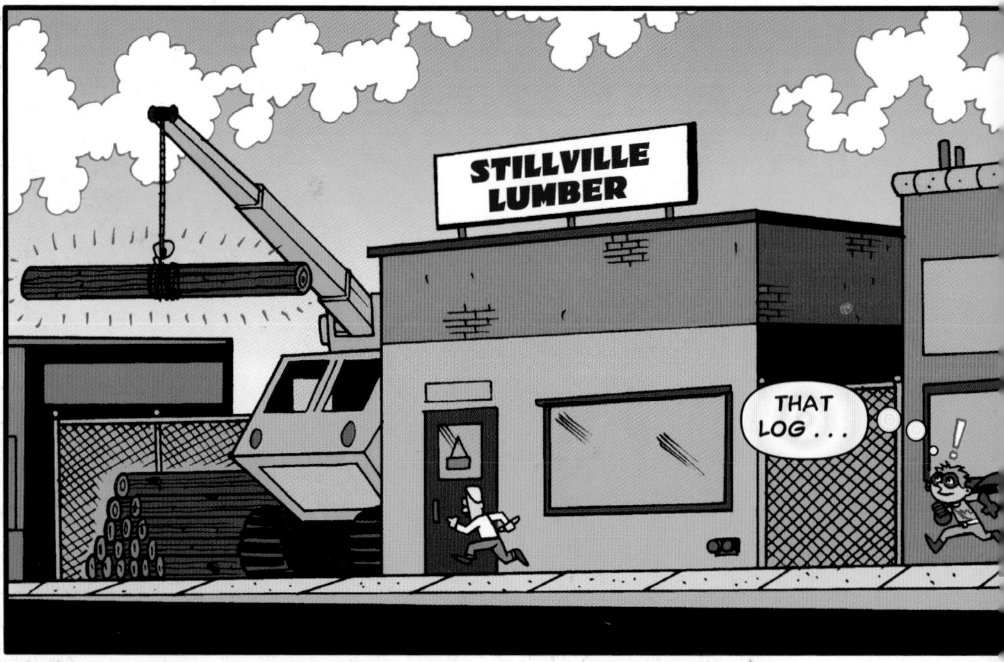
STILLVILLE LUMBER
THAT LOG . . .
!

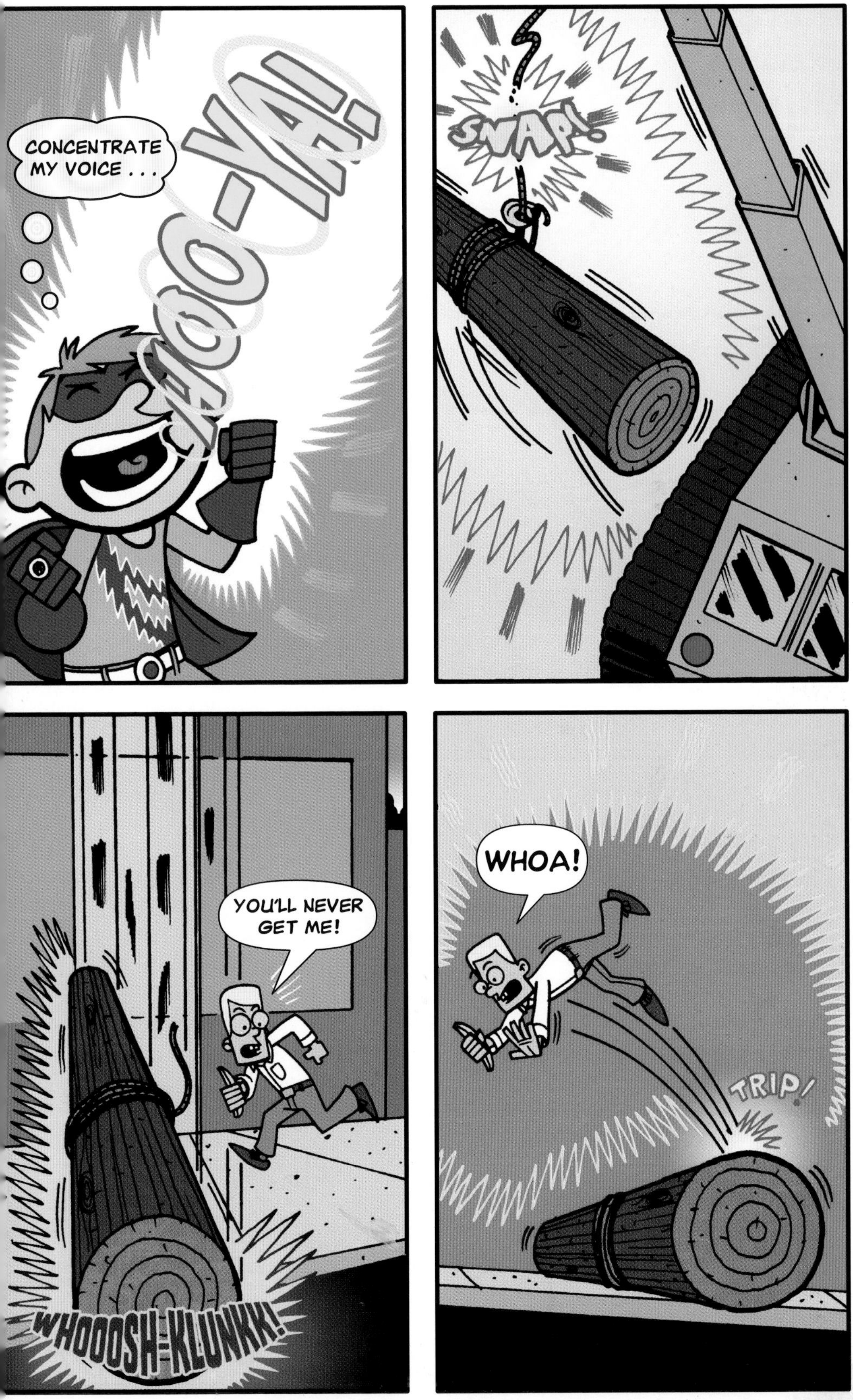
CONCENTRATE MY VOICE . . .
HOOO-YA!
SNAP!
YOU'LL NEVER GET ME!
WHOOOSH-KLUNKK!
WHOA!
TRIP!

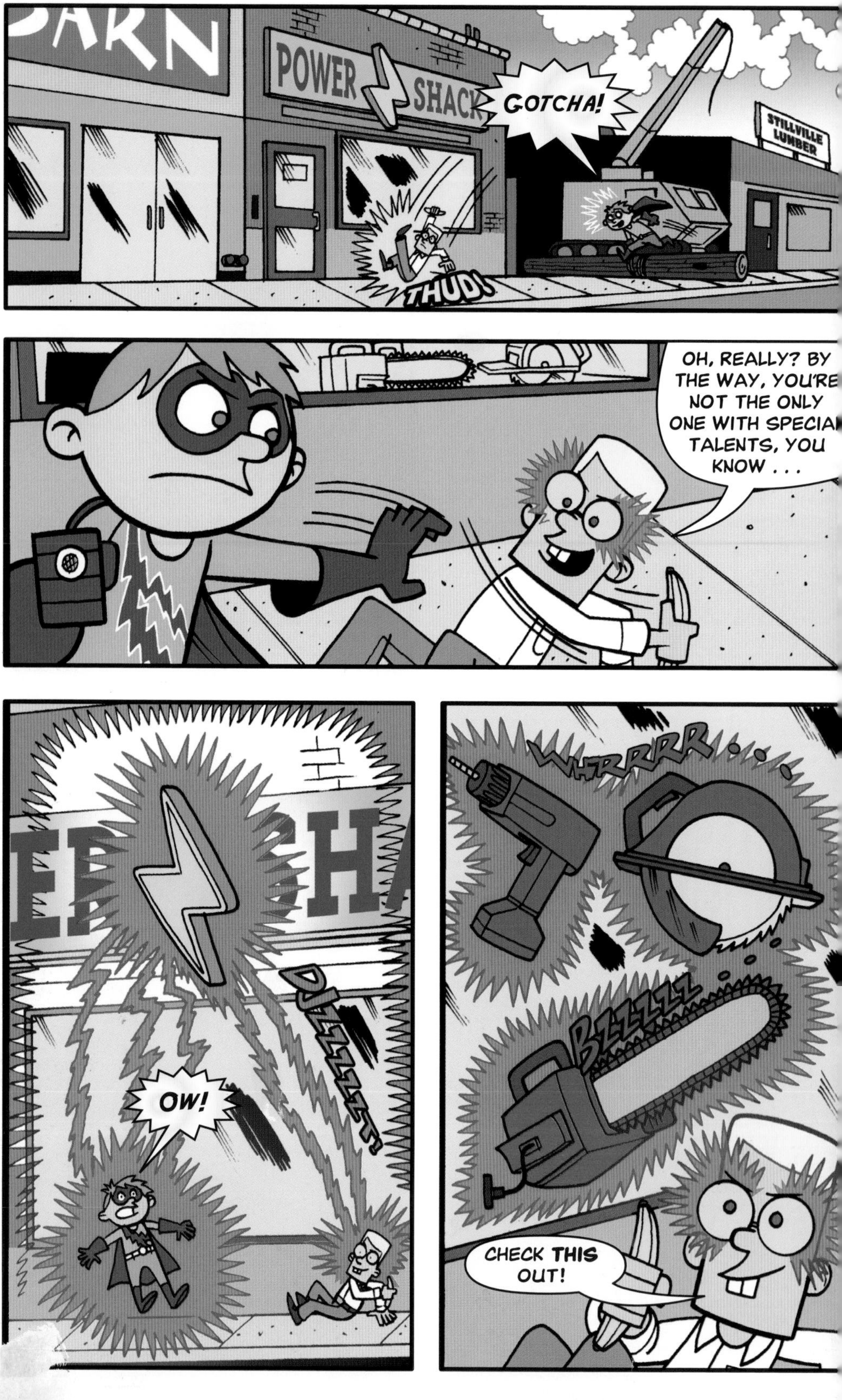
POWER SHACK
GOTCHA!
STILLVILLE LUMBER
THUD!
OH, REALLY? BY THE WAY, YOU'RE NOT THE ONLY ONE WITH SPECIAL TALENTS, YOU KNOW . . .
OW!
WHRRRR . . .
BZZZZZ
CHECK THIS OUT!

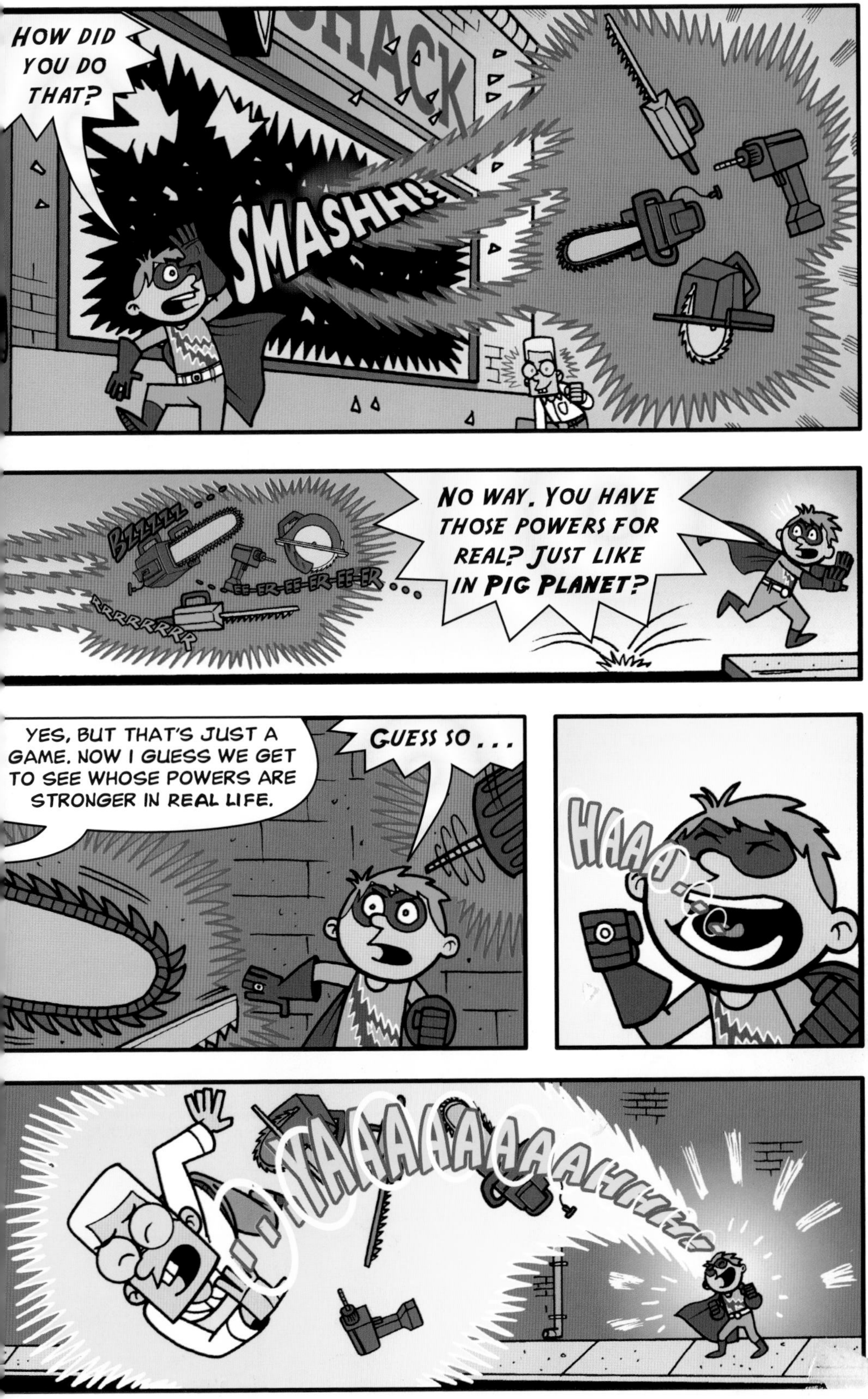
HOW DID YOU DO THAT?
SMASHH!
NO WAY. YOU HAVE THOSE POWERS FOR REAL? JUST LIKE IN PIG PLANET?
YES, BUT THAT'S JUST A GAME. NOW I GUESS WE GET TO SEE WHOSE POWERS ARE STRONGER IN REAL LIFE.
GUESS SO . . .

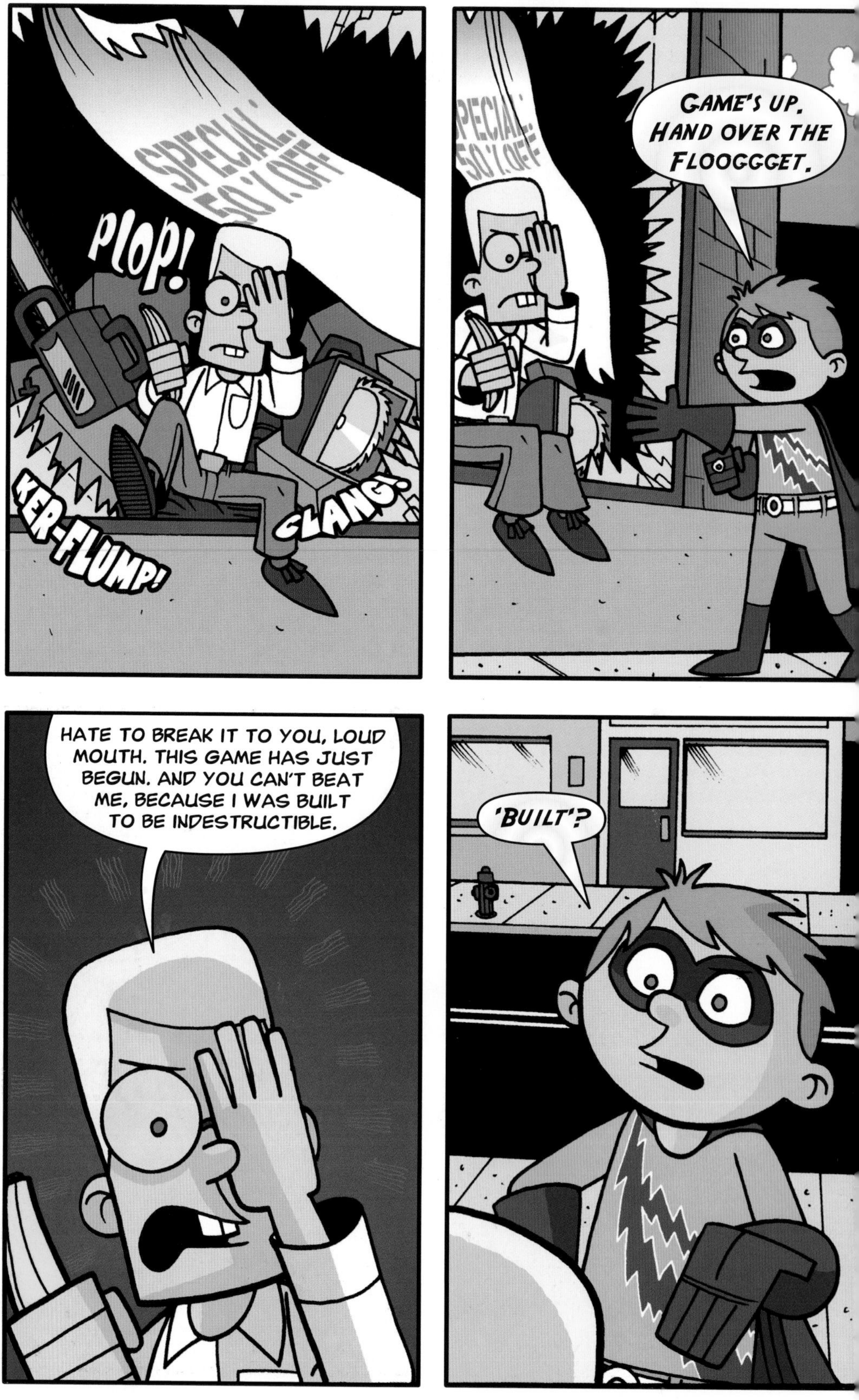
SPECIAL: 50% OFF
PLOP!
KER-FLUMP!
CLANG!
SPECIAL: 50% OFF
GAME'S UP. HAND OVER THE FLOOGGGET.
HATE TO BREAK IT TO YOU, LOUD MOUTH. THIS GAME HAS JUST BEGUN. AND YOU CAN'T BEAT ME, BECAUSE I WAS BUILT TO BE INDESTRUCTIBLE.
'BUILT'?

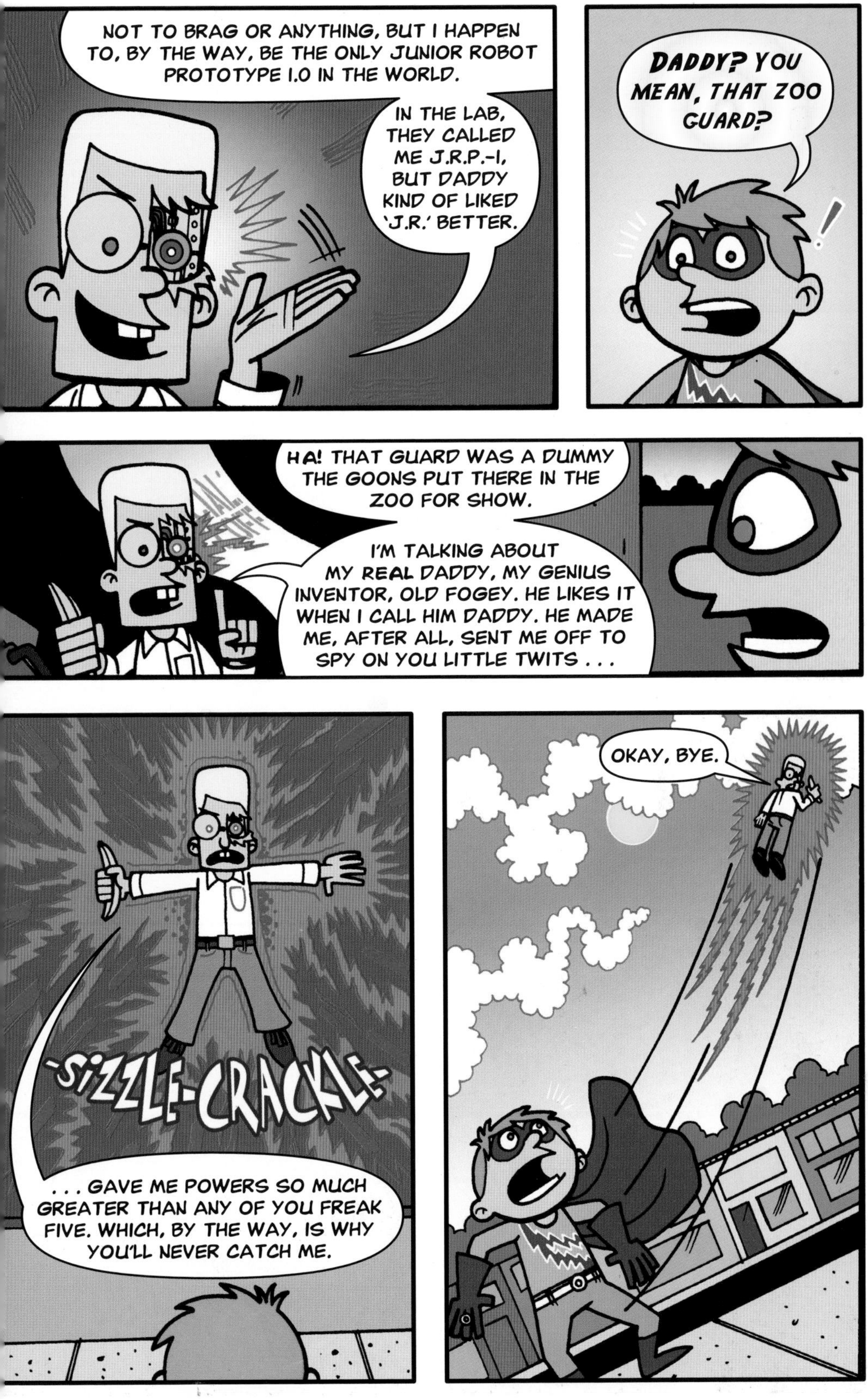
NOT TO BRAG OR ANYTHING, BUT I HAPPEN TO, BY THE WAY, BE THE ONLY JUNIOR ROBOT PROTOTYPE 1.0 IN THE WORLD.
IN THE LAB, THEY CALLED ME J.R.P.-1, BUT DADDY KIND OF LIKED 'J.R.' BETTER.
DADDY? YOU MEAN, THAT ZOO GUARD?
HA! THAT GUARD WAS A DUMMY THE GOONS PUT THERE IN THE ZOO FOR SHOW.
I'M TALKING ABOUT MY REAL DADDY, MY GENIUS INVENTOR, OLD FOGEY. HE LIKES IT WHEN I CALL HIM DADDY. HE MADE ME, AFTER ALL, SENT ME OFF TO SPY ON YOU LITTLE TWITS . . .
-SIZZLE-CRACKLE-
. . . GAVE ME POWERS SO MUCH GREATER THAN ANY OF YOU FREAK FIVE. WHICH, BY THE WAY, IS WHY YOU'LL NEVER CATCH ME.
OKAY, BYE.

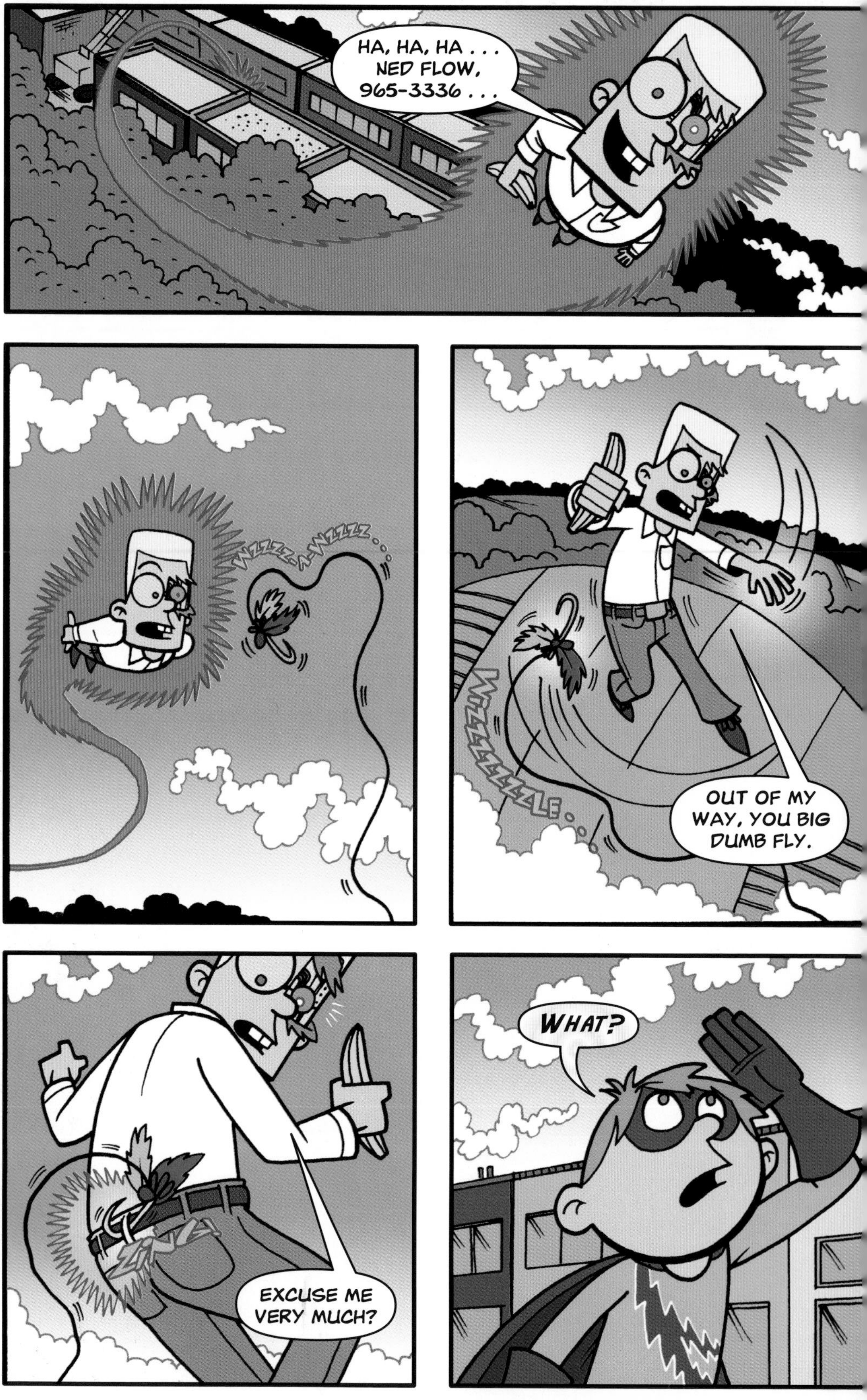

HA, HA, HA . . .
NED FLOW,
965-3336 . . .
WZZZZ-A-WZZZZ . . .
WIZZZZZLE . . .
OUT OF MY WAY, YOU BIG DUMB FLY.
EXCUSE ME VERY MUCH?
WHAT?

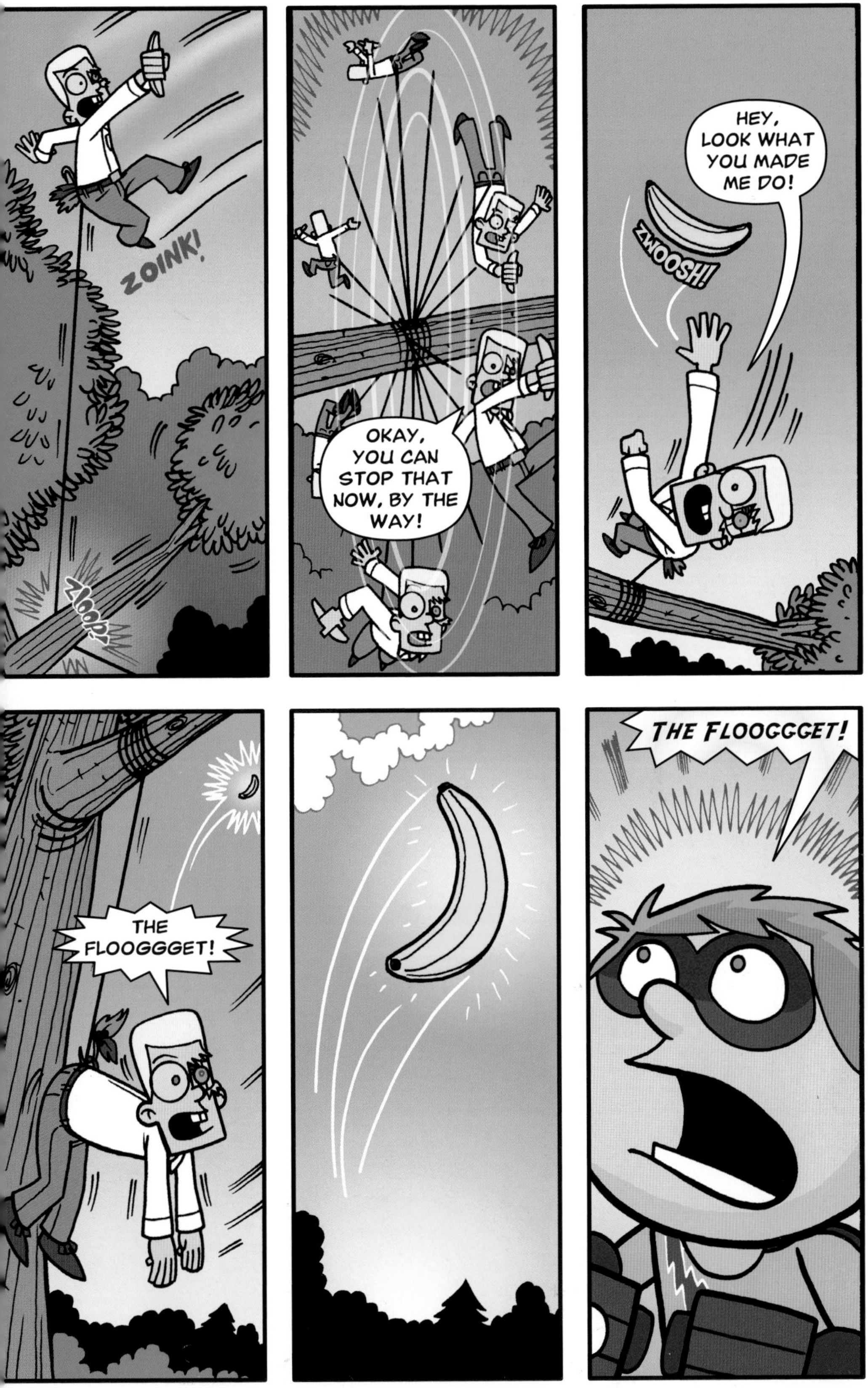
ZOINK!
ZLOOP!
OKAY, YOU CAN STOP THAT NOW, BY THE WAY!
HEY, LOOK WHAT YOU MADE ME DO!
ZWOOSH!
THE FLOOGGGET!
THE FLOOGGGET!

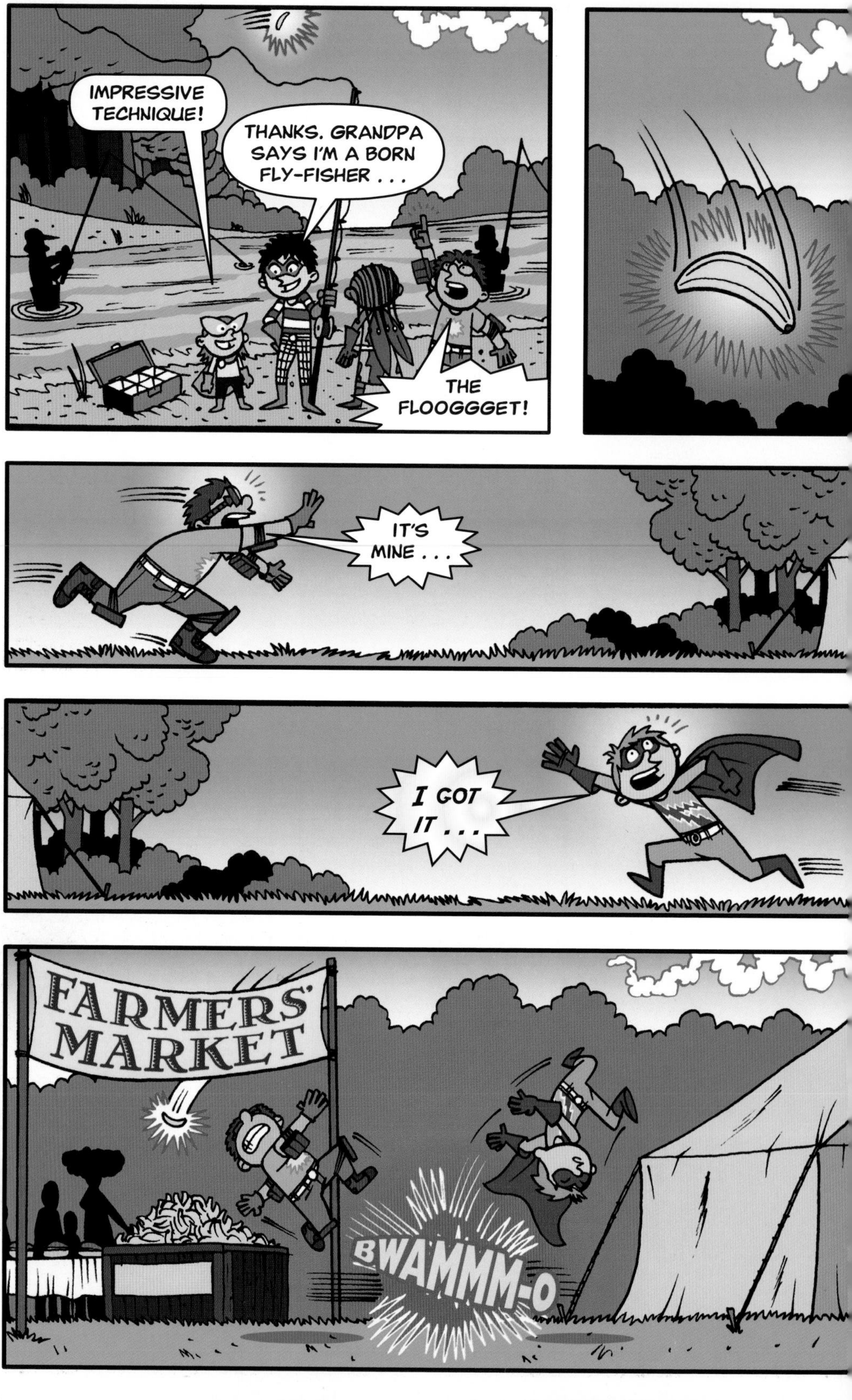
IMPRESSIVE TECHNIQUE!
THANKS. GRANDPA SAYS I'M A BORN FLY-FISHER . . .
THE FLOOGGGET!
IT'S MINE . . .
I GOT IT . . .
FARMERS' MARKET
BWAMMM-O

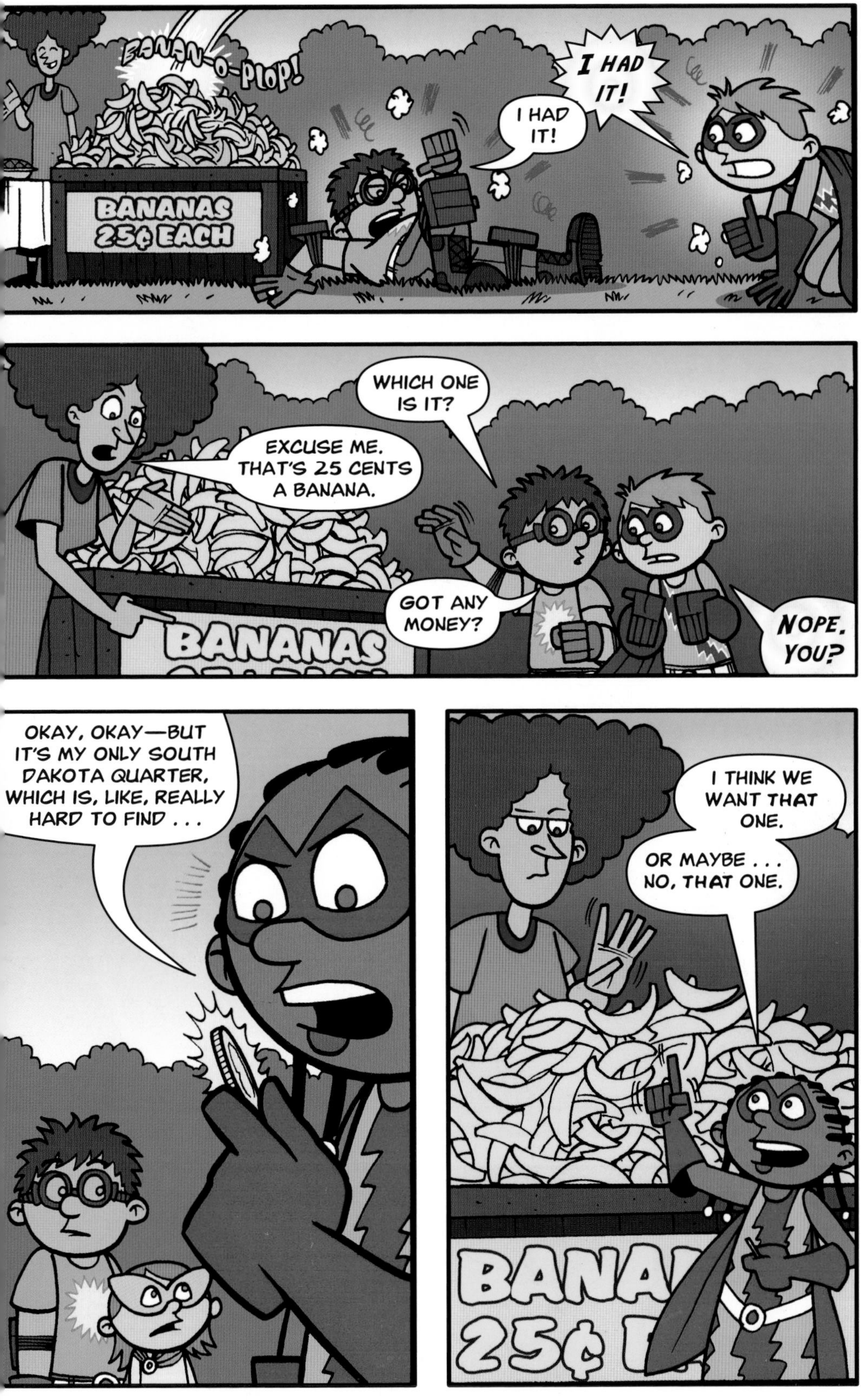
BANAN-O-PLOP!
BANANAS 25¢ EACH
I HAD IT!
I HAD IT!
WHICH ONE IS IT?
EXCUSE ME. THAT'S 25 CENTS A BANANA.
GOT ANY MONEY?
NOPE. YOU?
BANANAS
OKAY, OKAY—BUT IT'S MY ONLY SOUTH DAKOTA QUARTER, WHICH IS, LIKE, REALLY HARD TO FIND . . .
I THINK WE WANT THAT ONE.
OR MAYBE . . . NO, THAT ONE.

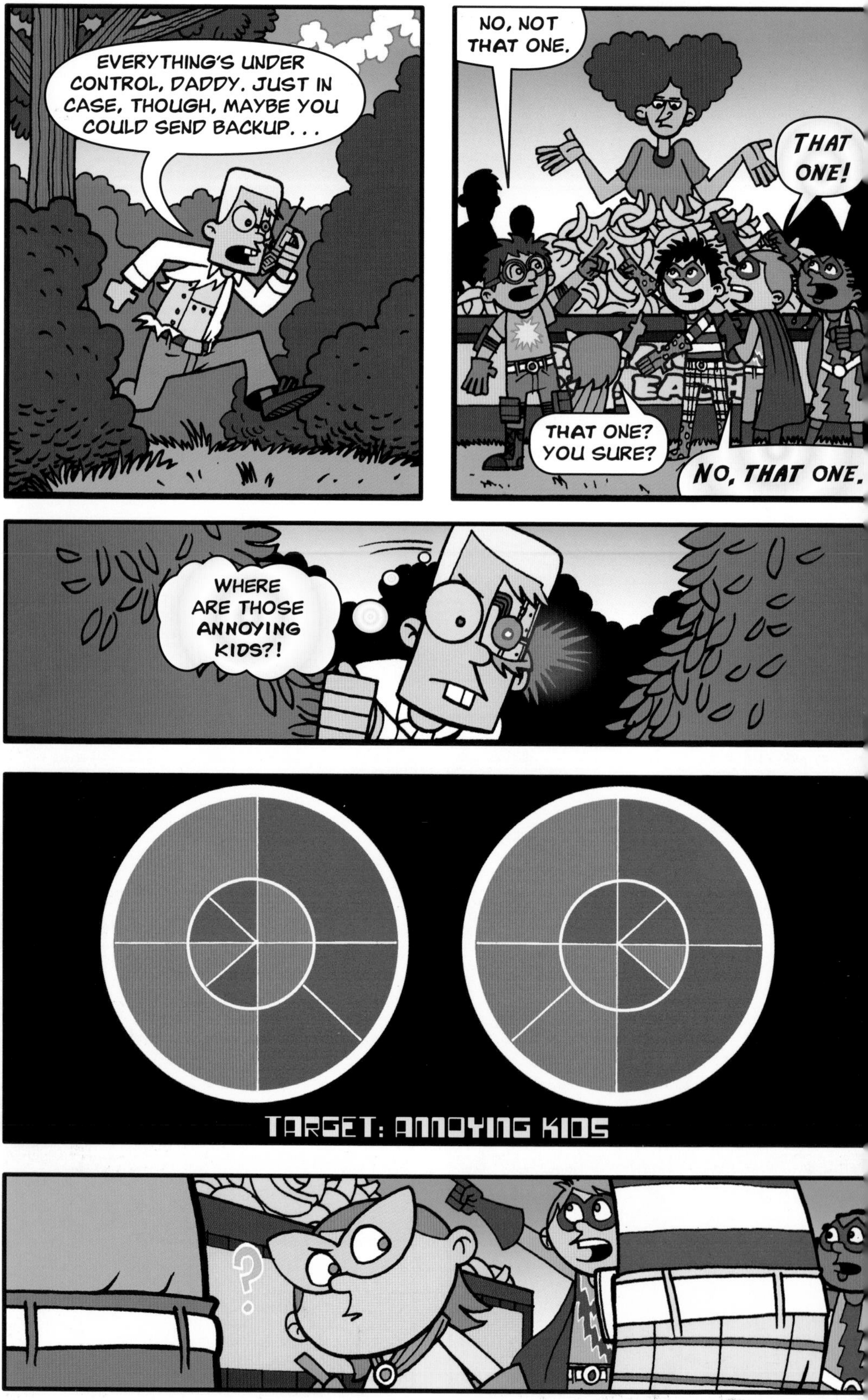
EVERYTHING'S UNDER CONTROL, DADDY. JUST IN CASE, THOUGH, MAYBE YOU COULD SEND BACKUP. . .
NO, NOT THAT ONE.
THAT ONE!
THAT ONE? YOU SURE?
NO, THAT ONE.
WHERE ARE THOSE ANNOYING KIDS?!
TARGET: ANNOYING KIDS
?

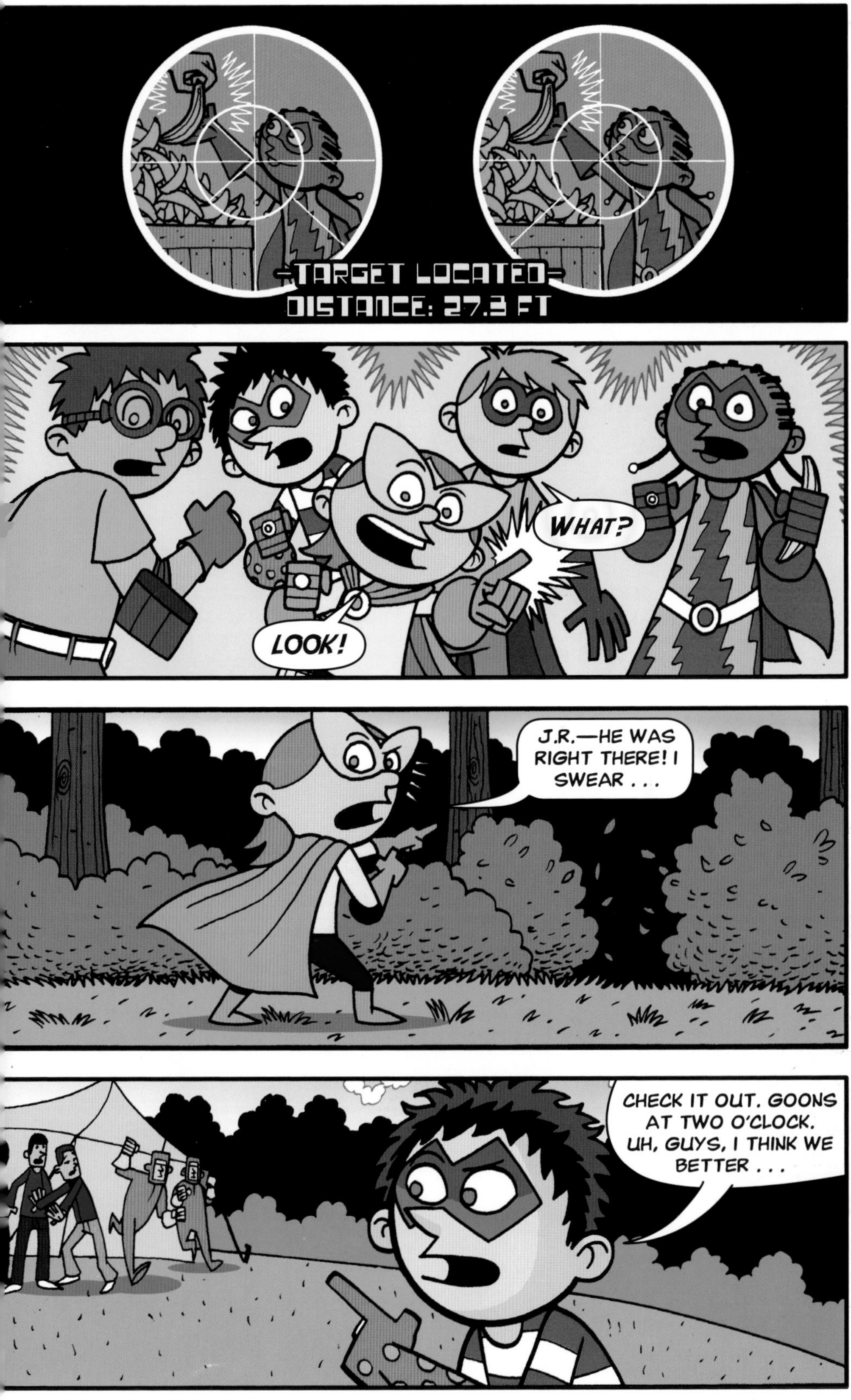
-TARGET LOCATED-
DISTANCE: 27.3 FT
LOOK!
WHAT?
J.R.—HE WAS RIGHT THERE! I SWEAR . . .
CHECK IT OUT. GOONS AT TWO O'CLOCK. UH, GUYS, I THINK WE BETTER . . .

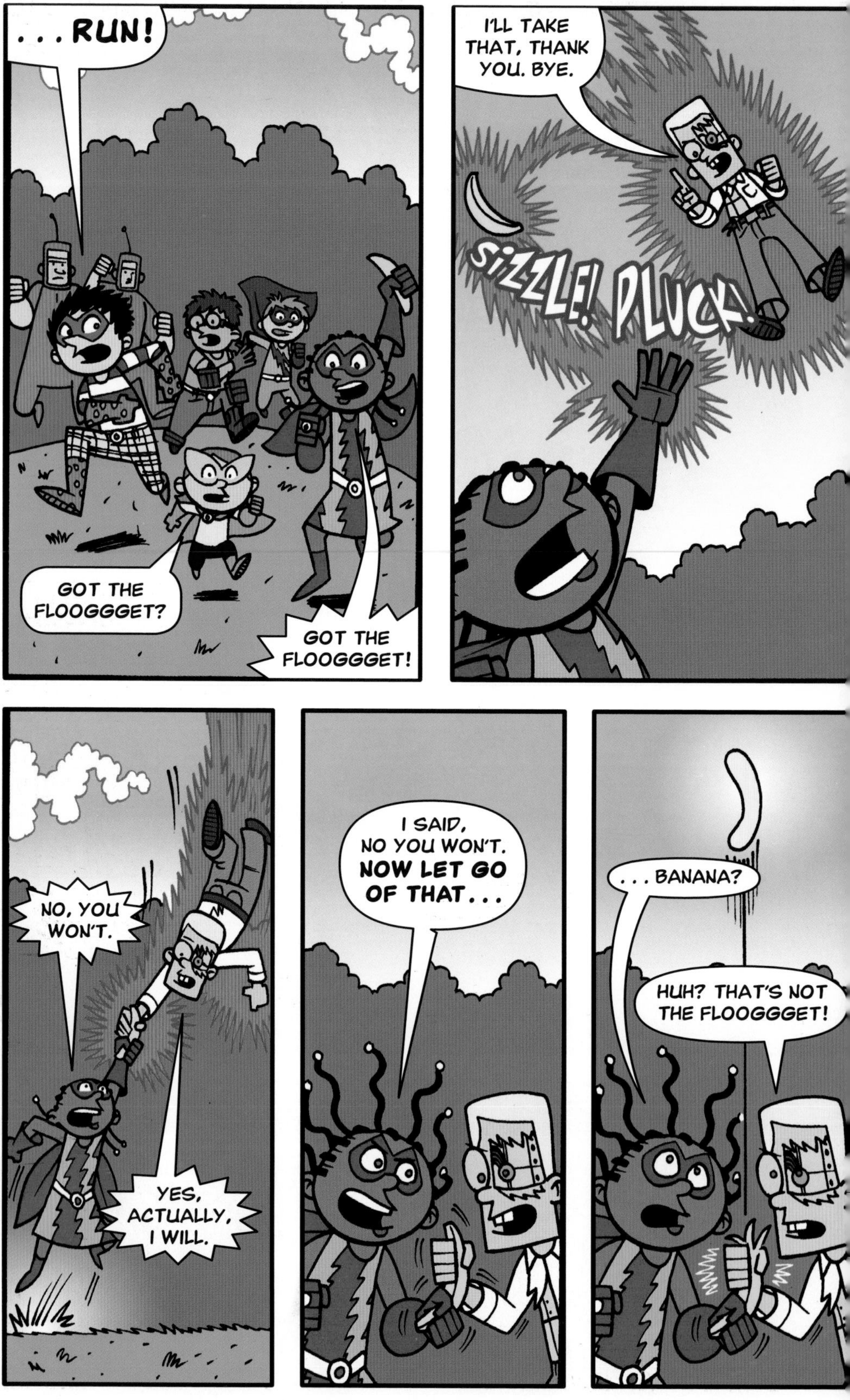
. . . RUN!
GOT THE FLOOGGGET?
GOT THE FLOOGGGET!
I'LL TAKE THAT, THANK YOU. BYE.
SIZZLE! PLUCK!
NO, YOU WON'T.
YES, ACTUALLY, I WILL.
I SAID, NO YOU WON'T. NOW LET GO OF THAT . . .
. . . BANANA?
HUH? THAT'S NOT THE FLOOGGGET!

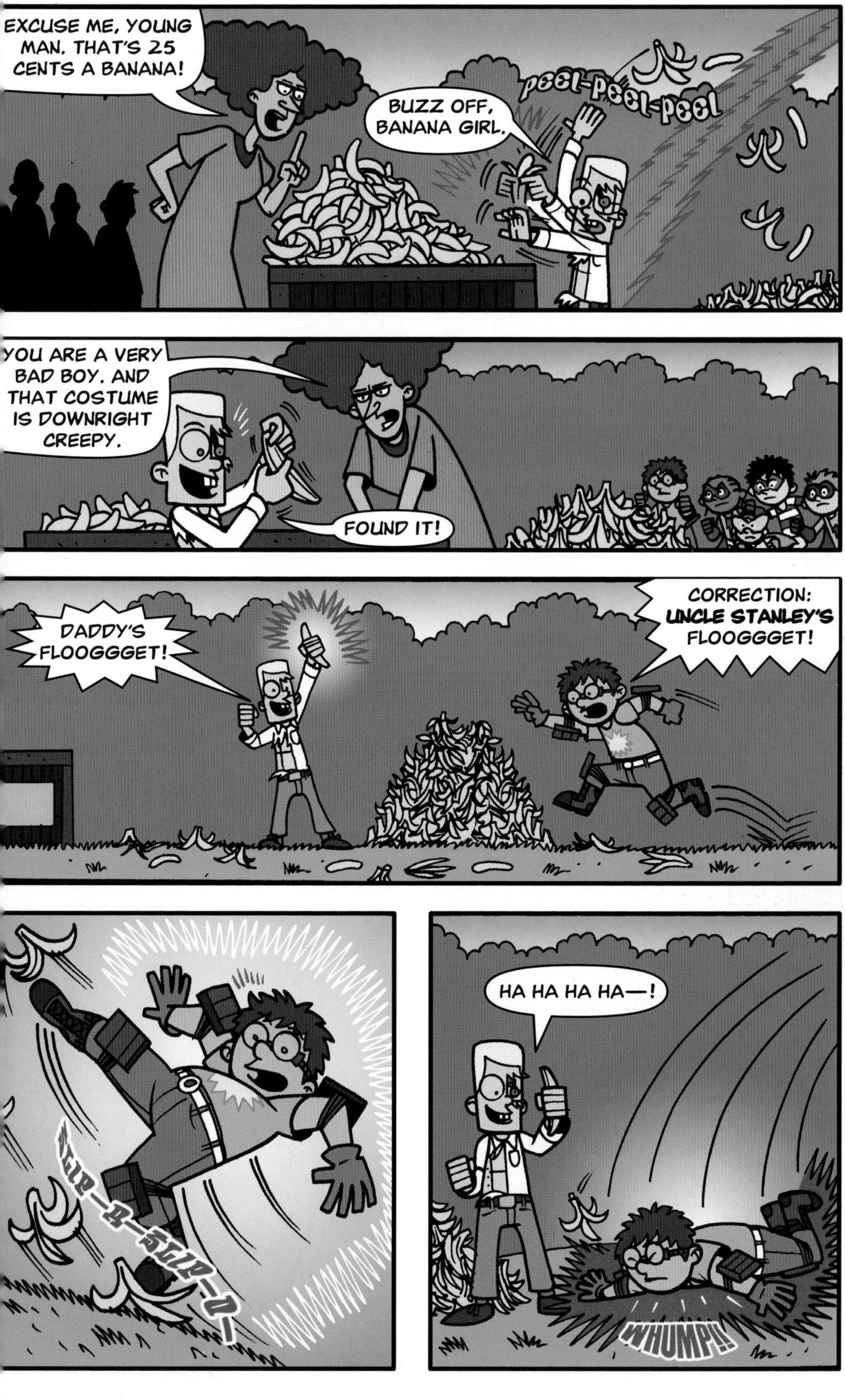
EXCUSE ME, YOUNG MAN. THAT'S 25 CENTS A BANANA!
BUZZ OFF, BANANA GIRL.
PEEL-PEEL-PEEL
YOU ARE A VERY BAD BOY. AND THAT COSTUME IS DOWNRIGHT CREEPY.
FOUND IT!
DADDY'S FLOOGGGET!
CORRECTION: UNCLE STANLEY'S FLOOGGGET!
SLIP—A—SLIP—O—
HA HA HA HA—!
WHUMP!!

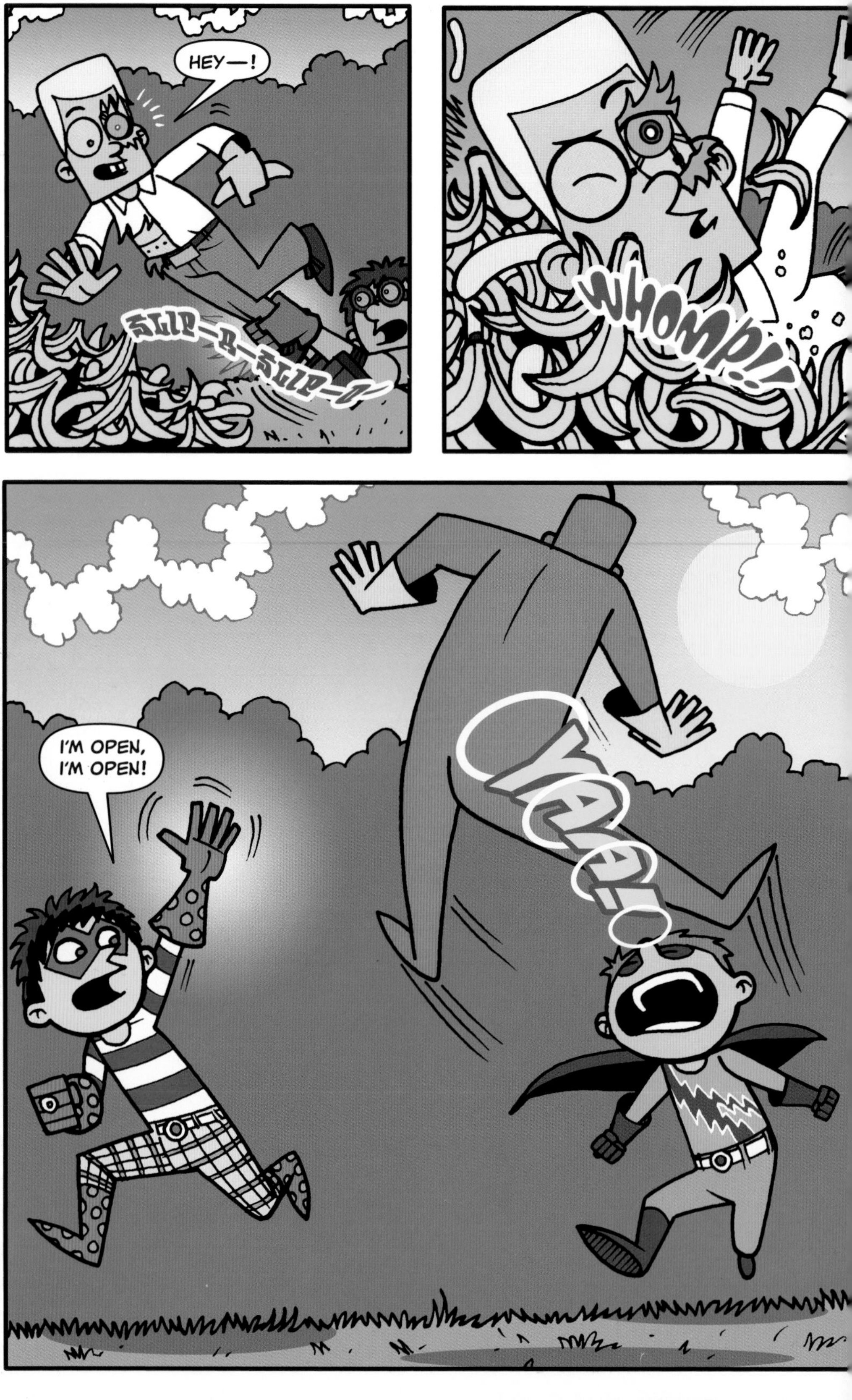
HEY—!
SLIP—A—SLIP—A
WHOMP!!
I'M OPEN, I'M OPEN!
YAAA!

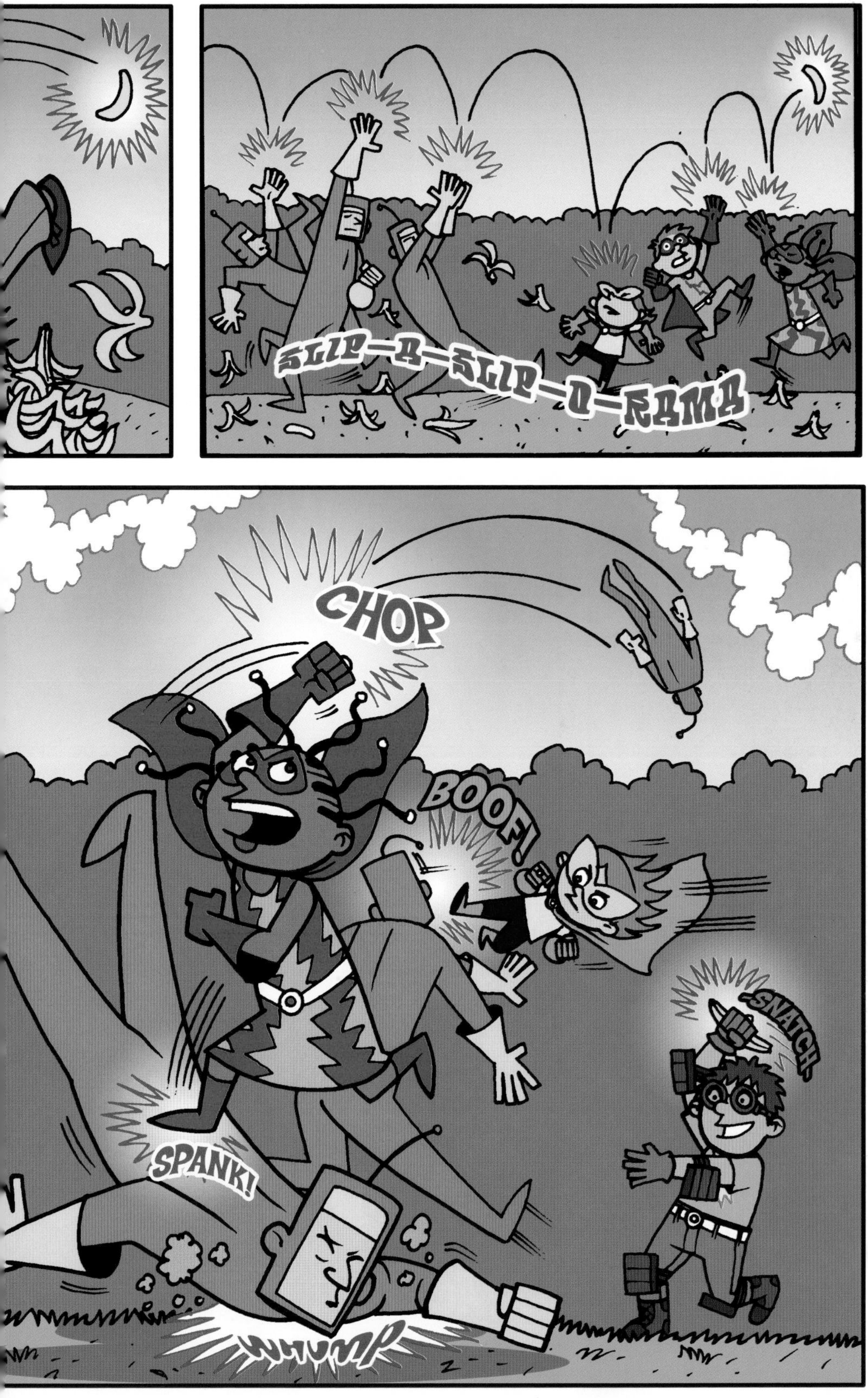
SLIP-A-SLIP-O-RAMA
CHOP
BOOF!
SNATCH
SPANK!
WHUMP

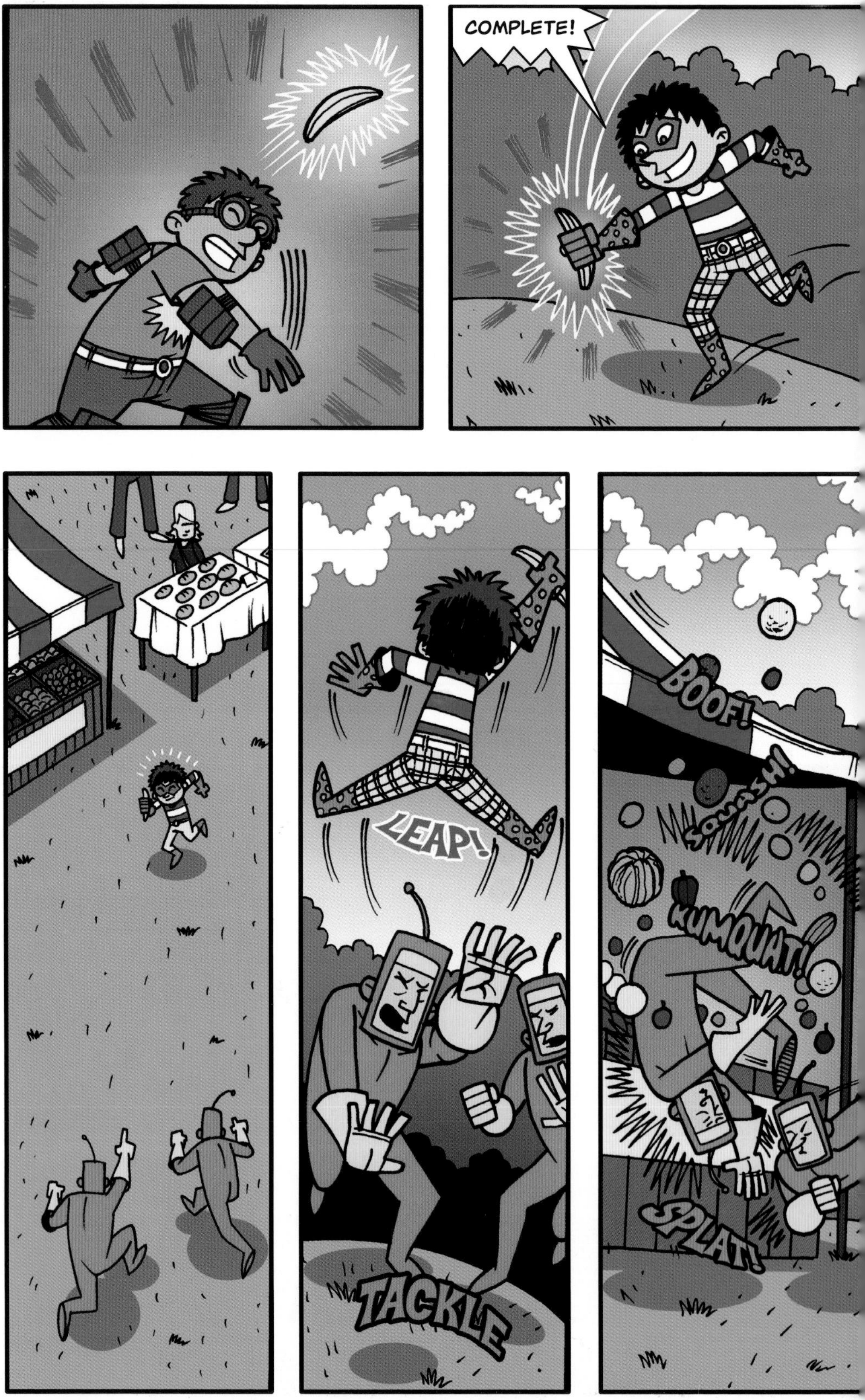
COMPLETE!
LEAP!
TACKLE
BOOF!
SQUASH!
KUMQUAT!
SPLAT!

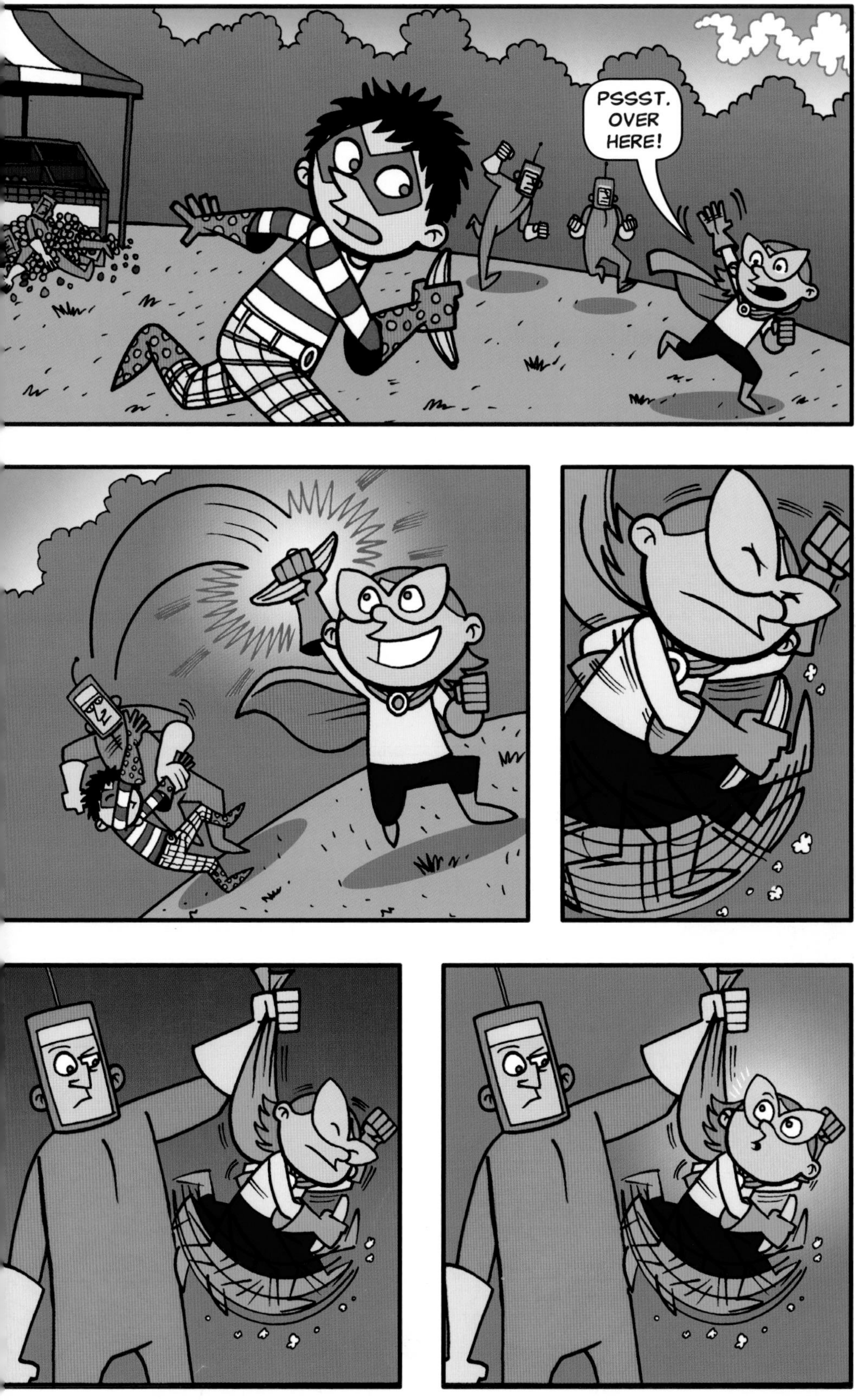
PSSST. OVER HERE!

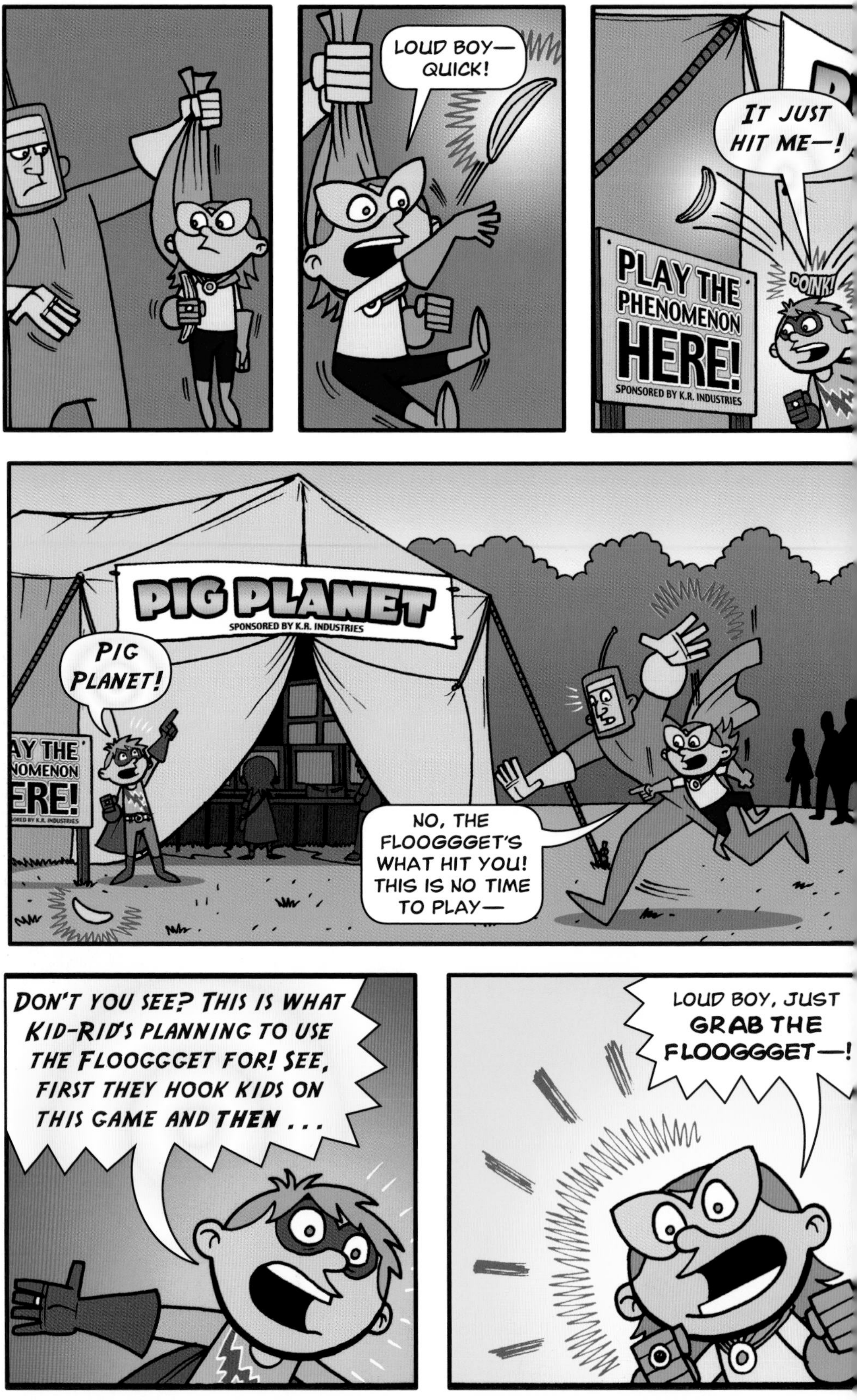
LOUD BOY—
QUICK!
IT JUST
HIT ME—!
PLAY THE PHENOMENON HERE!
SPONSORED BY K.R. INDUSTRIES
DOINK!
PIG PLANET
SPONSORED BY K.R. INDUSTRIES
PIG
PLANET!
NO, THE FLOOGGGET'S WHAT HIT YOU! THIS IS NO TIME TO PLAY—
DON'T YOU SEE? THIS IS WHAT KID-RID'S PLANNING TO USE THE FLOOGGGET FOR! SEE, FIRST THEY HOOK KIDS ON THIS GAME AND THEN . . .
LOUD BOY, JUST GRAB THE FLOOGGGET—!

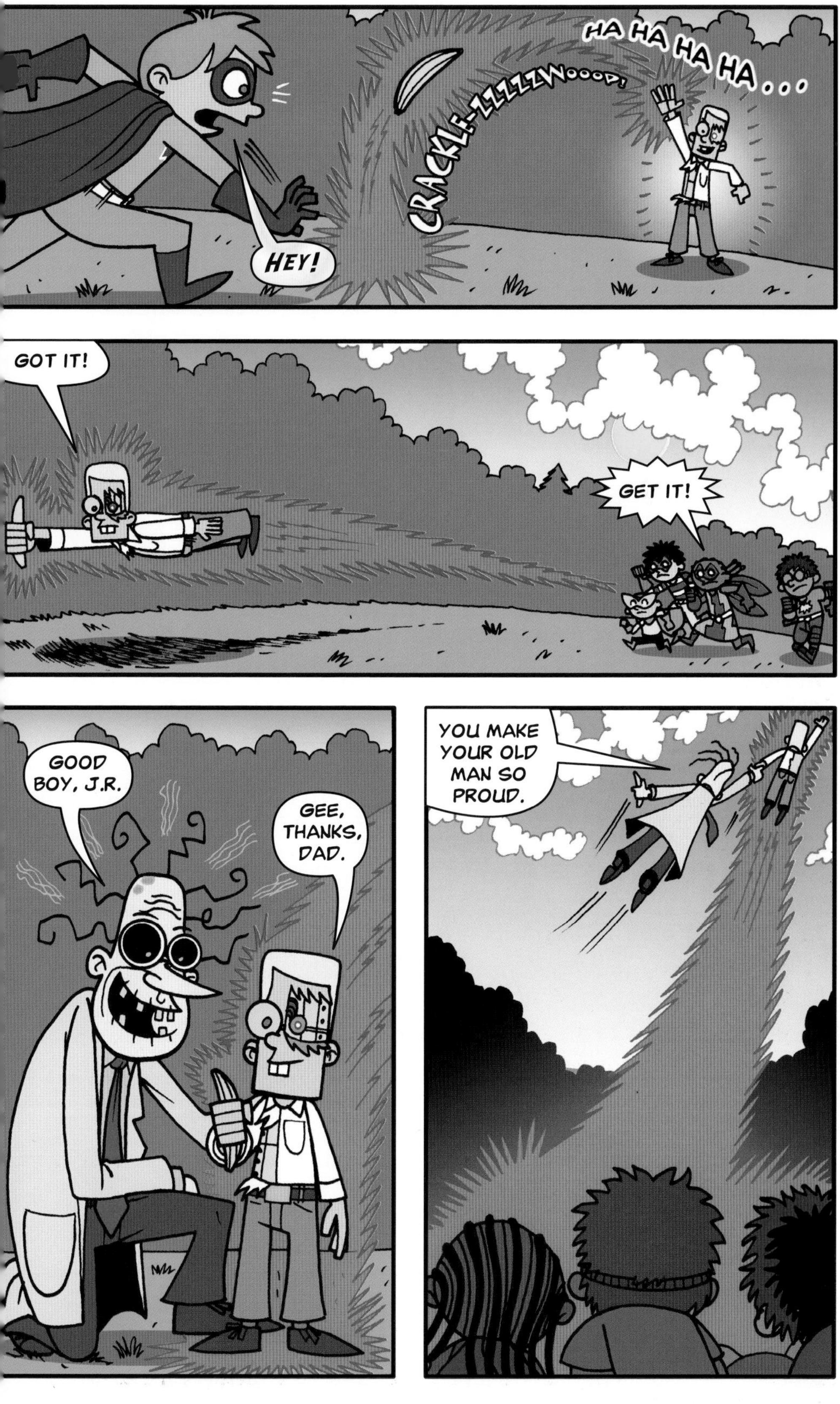
HEY!
CRACKLE-ZZZZZZWOOOP!
HA HA HA HA...
GOT IT!
GET IT!
GOOD BOY, J.R.
GEE, THANKS, DAD.
YOU MAKE YOUR OLD MAN SO PROUD.

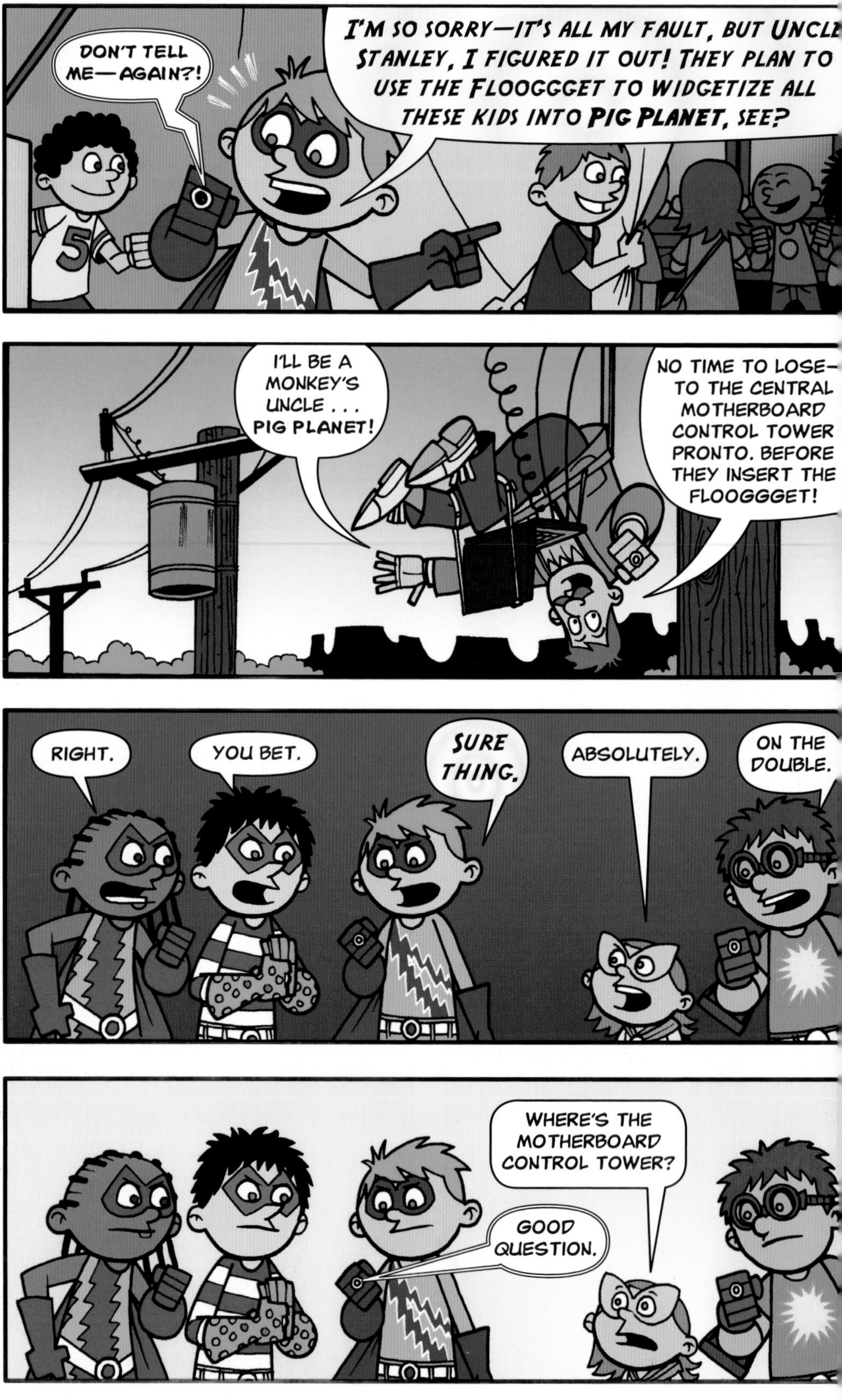
DON'T TELL ME—AGAIN?!
I'M SO SORRY—IT'S ALL MY FAULT, BUT UNCLE STANLEY, I FIGURED IT OUT! THEY PLAN TO USE THE FLOOGGGET TO WIDGETIZE ALL THESE KIDS INTO PIG PLANET, SEE?
I'LL BE A MONKEY'S UNCLE . . . PIG PLANET!
NO TIME TO LOSE—TO THE CENTRAL MOTHERBOARD CONTROL TOWER PRONTO. BEFORE THEY INSERT THE FLOOGGGET!
RIGHT.
YOU BET.
SURE THING.
ABSOLUTELY.
ON THE DOUBLE.
WHERE'S THE MOTHERBOARD CONTROL TOWER?
GOOD QUESTION.

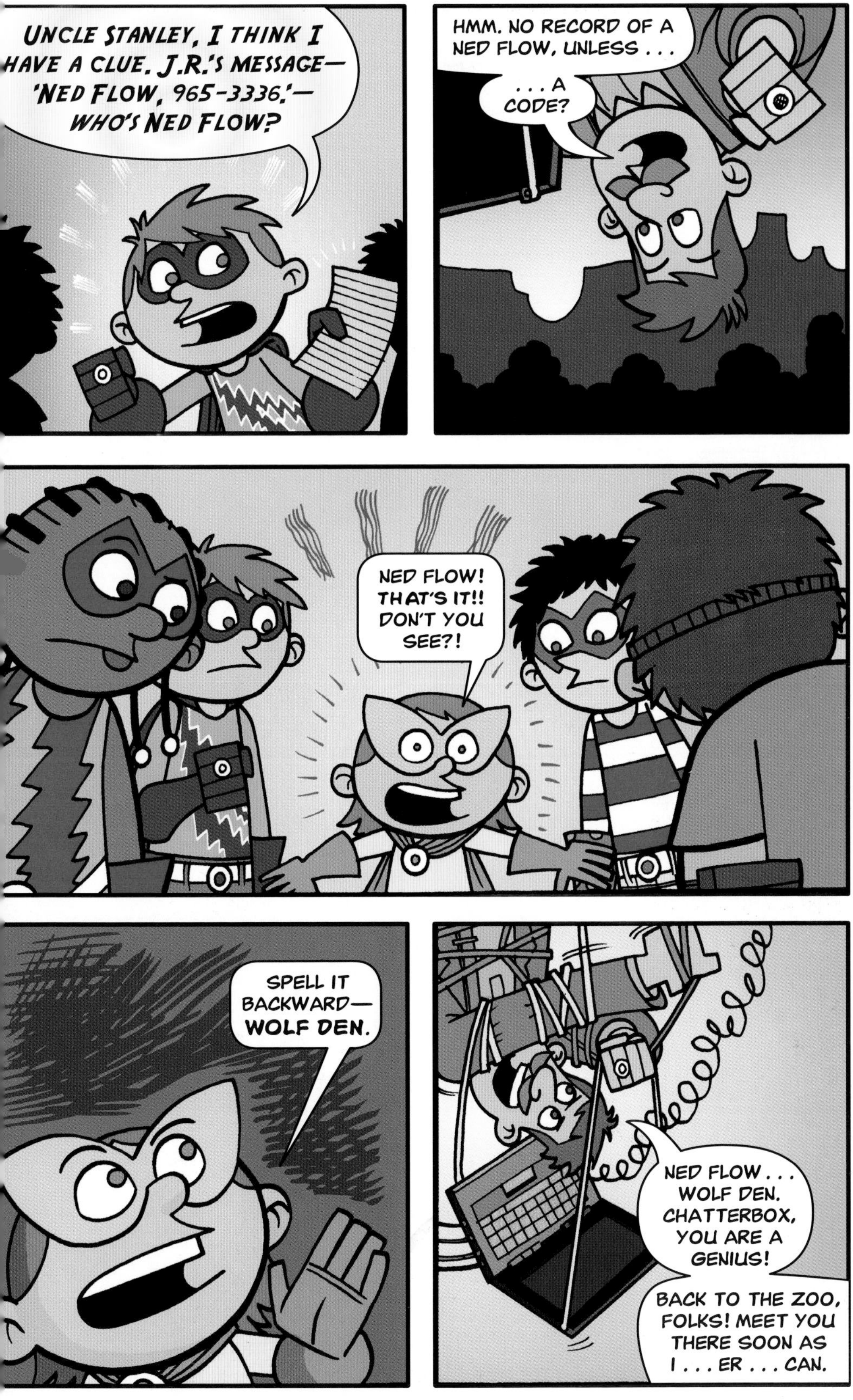
UNCLE STANLEY, I THINK I HAVE A CLUE. J.R.'S MESSAGE— 'NED FLOW, 965-3336.'— WHO'S NED FLOW?
HMM. NO RECORD OF A NED FLOW, UNLESS . . .
. . . A CODE?
NED FLOW! THAT'S IT!! DON'T YOU SEE?!
SPELL IT BACKWARD— WOLF DEN.
NED FLOW . . . WOLF DEN. CHATTERBOX, YOU ARE A GENIUS!
BACK TO THE ZOO, FOLKS! MEET YOU THERE SOON AS I . . . ER . . . CAN.

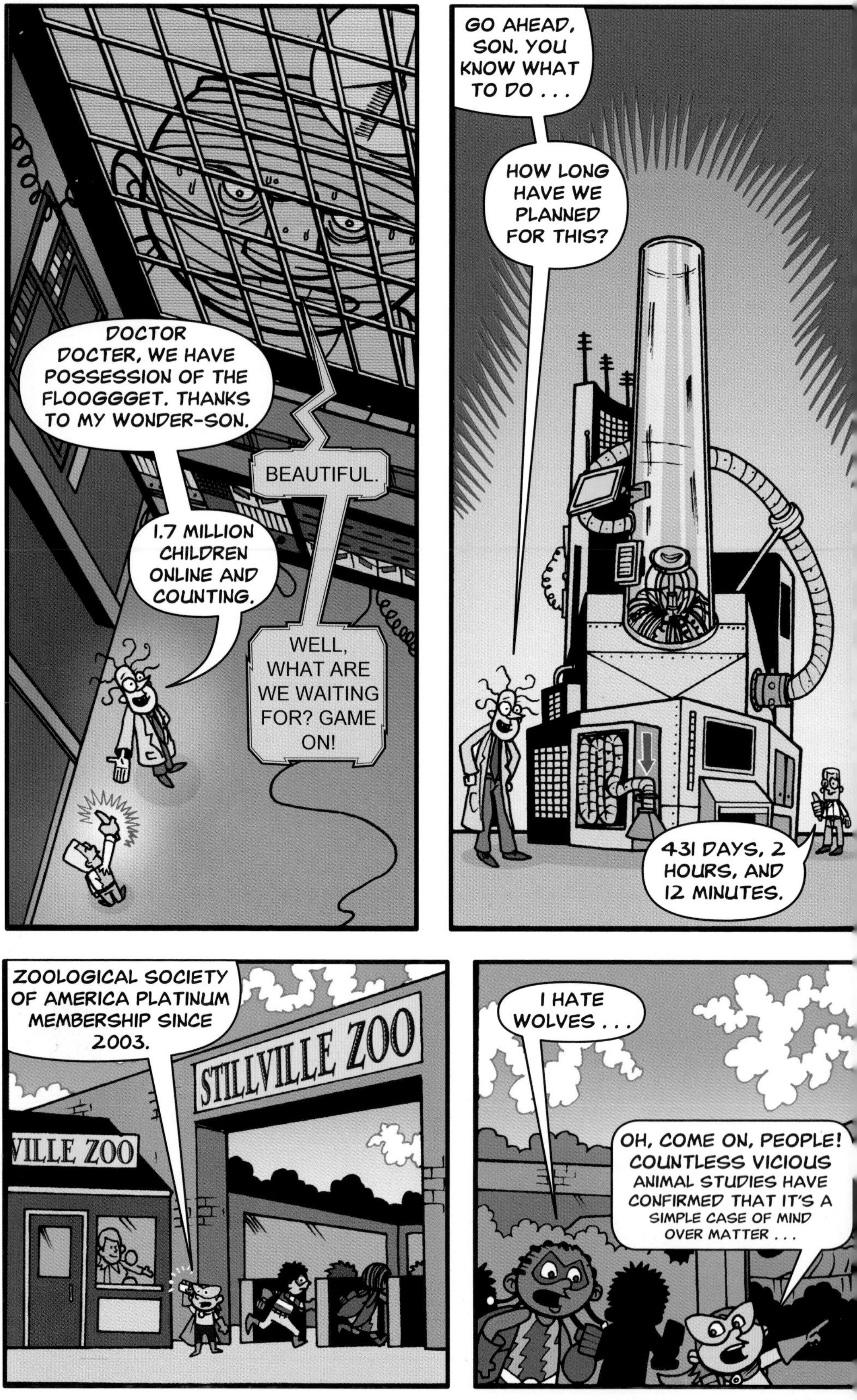
DOCTOR DOCTER, WE HAVE POSSESSION OF THE FLOOGGGET. THANKS TO MY WONDER-SON.
BEAUTIFUL.
1.7 MILLION CHILDREN ONLINE AND COUNTING.
WELL, WHAT ARE WE WAITING FOR? GAME ON!
GO AHEAD, SON. YOU KNOW WHAT TO DO . . .
HOW LONG HAVE WE PLANNED FOR THIS?
431 DAYS, 2 HOURS, AND 12 MINUTES.
ZOOLOGICAL SOCIETY OF AMERICA PLATINUM MEMBERSHIP SINCE 2003.
STILLVILLE ZOO
VILLE ZOO
I HATE WOLVES . . .
OH, COME ON, PEOPLE! COUNTLESS VICIOUS ANIMAL STUDIES HAVE CONFIRMED THAT IT'S A SIMPLE CASE OF MIND OVER MATTER . . .

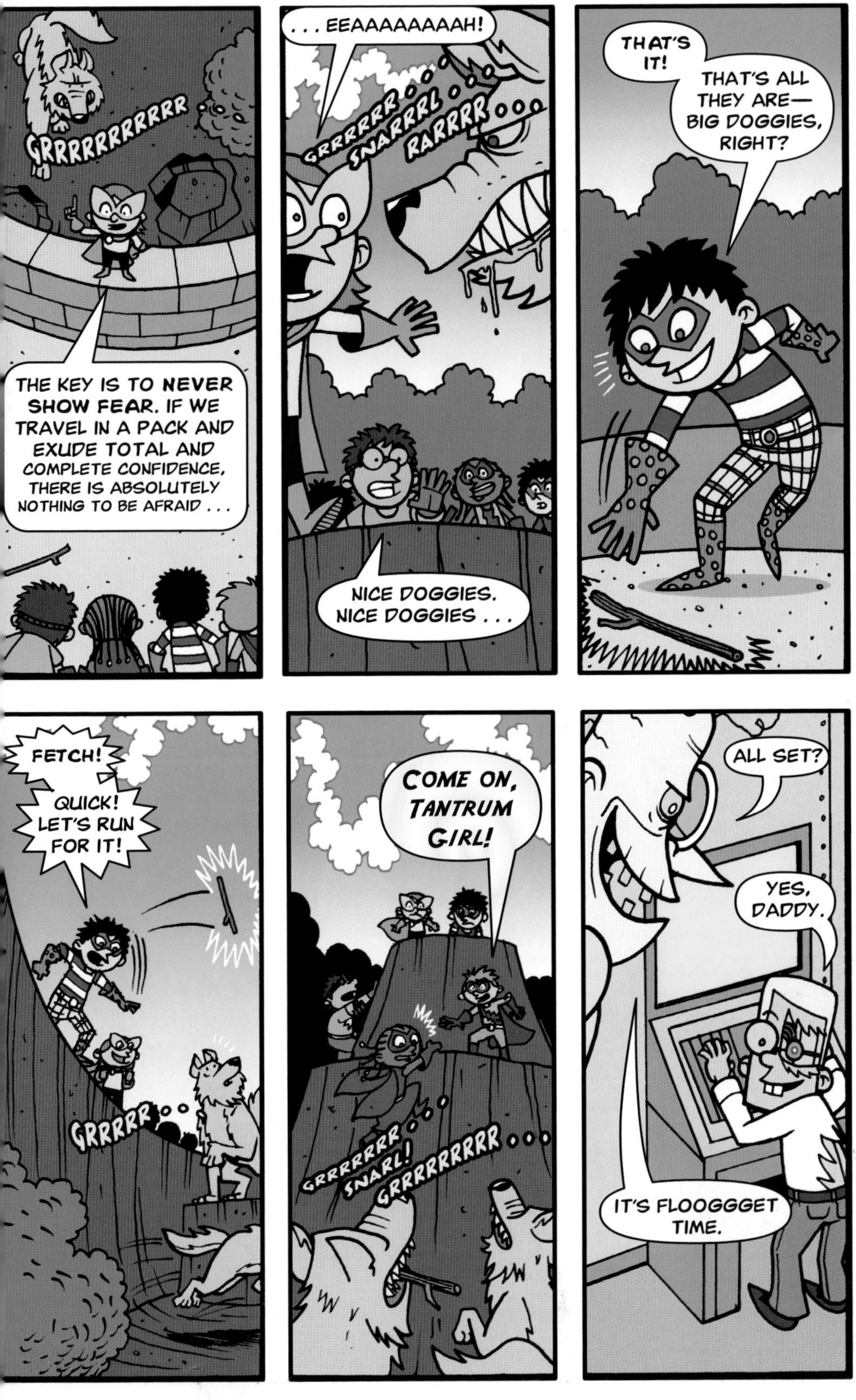
GRRRRRRRRRRR
THE KEY IS TO NEVER SHOW FEAR. IF WE TRAVEL IN A PACK AND EXUDE TOTAL AND COMPLETE CONFIDENCE, THERE IS ABSOLUTELY NOTHING TO BE AFRAID . . .
. . . EEAAAAAAAAAH!
GRRRRRR . . .
SNARRRL . . .
RARRRR . . .
NICE DOGGIES. NICE DOGGIES . . .
THAT'S IT!
THAT'S ALL THEY ARE— BIG DOGGIES, RIGHT?
FETCH!
QUICK! LET'S RUN FOR IT!
GRRRR . . .
COME ON, TANTRUM GIRL!
GRRRRRRR . . .
SNARL!
GRRRRRRRR . . .
ALL SET?
YES, DADDY.
IT'S FLOOGGGET TIME.

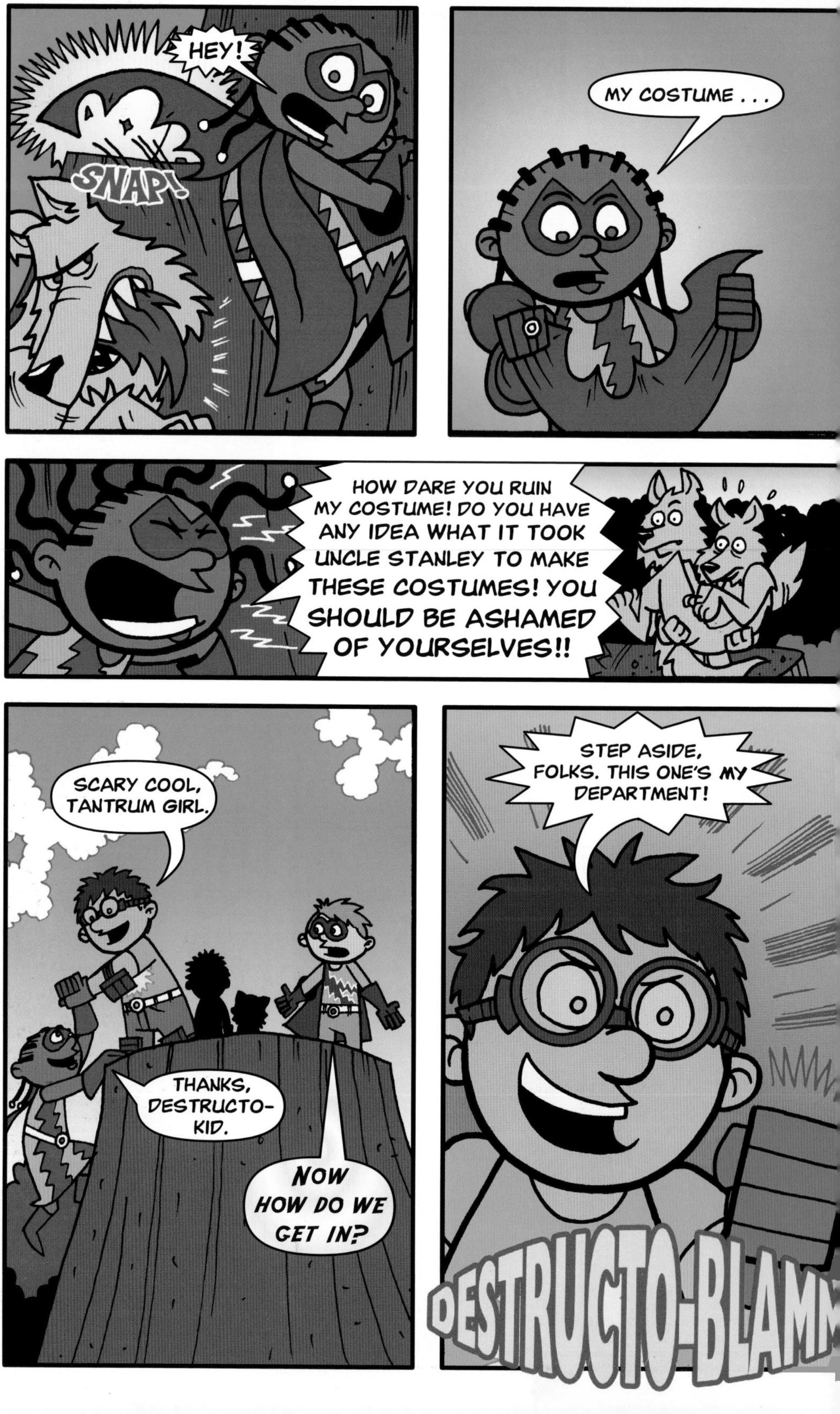
HEY!
SNAP!
MY COSTUME . . .
HOW DARE YOU RUIN MY COSTUME! DO YOU HAVE ANY IDEA WHAT IT TOOK UNCLE STANLEY TO MAKE THESE COSTUMES! YOU SHOULD BE ASHAMED OF YOURSELVES!!
SCARY COOL, TANTRUM GIRL.
THANKS, DESTRUCTO-KID.
NOW HOW DO WE GET IN?
STEP ASIDE, FOLKS. THIS ONE'S MY DEPARTMENT!
DESTRUCTO-BLAMM

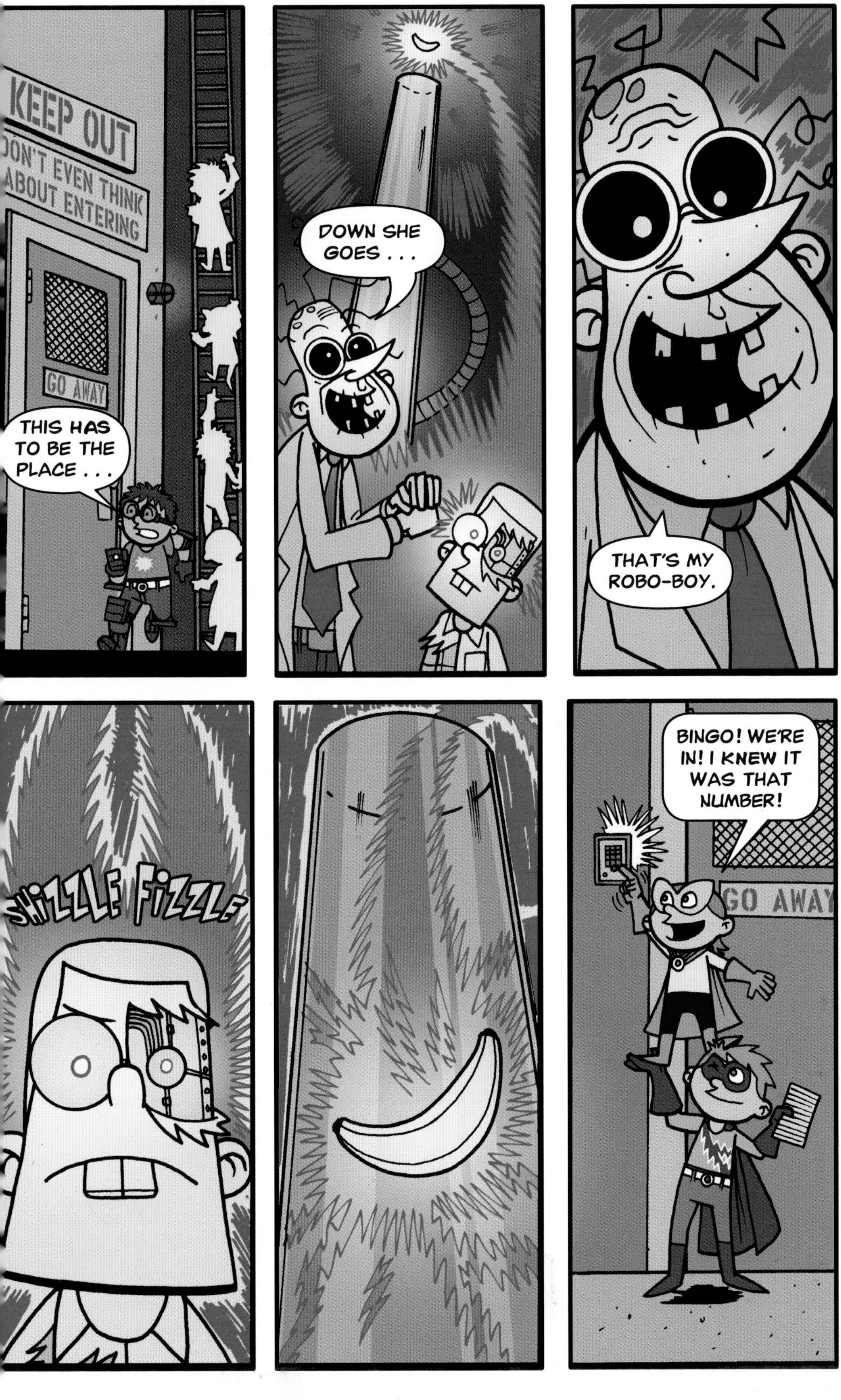
KEEP OUT
DON'T EVEN THINK ABOUT ENTERING
GO AWAY
THIS HAS TO BE THE PLACE . . .
DOWN SHE GOES . . .
THAT'S MY ROBO-BOY.
SHIZZLE FIZZLE
BINGO! WE'RE IN! I KNEW IT WAS THAT NUMBER!
GO AWAY

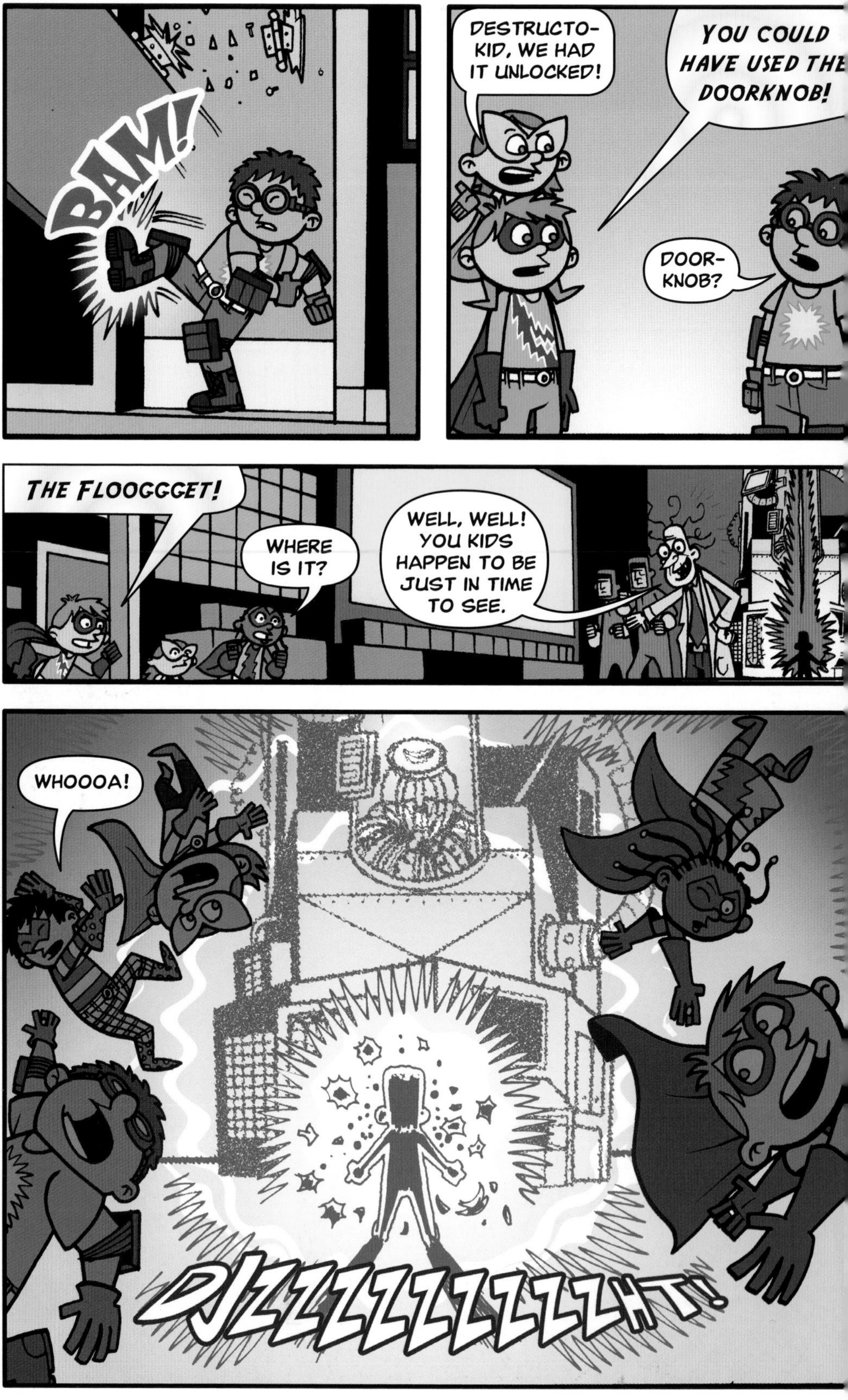
BAM!
DESTRUCTO-KID, WE HAD IT UNLOCKED!
YOU COULD HAVE USED THE DOORKNOB!
DOOR-KNOB?
THE FLOOGGGET!
WHERE IS IT?
WELL, WELL! YOU KIDS HAPPEN TO BE JUST IN TIME TO SEE.
WHOOOA!
DJZZZZZZZZZZHT!

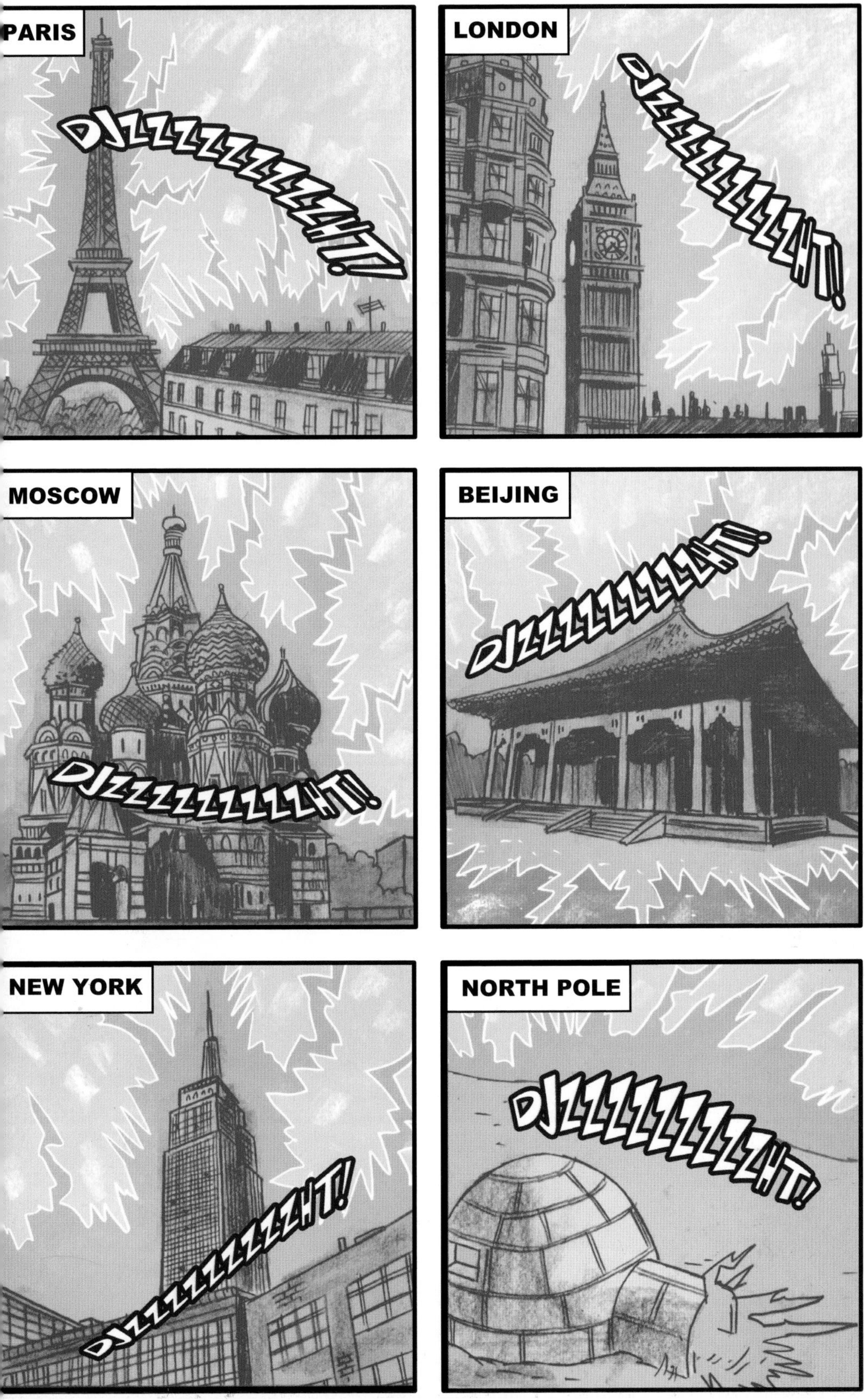
PARIS
DJZZZZZZZZZZHT!
LONDON
DJZZZZZZZZZZHT!
MOSCOW
DJZZZZZZZZZZHT!
BEIJING
DJZZZZZZZZZZHT!
NEW YORK
DJZZZZZZZZZZHT!
NORTH POLE
DJZZZZZZZZZZHT!

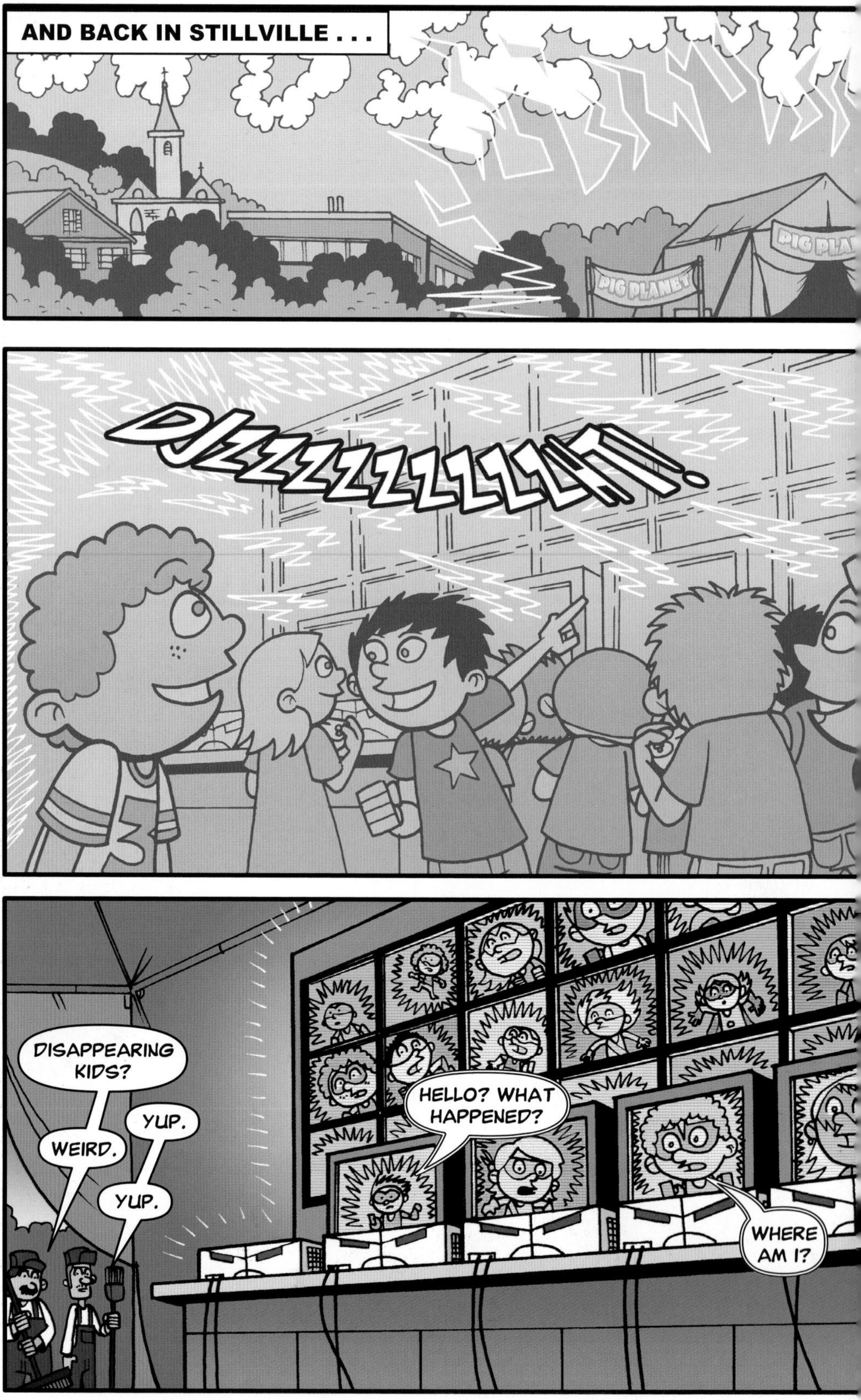
AND BACK IN STILLVILLE . . .
PIG PLANET
PIG PLANET
DJZZZZZZZZZZT!
DISAPPEARING KIDS?
WEIRD.
YUP.
YUP.
HELLO? WHAT HAPPENED?
WHERE AM I?

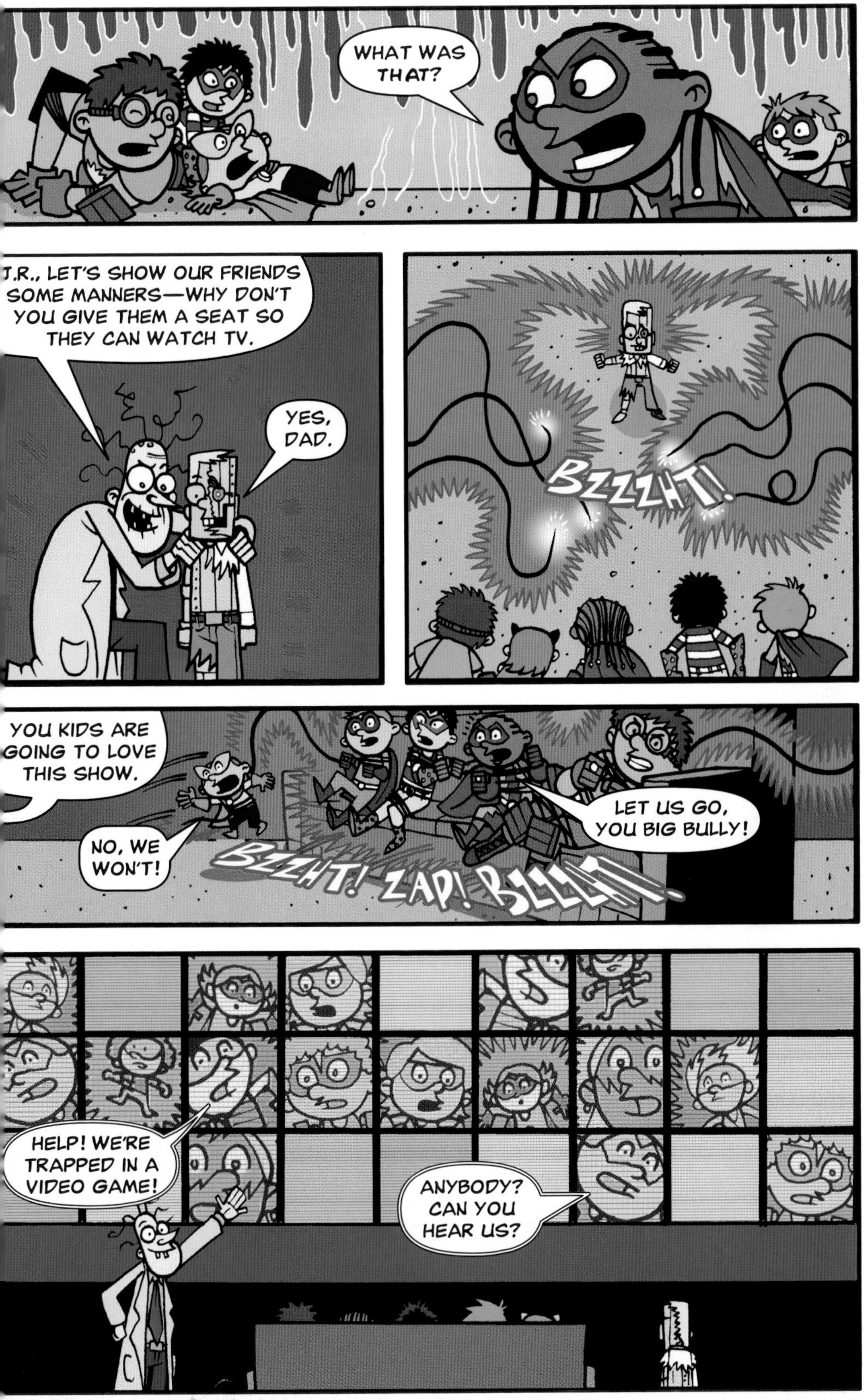
WHAT WAS THAT?
J.R., LET'S SHOW OUR FRIENDS SOME MANNERS—WHY DON'T YOU GIVE THEM A SEAT SO THEY CAN WATCH TV.
YES, DAD.
BZZZHT!
YOU KIDS ARE GOING TO LOVE THIS SHOW.
NO, WE WON'T!
LET US GO, YOU BIG BULLY!
BZZHT! ZAP!
HELP! WE'RE TRAPPED IN A VIDEO GAME!
ANYBODY? CAN YOU HEAR US?

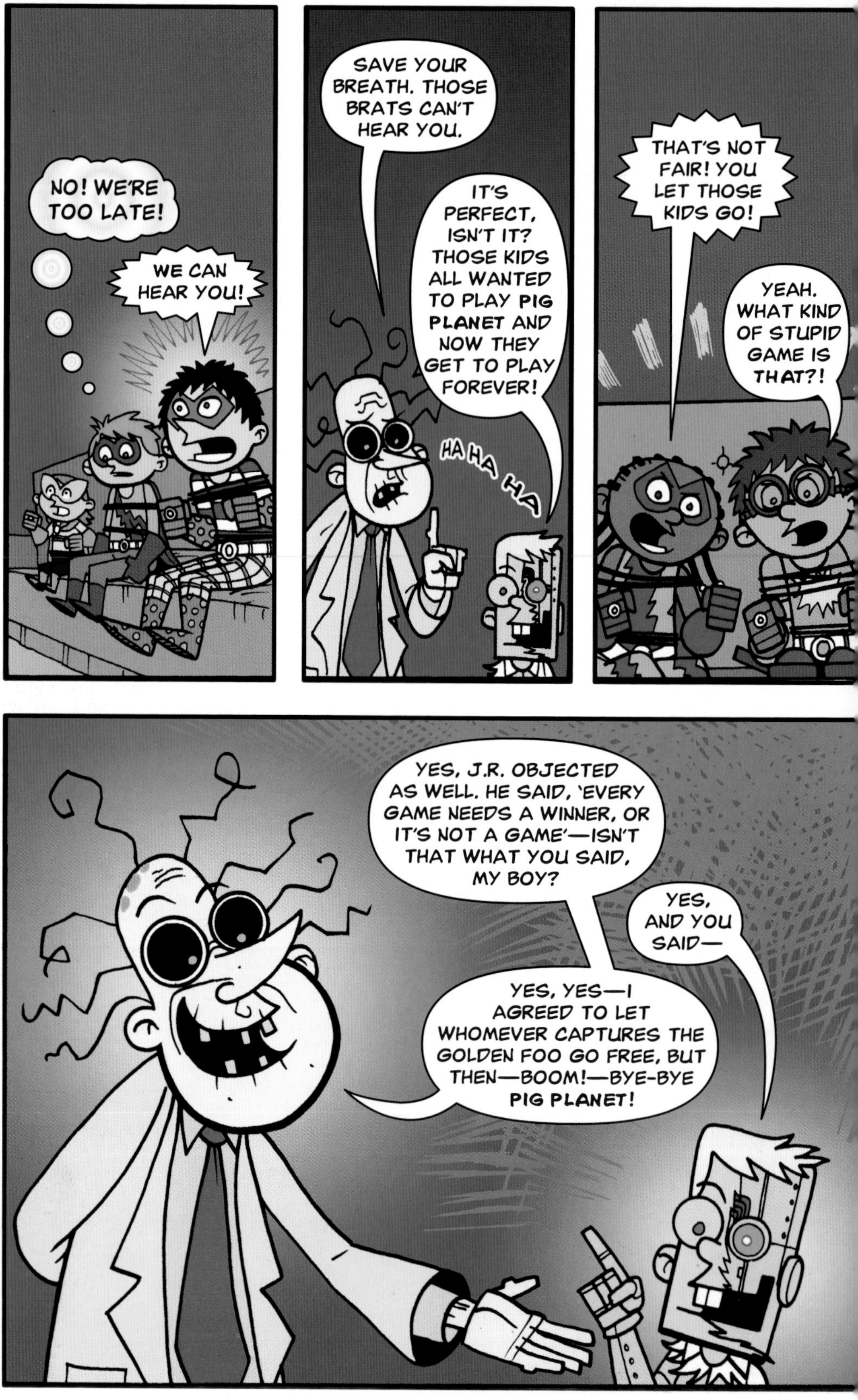
NO! WE'RE TOO LATE!
WE CAN HEAR YOU!
SAVE YOUR BREATH. THOSE BRATS CAN'T HEAR YOU.
IT'S PERFECT, ISN'T IT? THOSE KIDS ALL WANTED TO PLAY PIG PLANET AND NOW THEY GET TO PLAY FOREVER!
HA HA HA
THAT'S NOT FAIR! YOU LET THOSE KIDS GO!
YEAH. WHAT KIND OF STUPID GAME IS THAT?!
YES, J.R. OBJECTED AS WELL. HE SAID, 'EVERY GAME NEEDS A WINNER, OR IT'S NOT A GAME'—ISN'T THAT WHAT YOU SAID, MY BOY?
YES, AND YOU SAID—
YES, YES—I AGREED TO LET WHOMEVER CAPTURES THE GOLDEN FOO GO FREE, BUT THEN—BOOM!—BYE-BYE PIG PLANET!

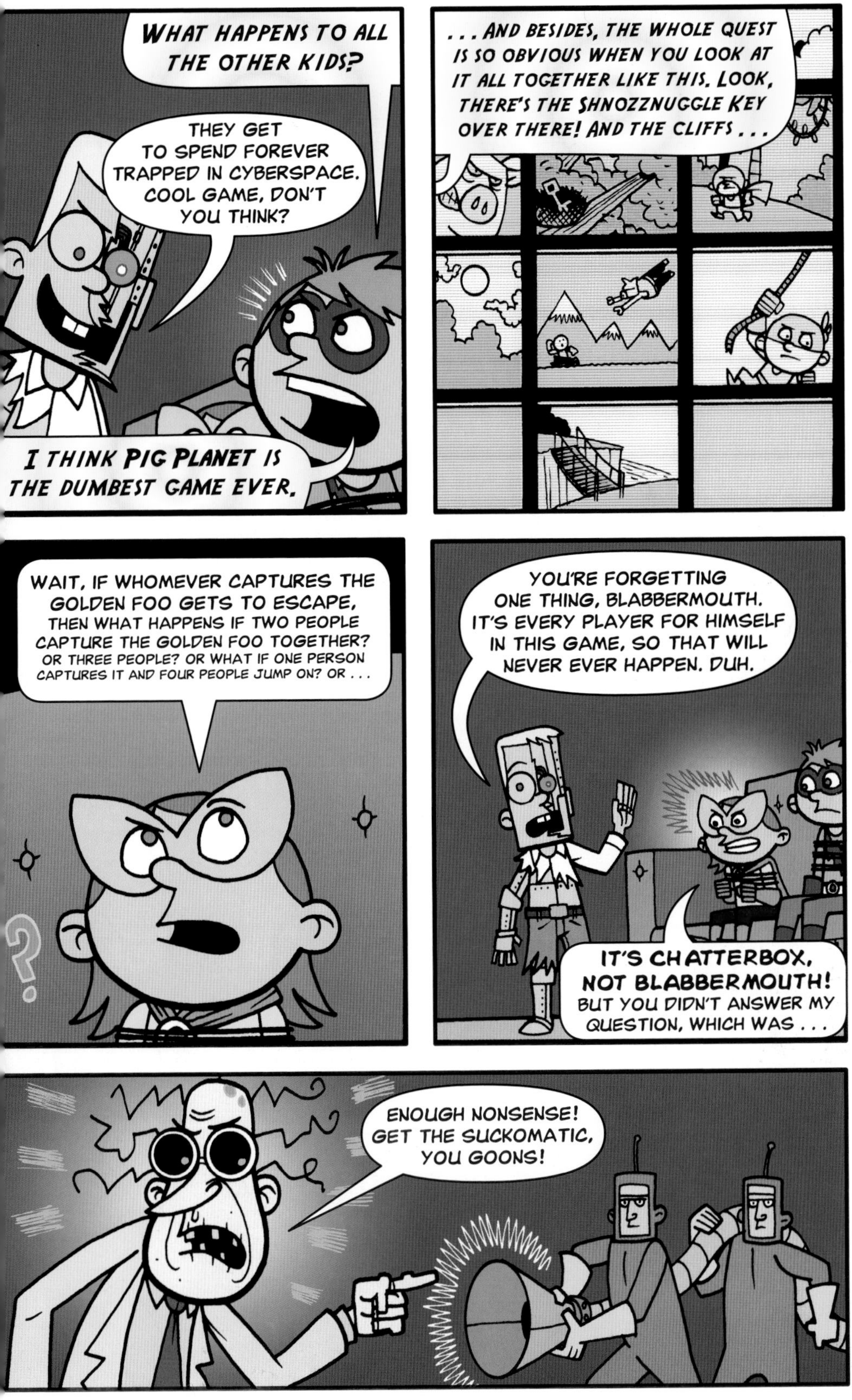
WHAT HAPPENS TO ALL THE OTHER KIDS?
THEY GET TO SPEND FOREVER TRAPPED IN CYBERSPACE. COOL GAME, DON'T YOU THINK?
I THINK PIG PLANET IS THE DUMBEST GAME EVER.
. . . AND BESIDES, THE WHOLE QUEST IS SO OBVIOUS WHEN YOU LOOK AT IT ALL TOGETHER LIKE THIS. LOOK, THERE'S THE SHNOZZNUGGLE KEY OVER THERE! AND THE CLIFFS . . .
WAIT, IF WHOMEVER CAPTURES THE GOLDEN FOO GETS TO ESCAPE, THEN WHAT HAPPENS IF TWO PEOPLE CAPTURE THE GOLDEN FOO TOGETHER? OR THREE PEOPLE? OR WHAT IF ONE PERSON CAPTURES IT AND FOUR PEOPLE JUMP ON? OR . . .
YOU'RE FORGETTING ONE THING, BLABBERMOUTH. IT'S EVERY PLAYER FOR HIMSELF IN THIS GAME, SO THAT WILL NEVER EVER HAPPEN. DUH.
IT'S CHATTERBOX, NOT BLABBERMOUTH! BUT YOU DIDN'T ANSWER MY QUESTION, WHICH WAS . . .
ENOUGH NONSENSE! GET THE SUCKOMATIC, YOU GOONS!

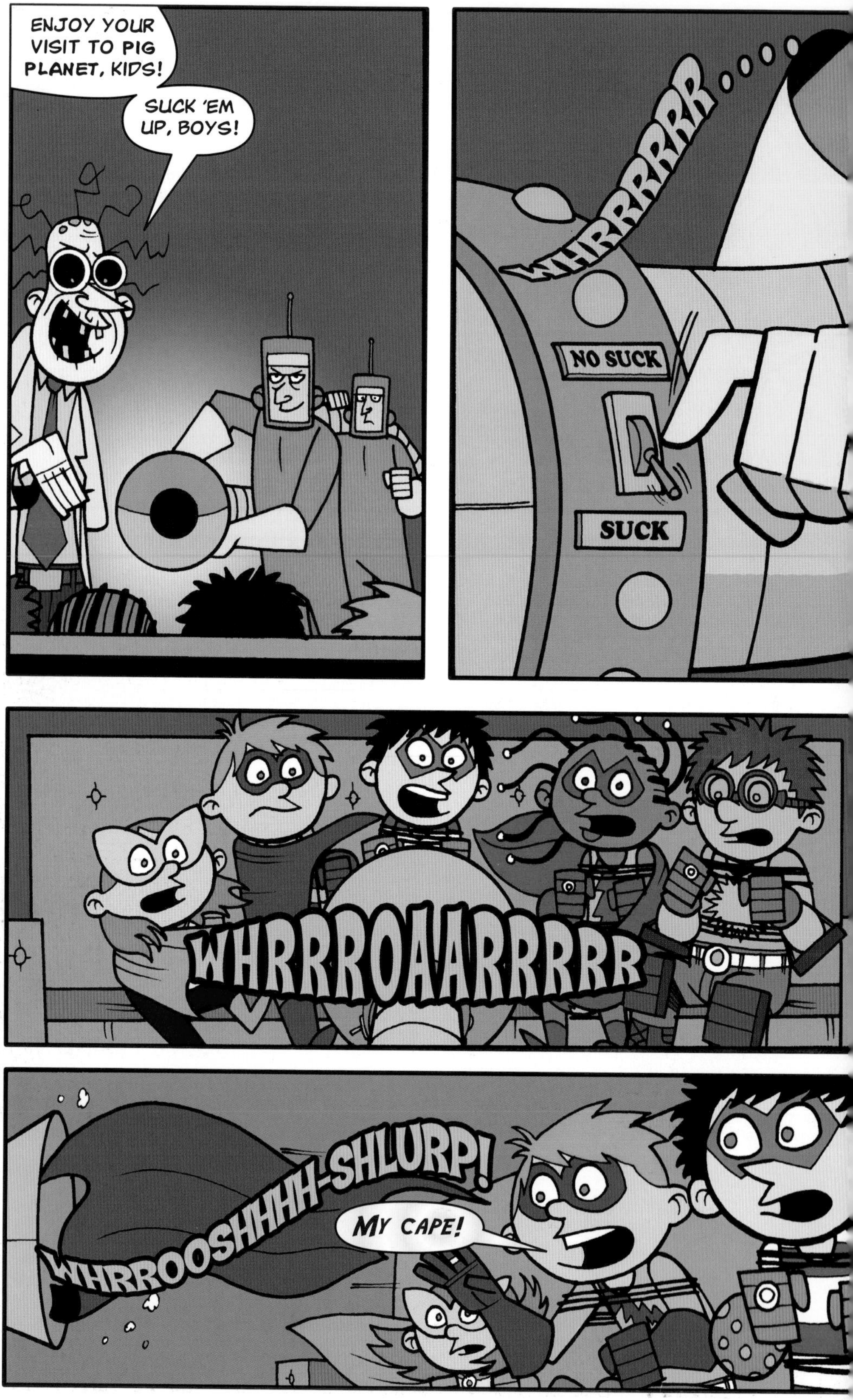

ENJOY YOUR VISIT TO PIG PLANET, KIDS!
SUCK 'EM UP, BOYS!
WHRRRRRR....
NO SUCK
SUCK
WHRRROAARRRRR
WHRROOSHHHH-SHLURP!
MY CAPE!

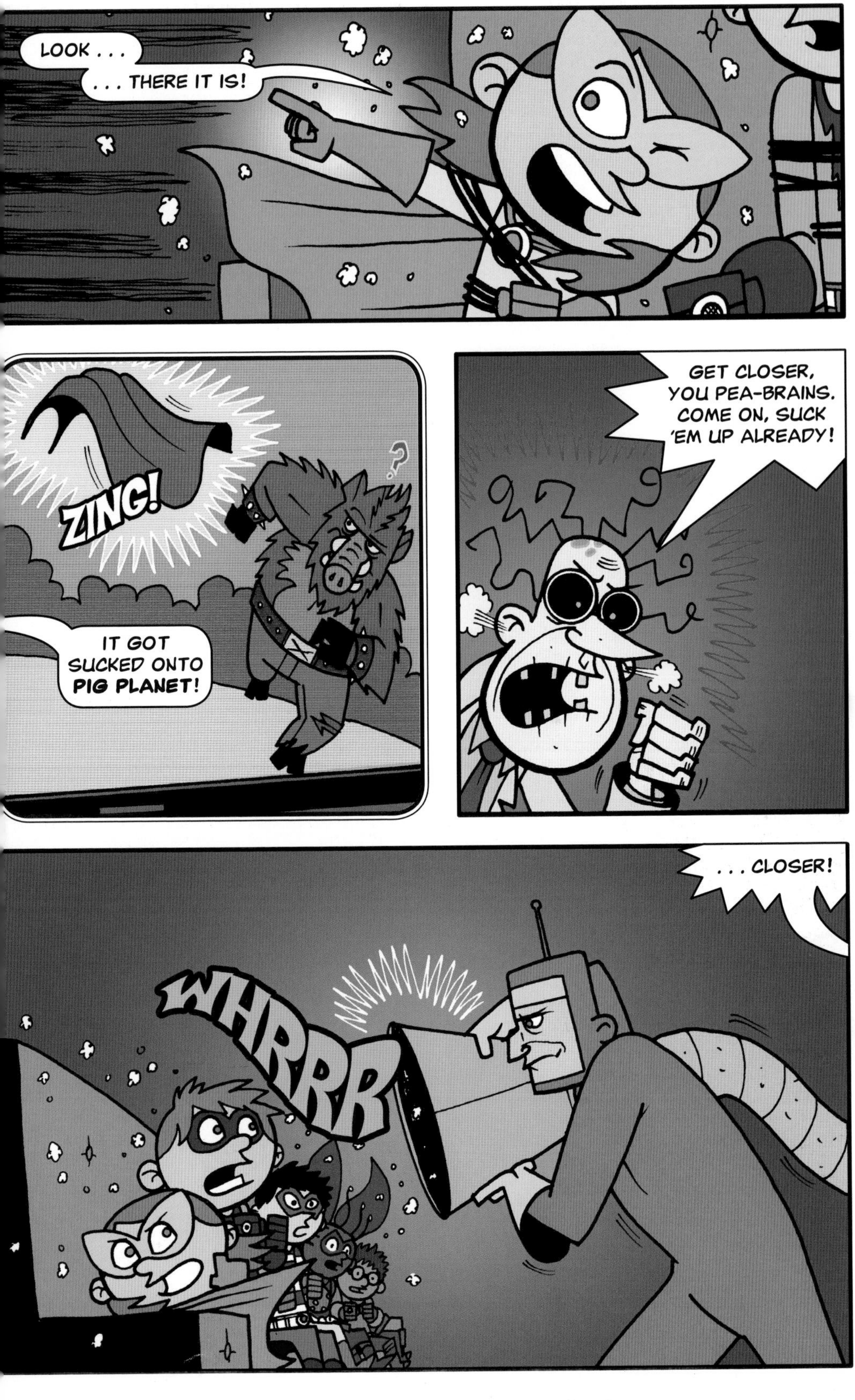
LOOK . . .
. . . THERE IT IS!
ZING!
IT GOT SUCKED ONTO PIG PLANET!
GET CLOSER, YOU PEA-BRAINS. COME ON, SUCK 'EM UP ALREADY!
. . . CLOSER!
WHRRR

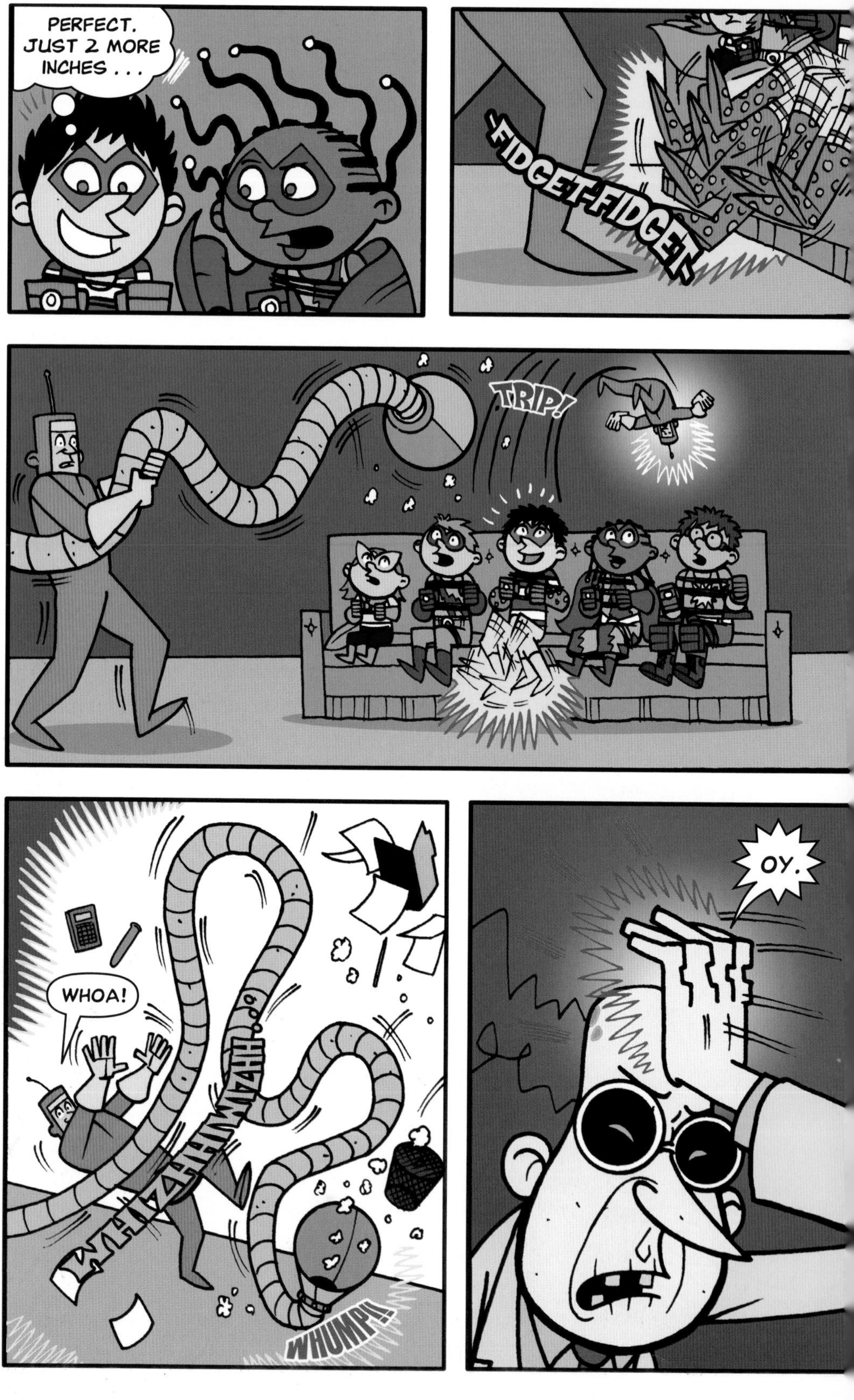
PERFECT. JUST 2 MORE INCHES . . .
FIDGET FIDGET
TRIP!
WHOA!
WHIZAHHWHIZAHH...
WHUMP!
OY.

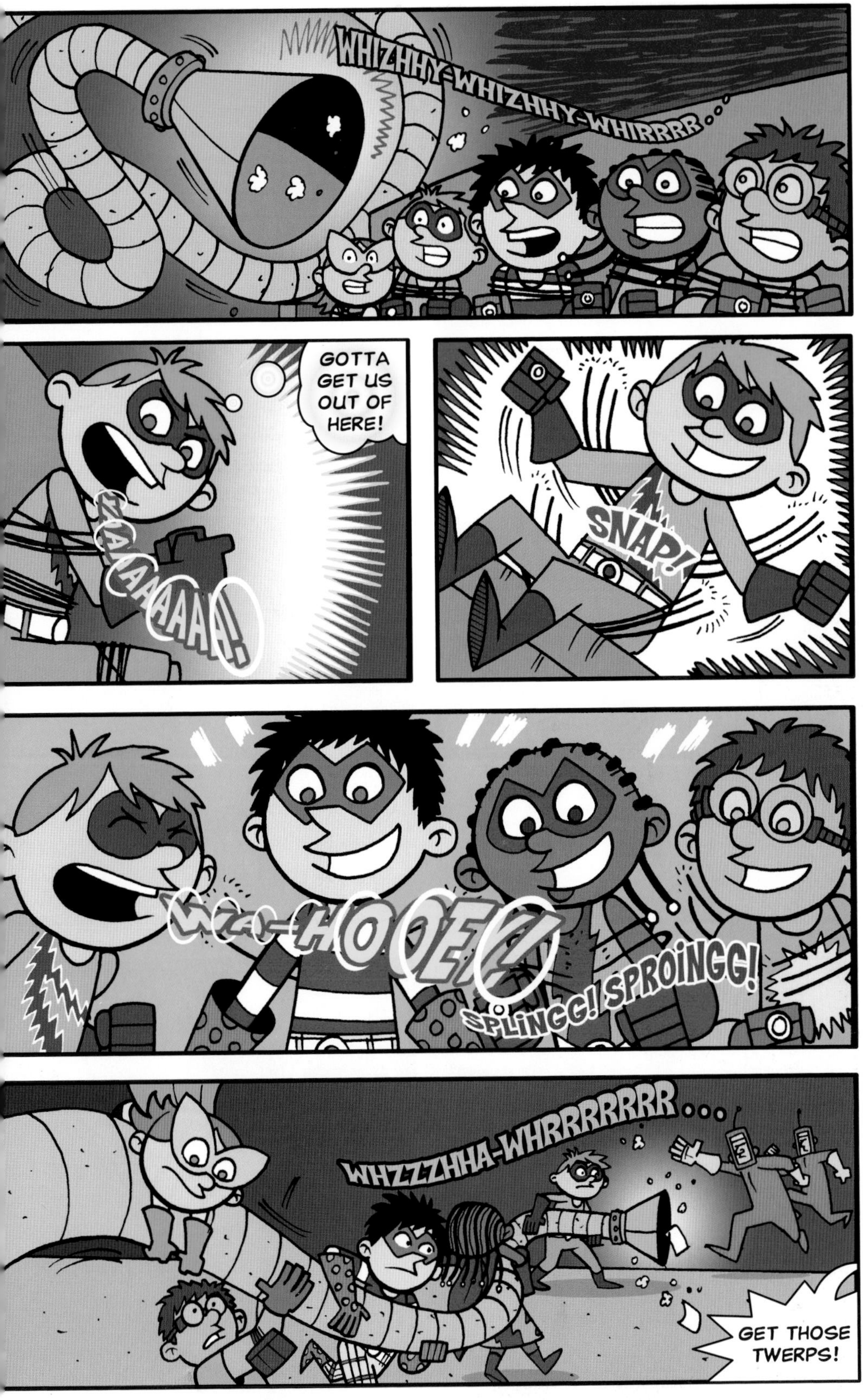
WHIZHHY-WHIZHHY-WHIRRRR...
GOTTA GET US OUT OF HERE!
AAAAAAA!
SNAP!
WA-HOOEY!
SPLINGG! SPROINGG!
WHZZZHHA-WHRRRRRRR...
GET THOSE TWERPS!

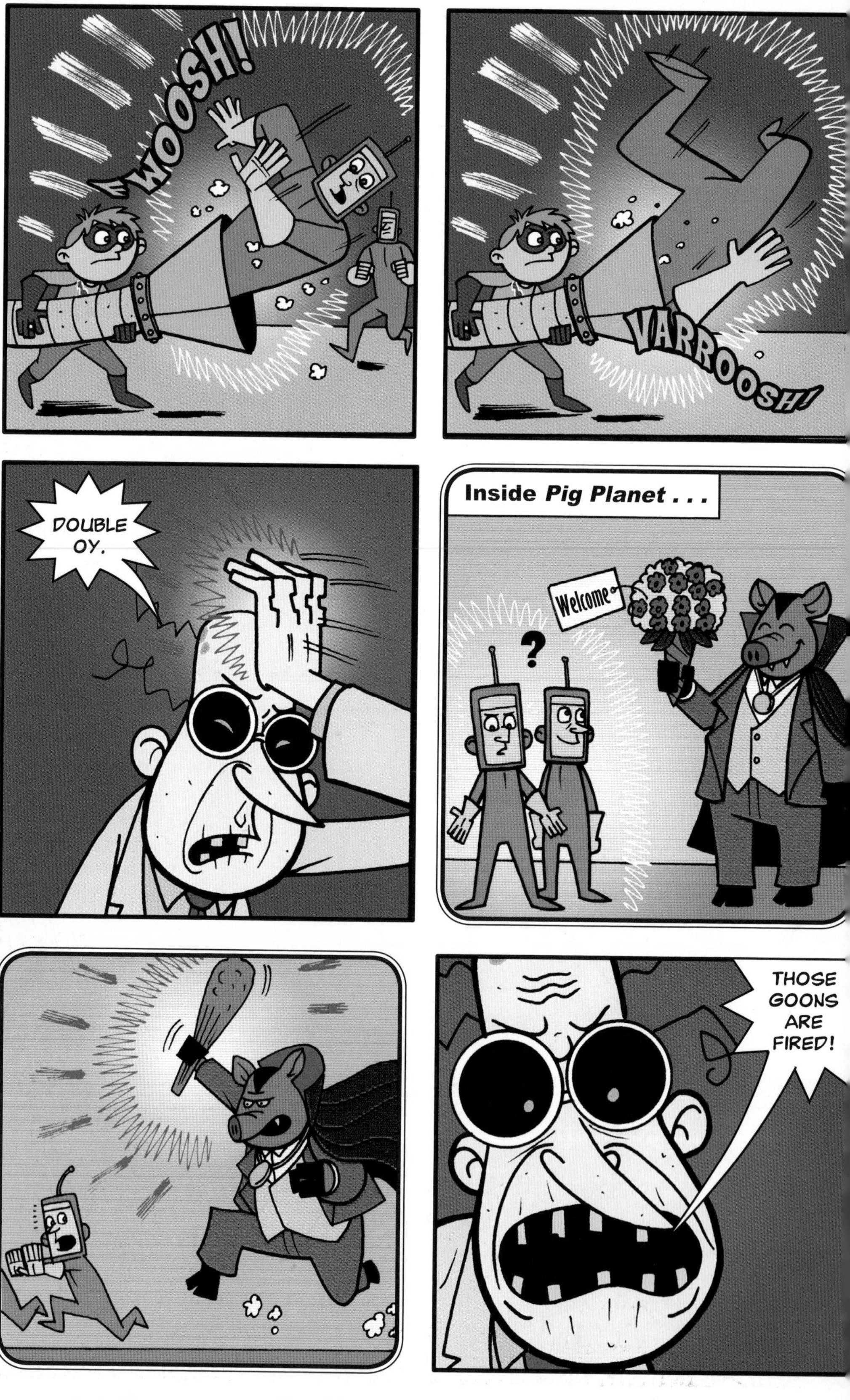
WOOSH!
VARROOSH!
DOUBLE OY.
Inside Pig Planet . . .
Welcome
?
THOSE GOONS ARE FIRED!

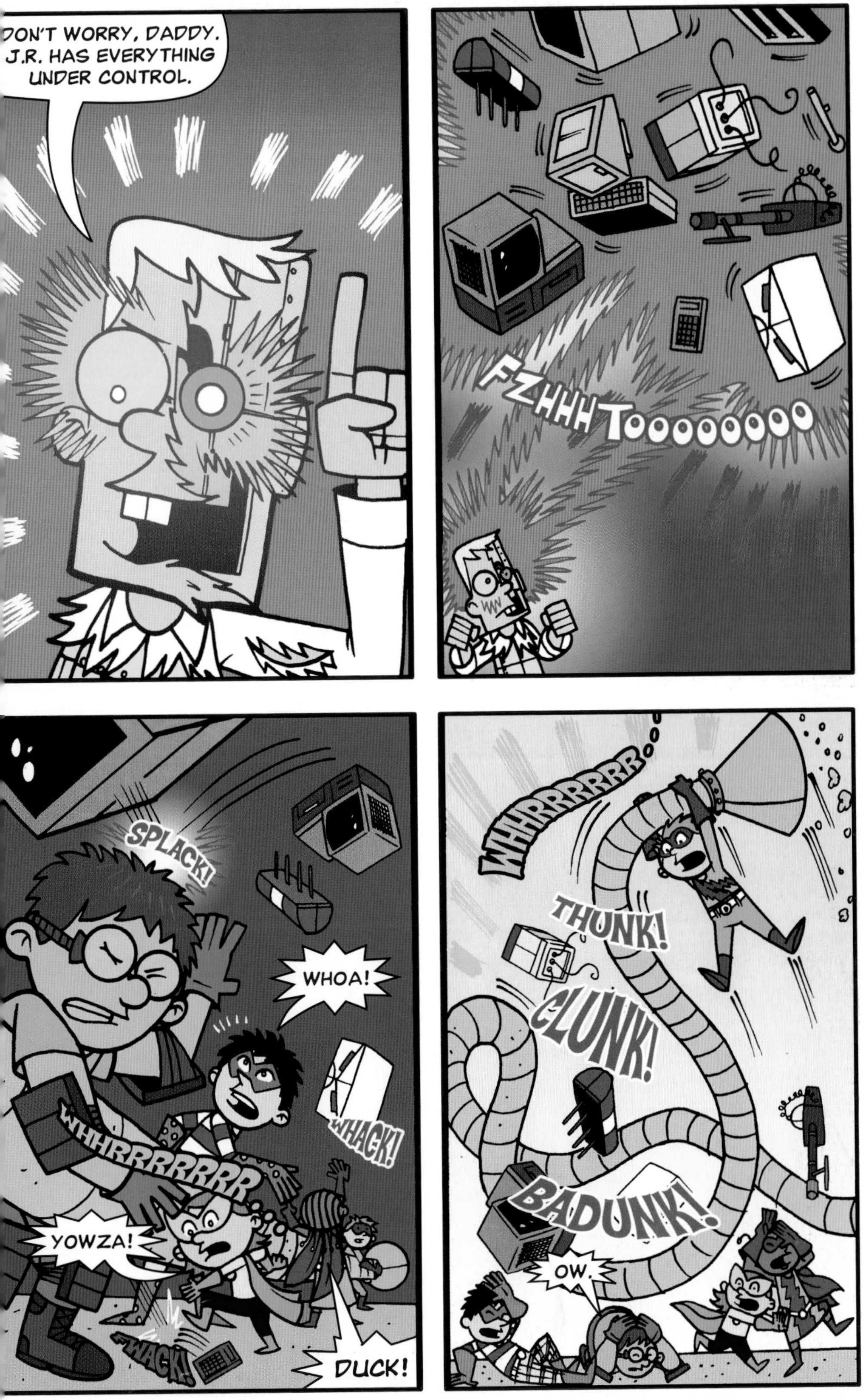
DON'T WORRY, DADDY. J.R. HAS EVERYTHING UNDER CONTROL.
FZHHHTOOOOOOOO
SPLACK!
WHOA!
WHHRRRRRRRR
WHACK!
YOWZA!
WACK!
DUCK!
WHHRRRRRRR
THUNK!
CLUNK!
BADUNK!
OW.

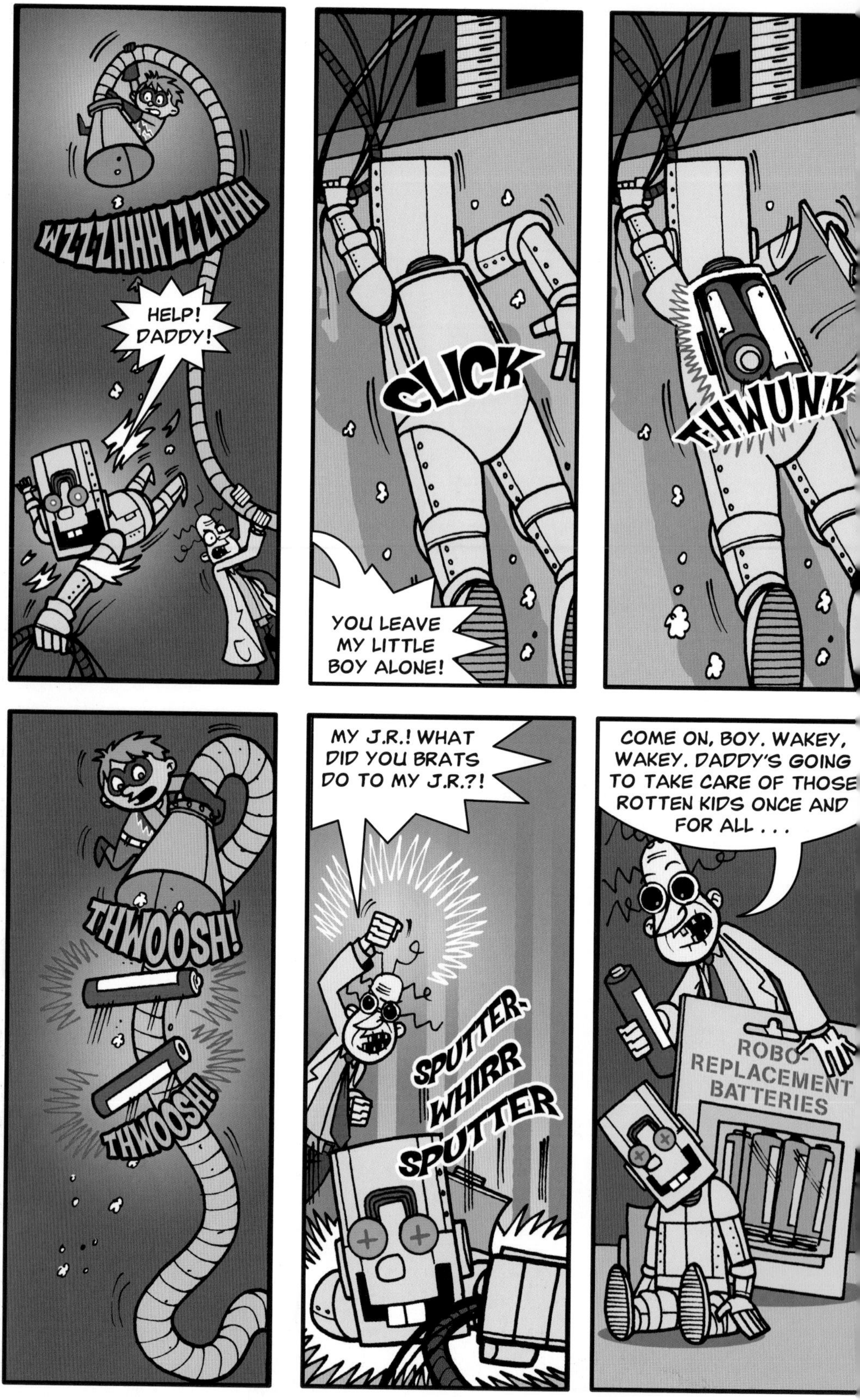
WZZZZHHHZZZZHHH
HELP! DADDY!
CLICK
YOU LEAVE MY LITTLE BOY ALONE!
THWUNK
THWOOSH!
THWOOSH!
MY J.R.! WHAT DID YOU BRATS DO TO MY J.R.?!
SPUTTER-WHIRR SPUTTER
COME ON, BOY. WAKEY, WAKEY. DADDY'S GOING TO TAKE CARE OF THOSE ROTTEN KIDS ONCE AND FOR ALL . . .
ROBO-REPLACEMENT BATTERIES

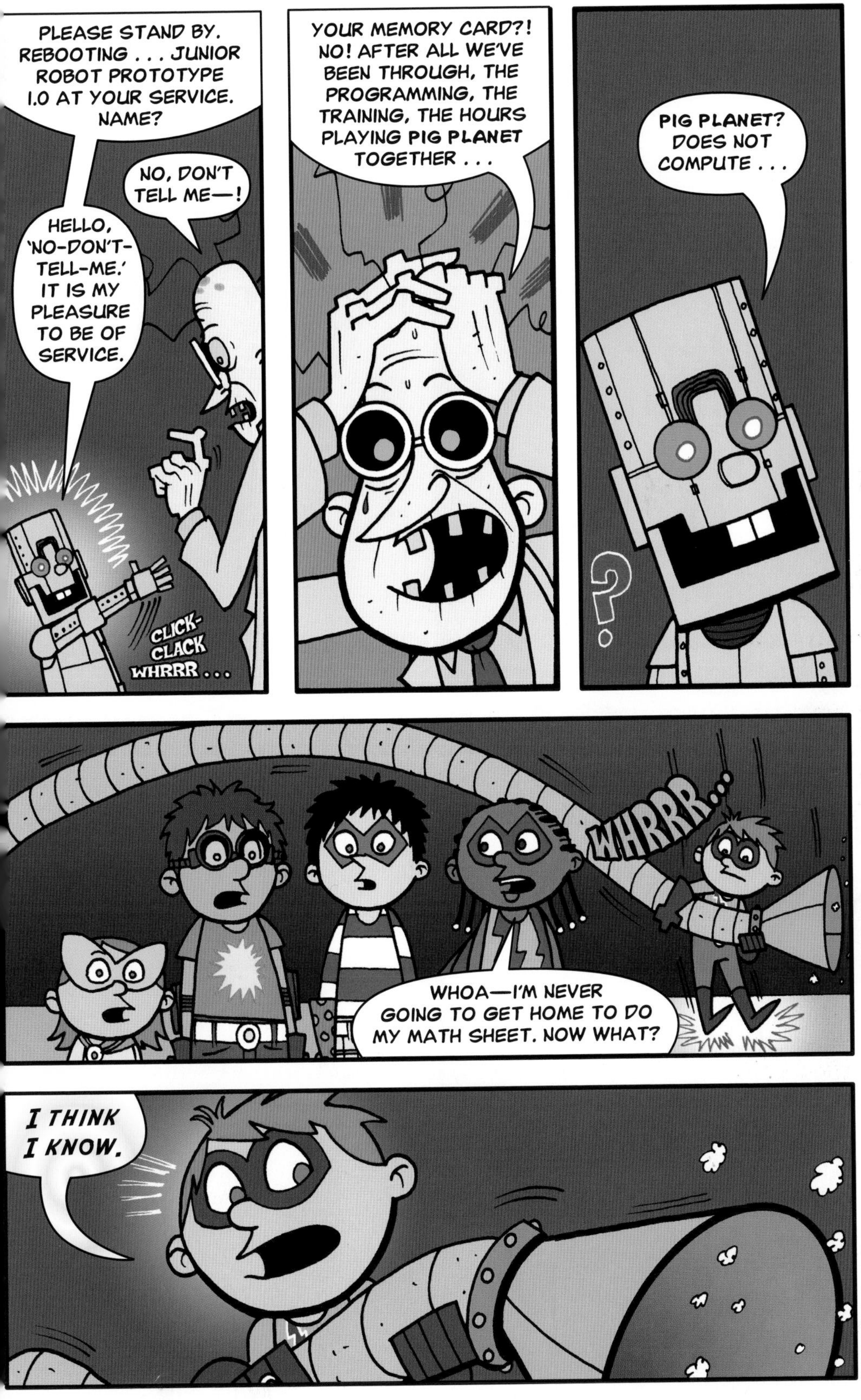

PLEASE STAND BY. REBOOTING . . . JUNIOR ROBOT PROTOTYPE 1.0 AT YOUR SERVICE. NAME?
NO, DON'T TELL ME—!
HELLO, 'NO-DON'T-TELL-ME.' IT IS MY PLEASURE TO BE OF SERVICE.
CLICK-CLACK WHRRR . . .
YOUR MEMORY CARD?! NO! AFTER ALL WE'VE BEEN THROUGH, THE PROGRAMMING, THE TRAINING, THE HOURS PLAYING PIG PLANET TOGETHER . . .
PIG PLANET? DOES NOT COMPUTE . . .
WHRRR . . .
WHOA—I'M NEVER GOING TO GET HOME TO DO MY MATH SHEET. NOW WHAT?
I THINK I KNOW.

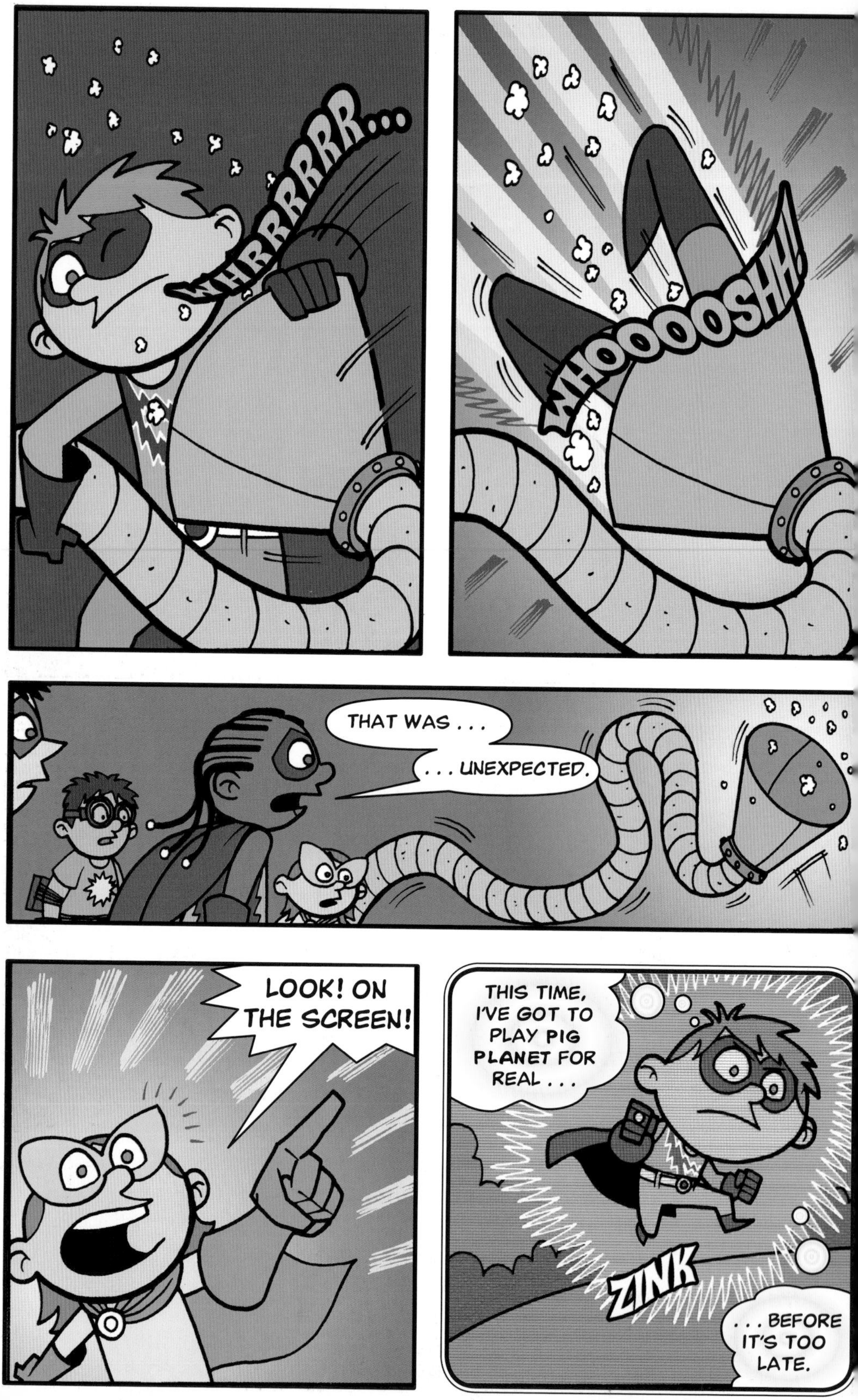
WHRRRRRR...
WHOOOOSHH!
THAT WAS . . .
. . . UNEXPECTED.
LOOK! ON THE SCREEN!
THIS TIME, I'VE GOT TO PLAY PIG PLANET FOR REAL . . .
ZINK
. . . BEFORE IT'S TOO LATE.

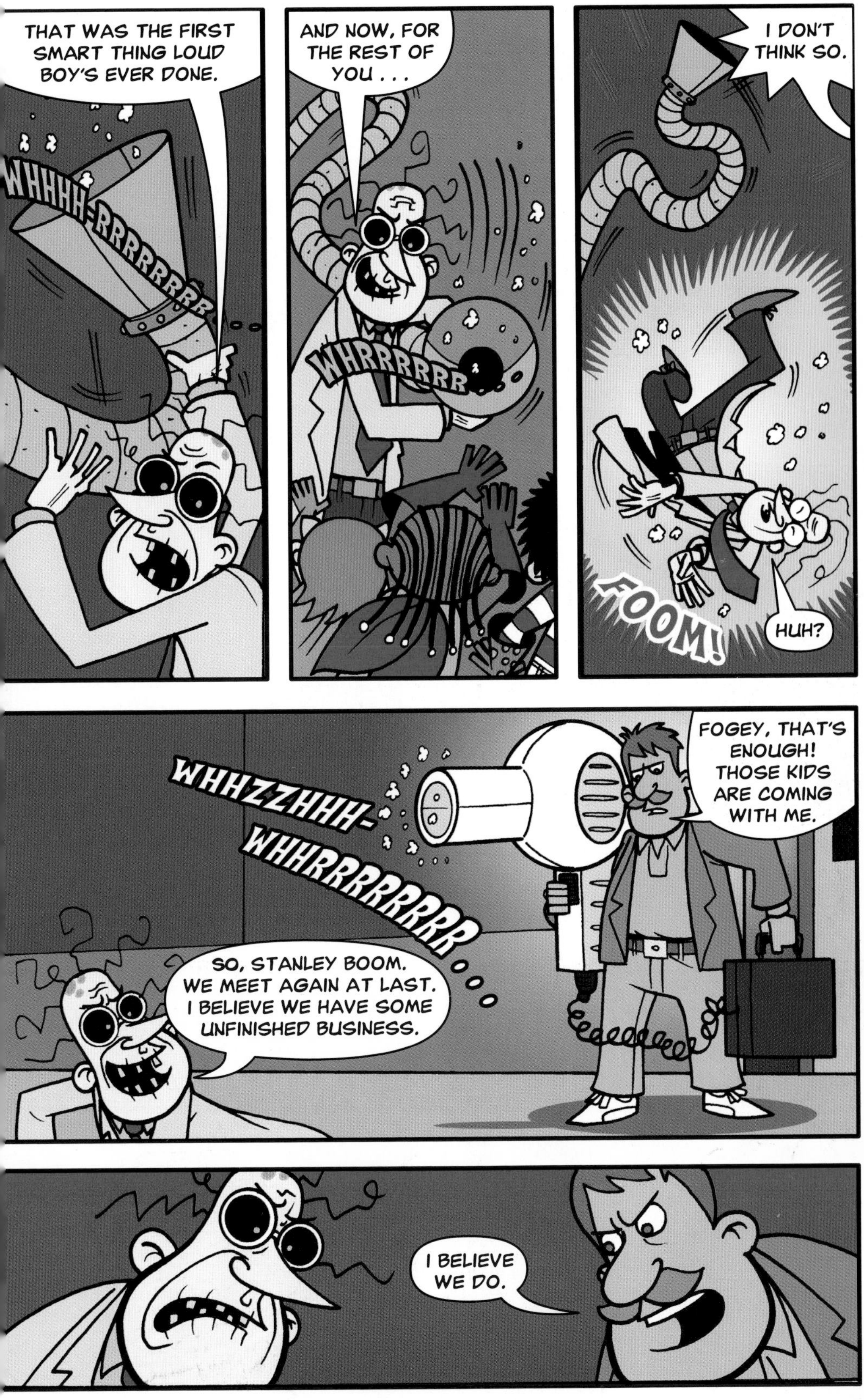
THAT WAS THE FIRST SMART THING LOUD BOY'S EVER DONE.
WHHHH-RRRRRRRRR
AND NOW, FOR THE REST OF YOU . . .
WHRRRRRRR
I DON'T THINK SO.
FOOM!
HUH?
WHHZZHHH-WHHRRRRRRRRRR
FOGEY, THAT'S ENOUGH! THOSE KIDS ARE COMING WITH ME.
SO, STANLEY BOOM. WE MEET AGAIN AT LAST. I BELIEVE WE HAVE SOME UNFINISHED BUSINESS.
I BELIEVE WE DO.

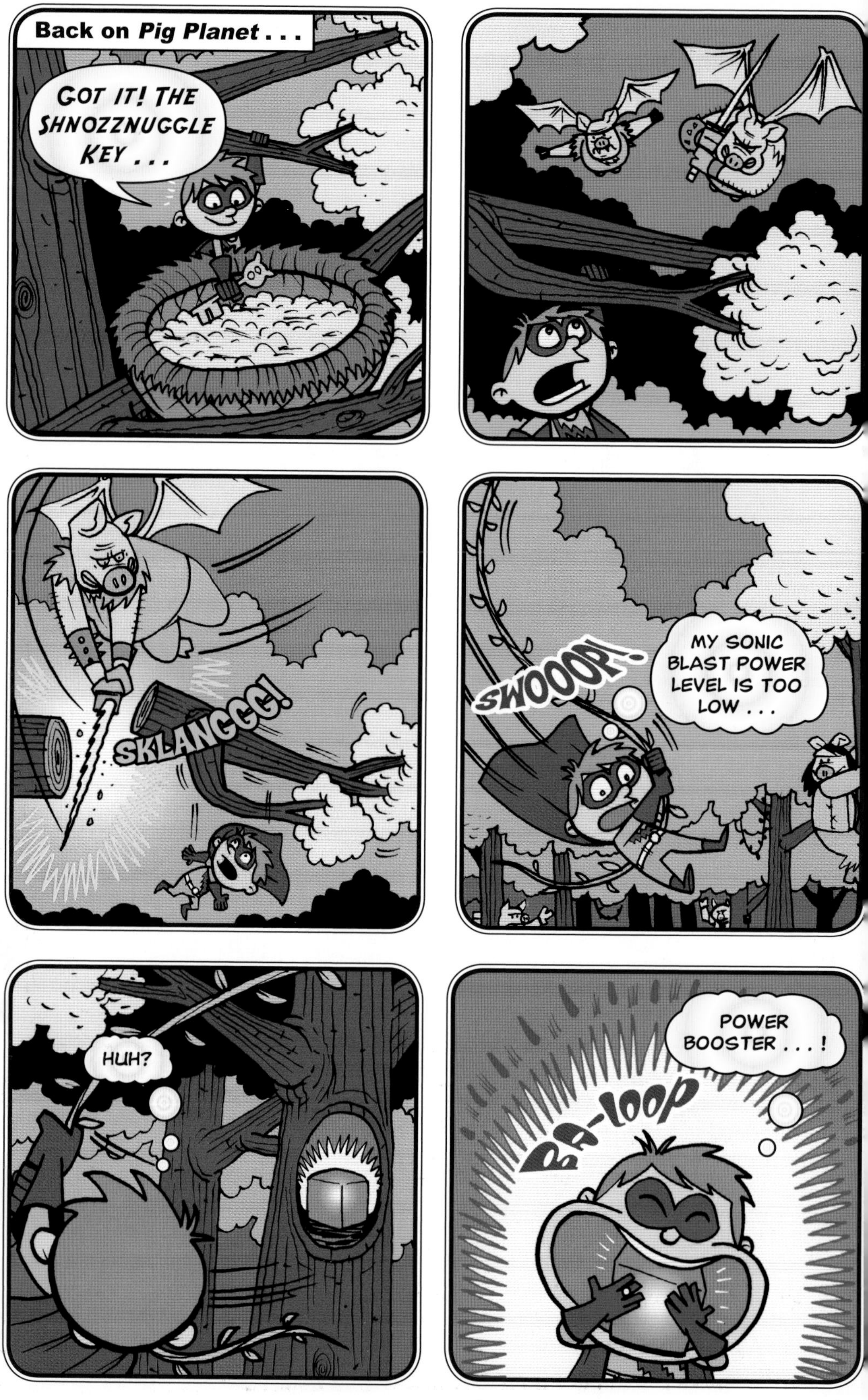
Back on Pig Planet . . .
GOT IT! THE SHNOZZNUGGLE KEY . . .
SKLANGGG!
SWOOOP!
MY SONIC BLAST POWER LEVEL IS TOO LOW . . .
HUH?
POWER BOOSTER . . . !
BA-LOOP

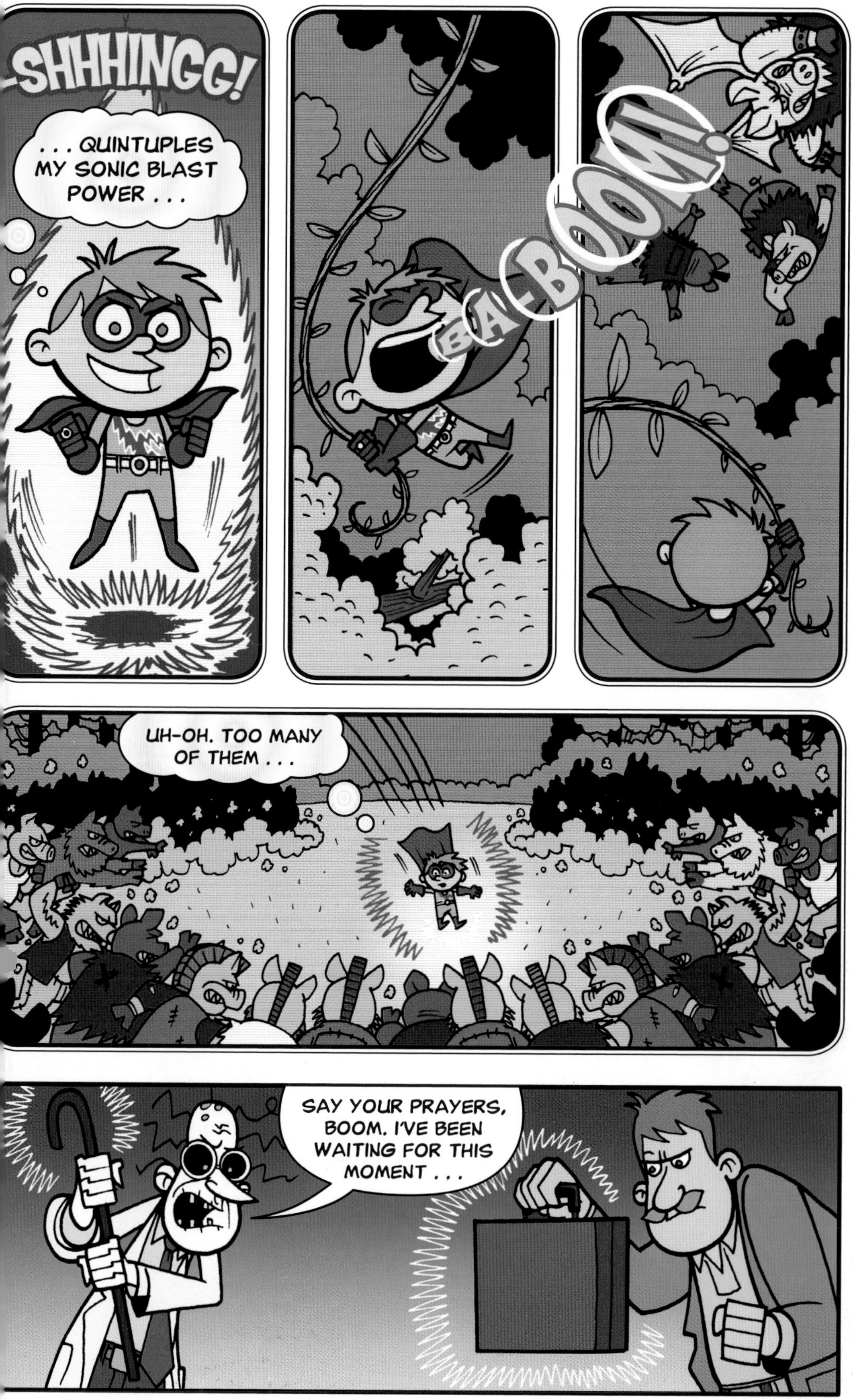
SHHHINGG!
. . . QUINTUPLES MY SONIC BLAST POWER . . .
BA-BOOM!
UH-OH. TOO MANY OF THEM . . .
SAY YOUR PRAYERS, BOOM. I'VE BEEN WAITING FOR THIS MOMENT . . .

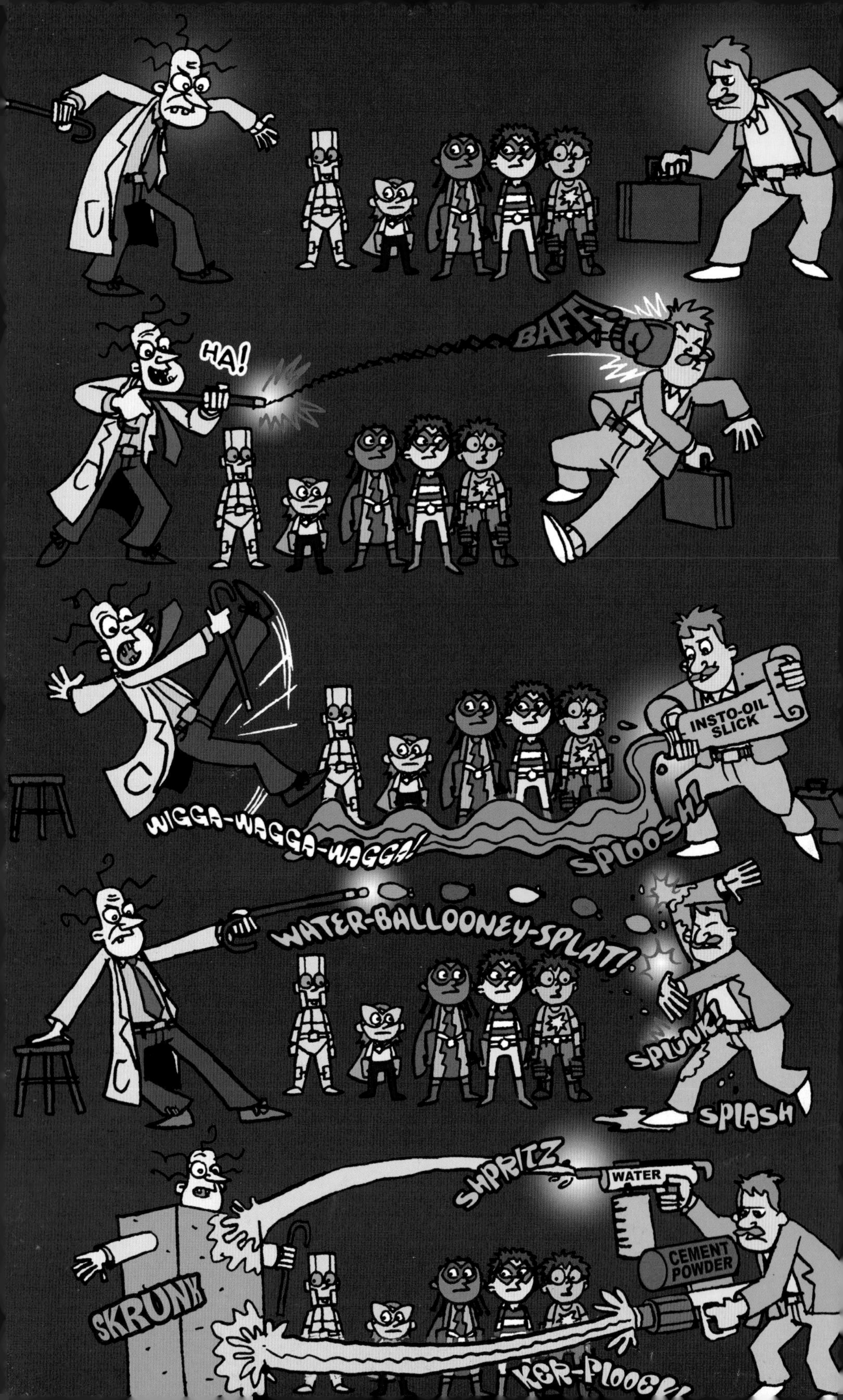

HA!
BAFF!
INSTO-OIL SLICK
WIGGA-WAGGA-WAGGA!
SPLOOSH!
WATER-BALLOONEY-SPLAT!
SPLUNK!
SPLASH
SHPRITZ
WATER
CEMENT POWDER
SKRUNK
KER-PLOOEY!

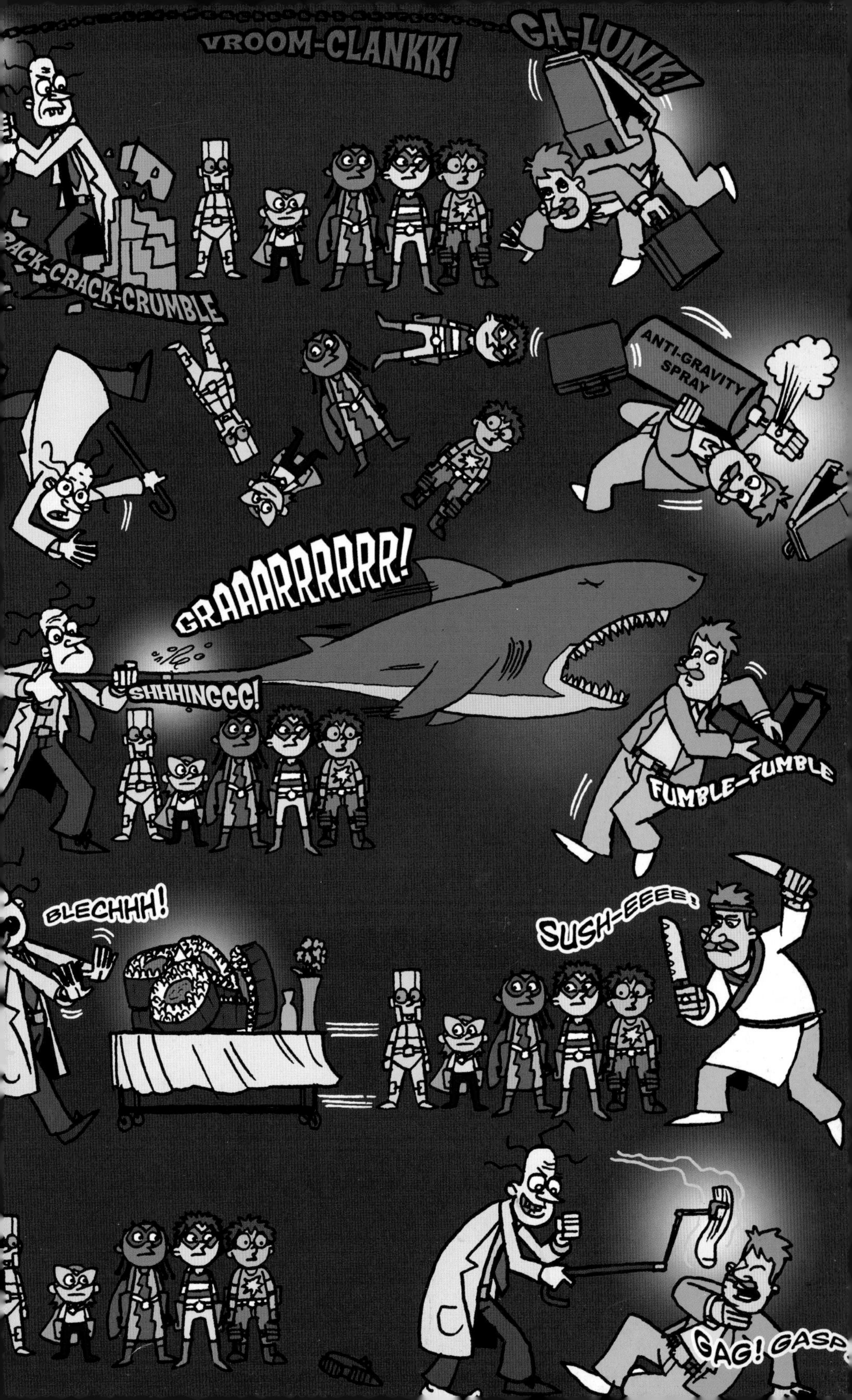
VROOM-CLANKK!
GA-LUNK!
CRACK-CRACK-CRUMBLE
ANTI-GRAVITY SPRAY
GRAAARRRRRR!
SHHHINGGG!
FUMBLE-FUMBLE
BLECHHH!
SUSH-EEEE!
GAG! GASP

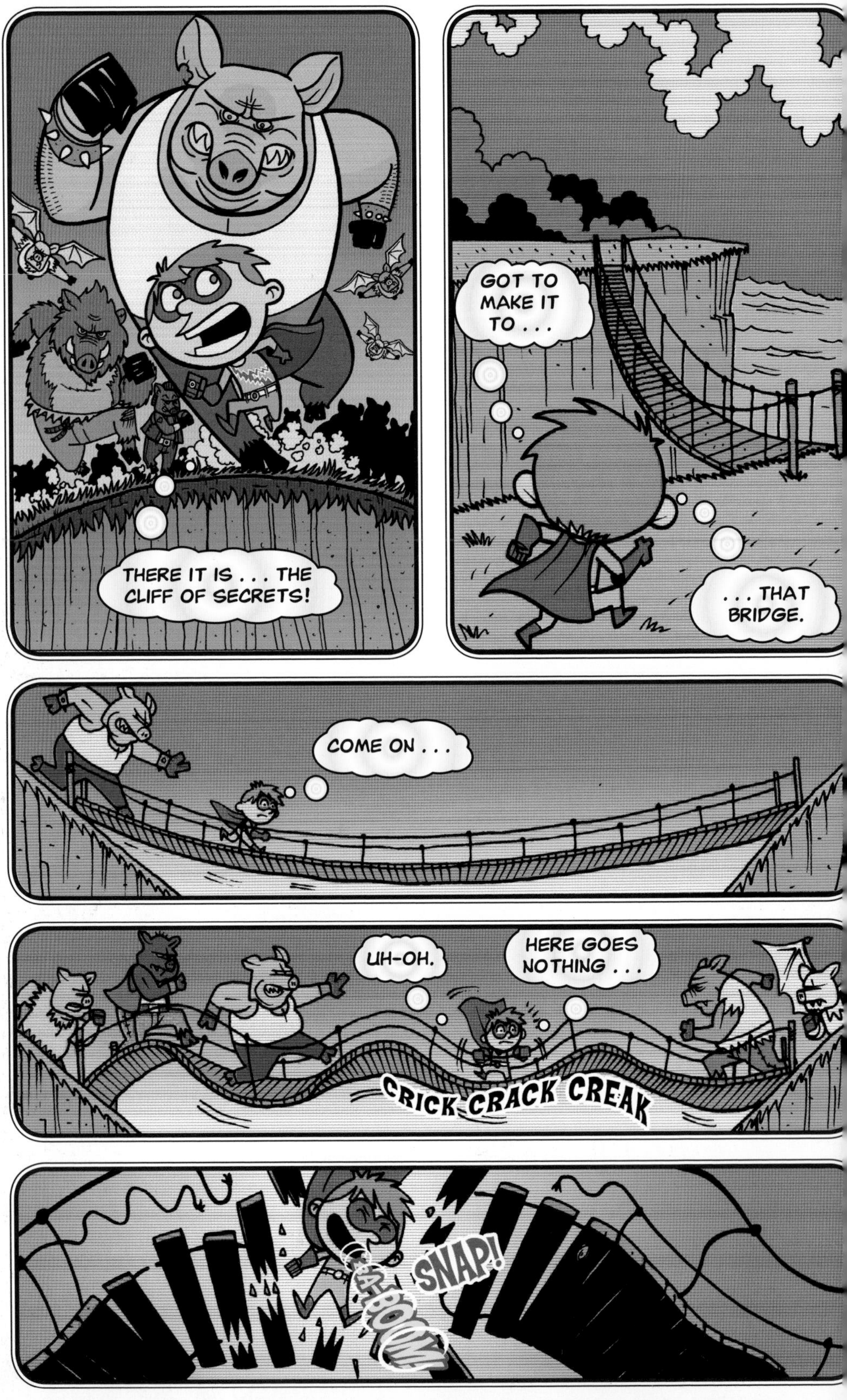
THERE IT IS . . . THE CLIFF OF SECRETS!
GOT TO MAKE IT TO . . .
. . . THAT BRIDGE.
COME ON . . .
UH-OH.
HERE GOES NOTHING . . .
CRICK CRACK CREAK
SNAP!

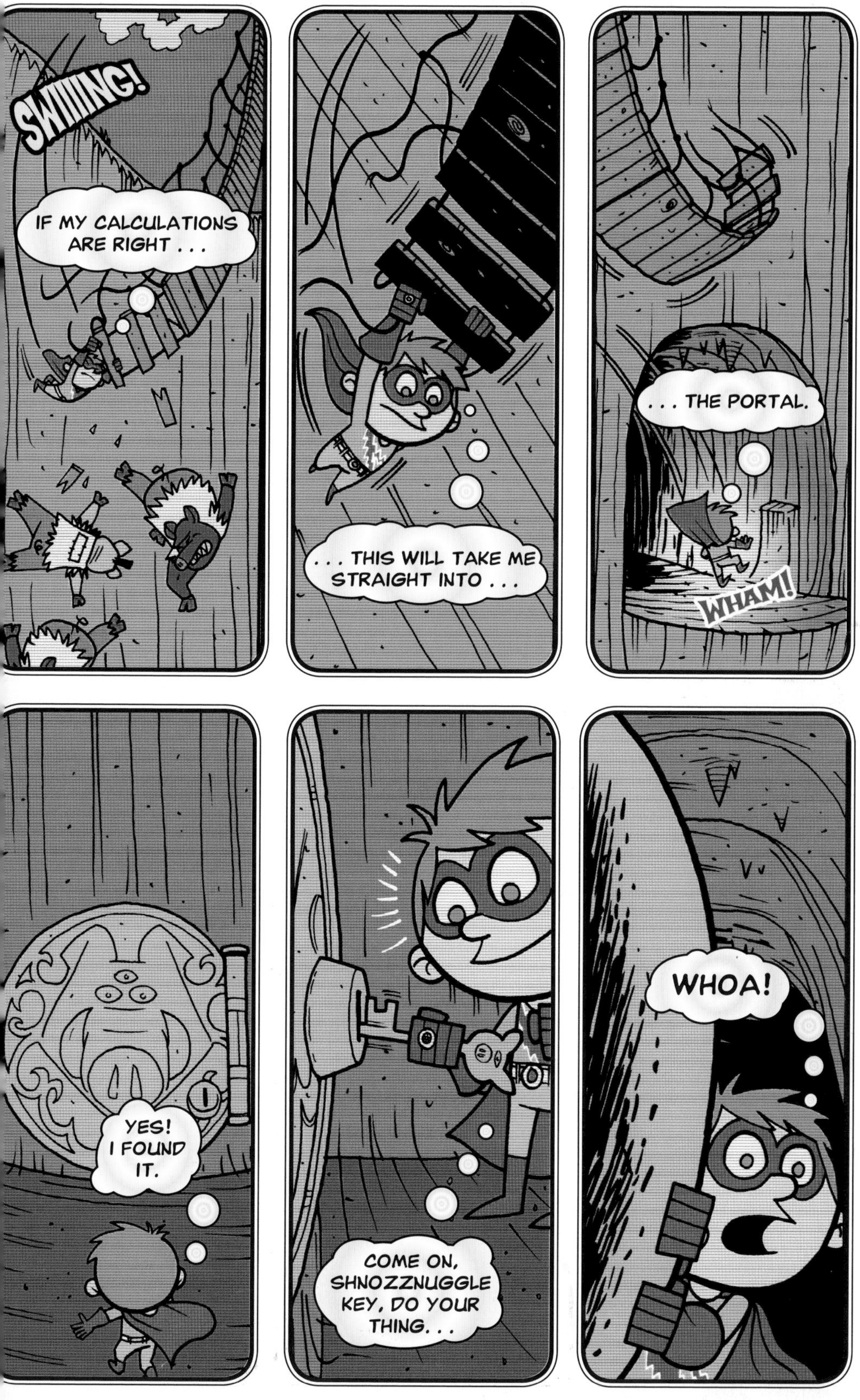
SWIIIING!
IF MY CALCULATIONS ARE RIGHT . . .
. . . THIS WILL TAKE ME STRAIGHT INTO . . .
. . . THE PORTAL.
WHAM!
YES! I FOUND IT.
COME ON, SHNOZZNUGGLE KEY, DO YOUR THING. . .
WHOA!

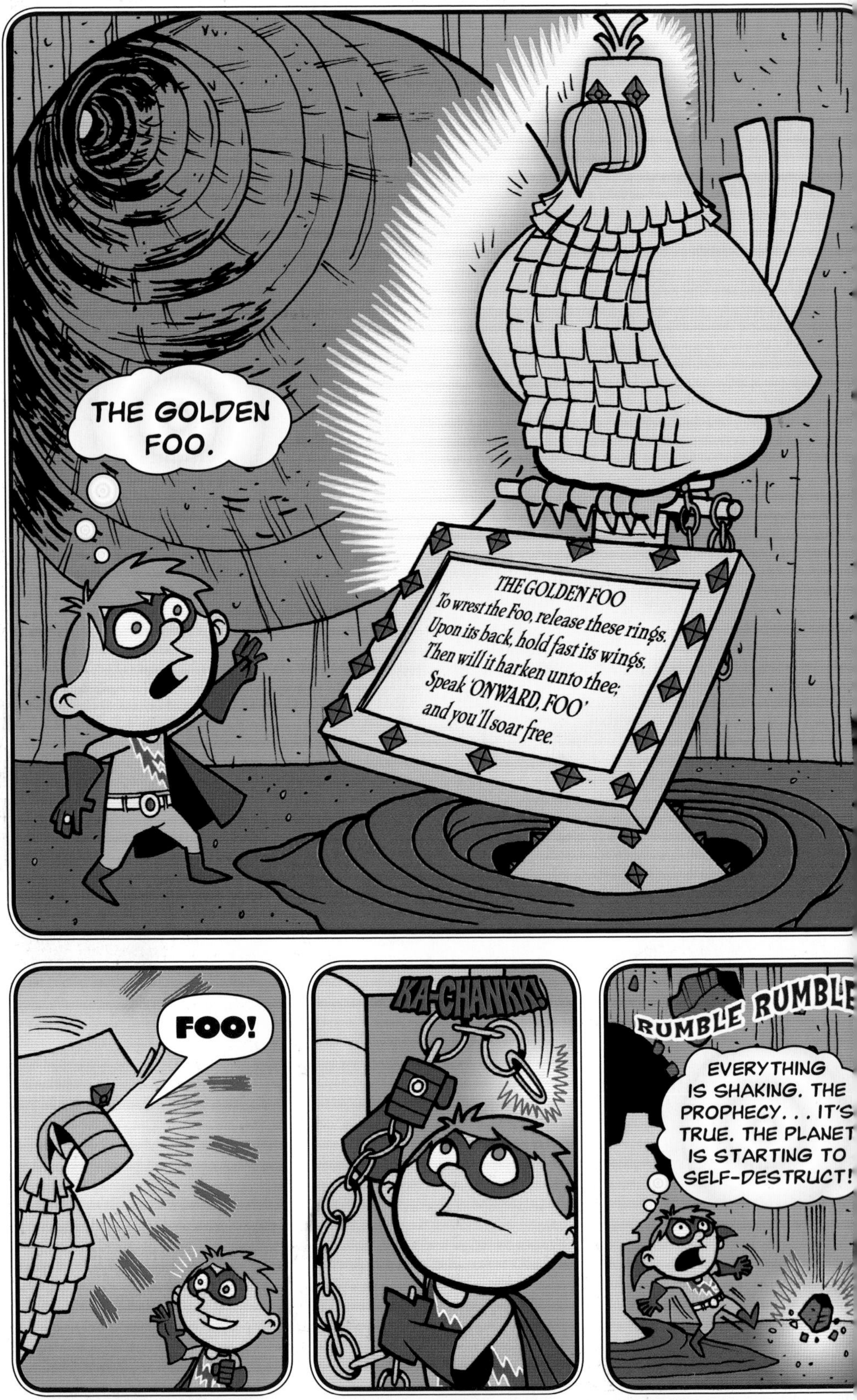
THE GOLDEN FOO.
THE GOLDEN FOO
To wrest the Foo, release these rings.
Upon its back, hold fast its wings.
Then will it harken unto thee;
Speak 'ONWARD, FOO'
and you'll soar free.
FOO!
KA-CHANKK!
RUMBLE RUMBLE
EVERYTHING IS SHAKING. THE PROPHECY. . . IT'S TRUE. THE PLANET IS STARTING TO SELF-DESTRUCT!

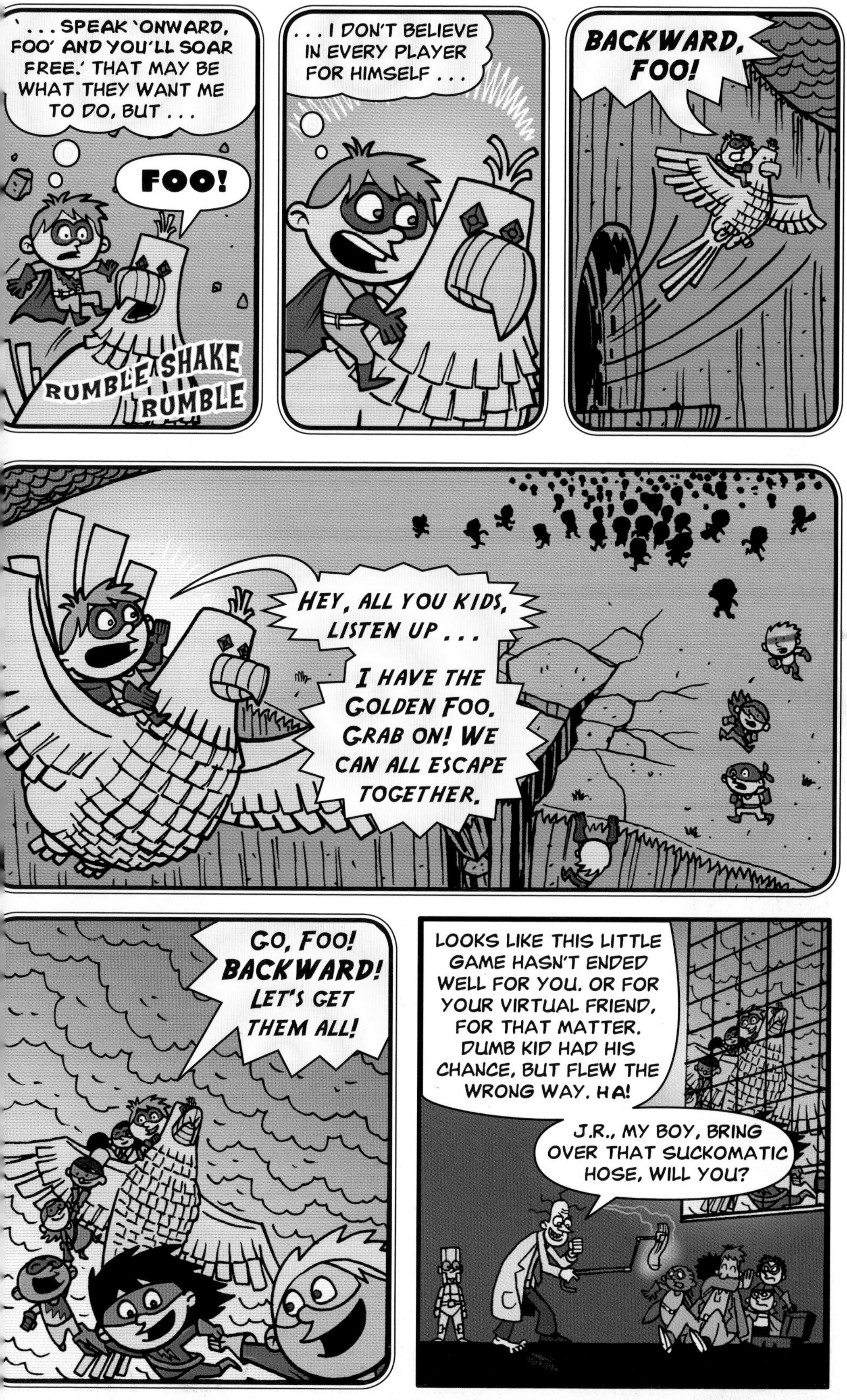

` . . . SPEAK 'ONWARD, FOO' AND YOU'LL SOAR FREE.' THAT MAY BE WHAT THEY WANT ME TO DO, BUT . . .
FOO!
RUMBLE SHAKE RUMBLE
. . . I DON'T BELIEVE IN EVERY PLAYER FOR HIMSELF . . .
BACKWARD, FOO!
HEY, ALL YOU KIDS, LISTEN UP . . .
I HAVE THE GOLDEN FOO. GRAB ON! WE CAN ALL ESCAPE TOGETHER.
GO, FOO! BACKWARD! LET'S GET THEM ALL!
LOOKS LIKE THIS LITTLE GAME HASN'T ENDED WELL FOR YOU. OR FOR YOUR VIRTUAL FRIEND, FOR THAT MATTER. DUMB KID HAD HIS CHANCE, BUT FLEW THE WRONG WAY. HA!
J.R., MY BOY, BRING OVER THAT SUCKOMATIC HOSE, WILL YOU?

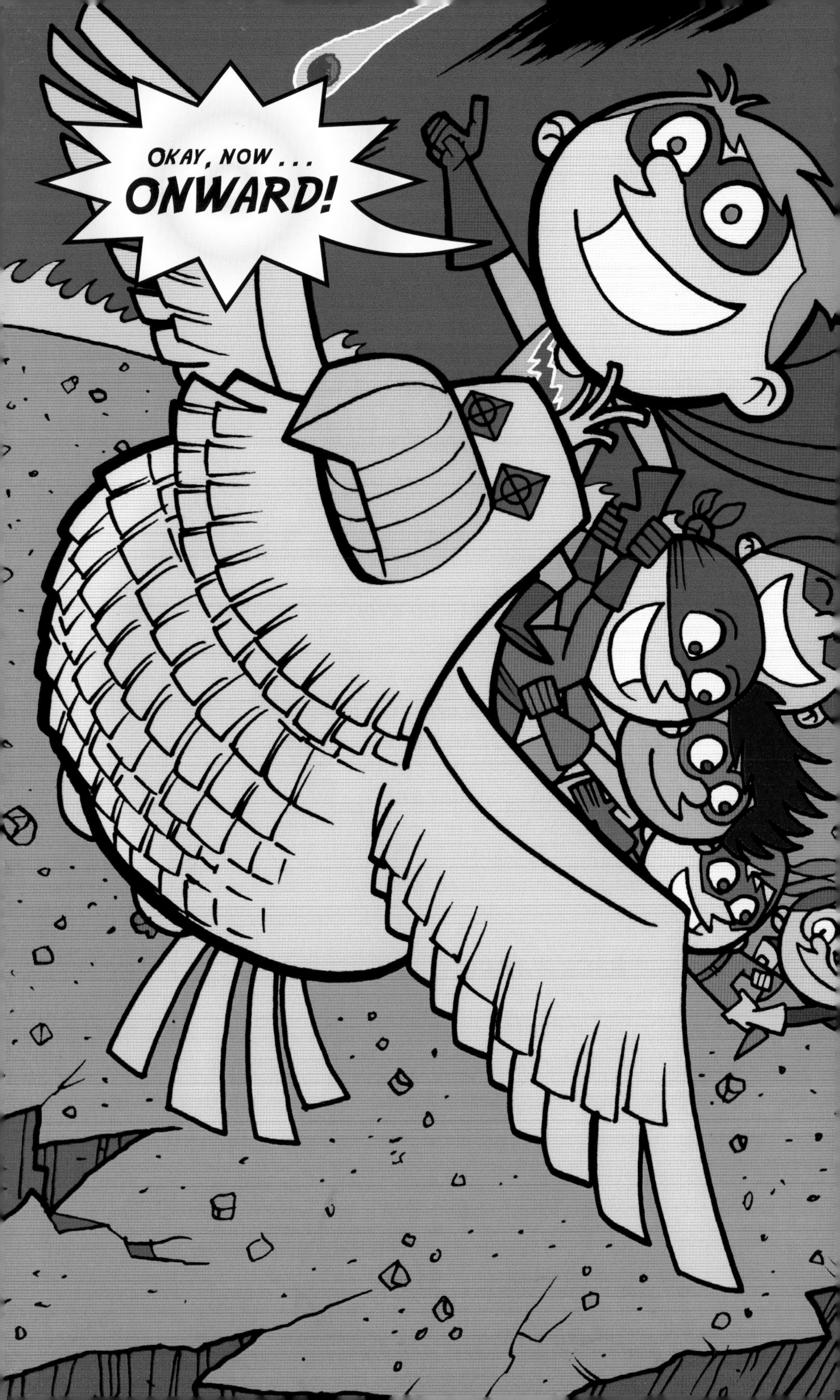
OKAY, NOW . . .
ONWARD!

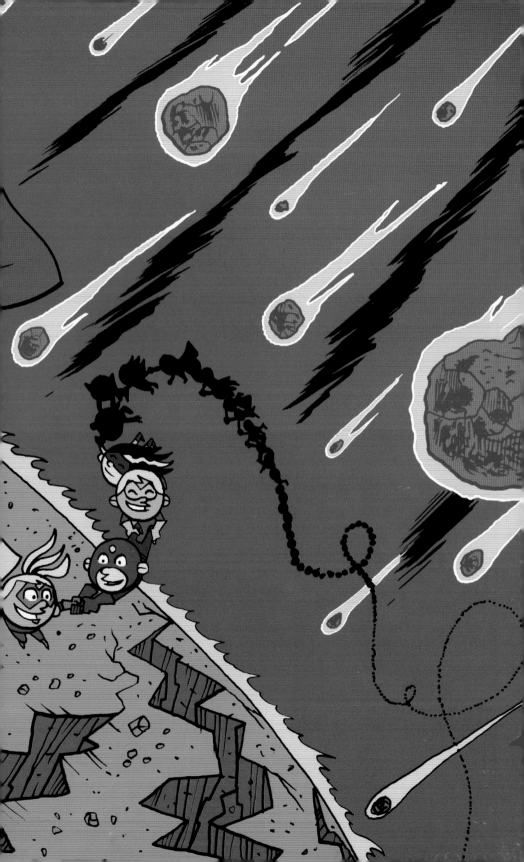

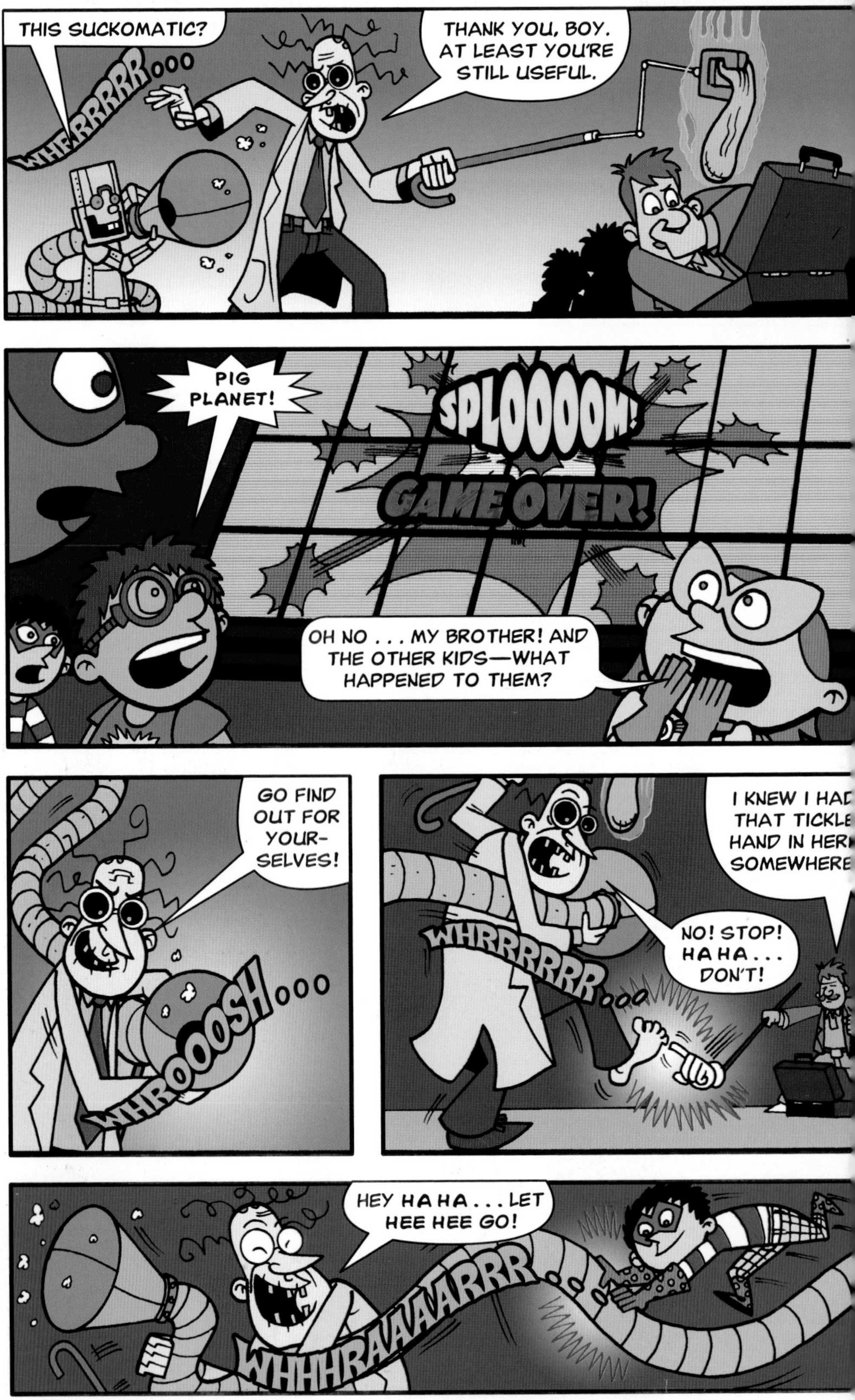
THIS SUCKOMATIC?
WHRRRRRooo
THANK YOU, BOY. AT LEAST YOU'RE STILL USEFUL.
PIG PLANET!
SPLOOOOM!
GAME OVER!
OH NO . . . MY BROTHER! AND THE OTHER KIDS—WHAT HAPPENED TO THEM?
GO FIND OUT FOR YOUR-SELVES!
WHROOOOSHooo
I KNEW I HAD THAT TICKLE HAND IN HER SOMEWHERE
WHRRRRRRRooo
NO! STOP! HA HA . . . DON'T!
HEY HA HA . . . LET HEE HEE GO!
WHHHRAAAAARRR . . .

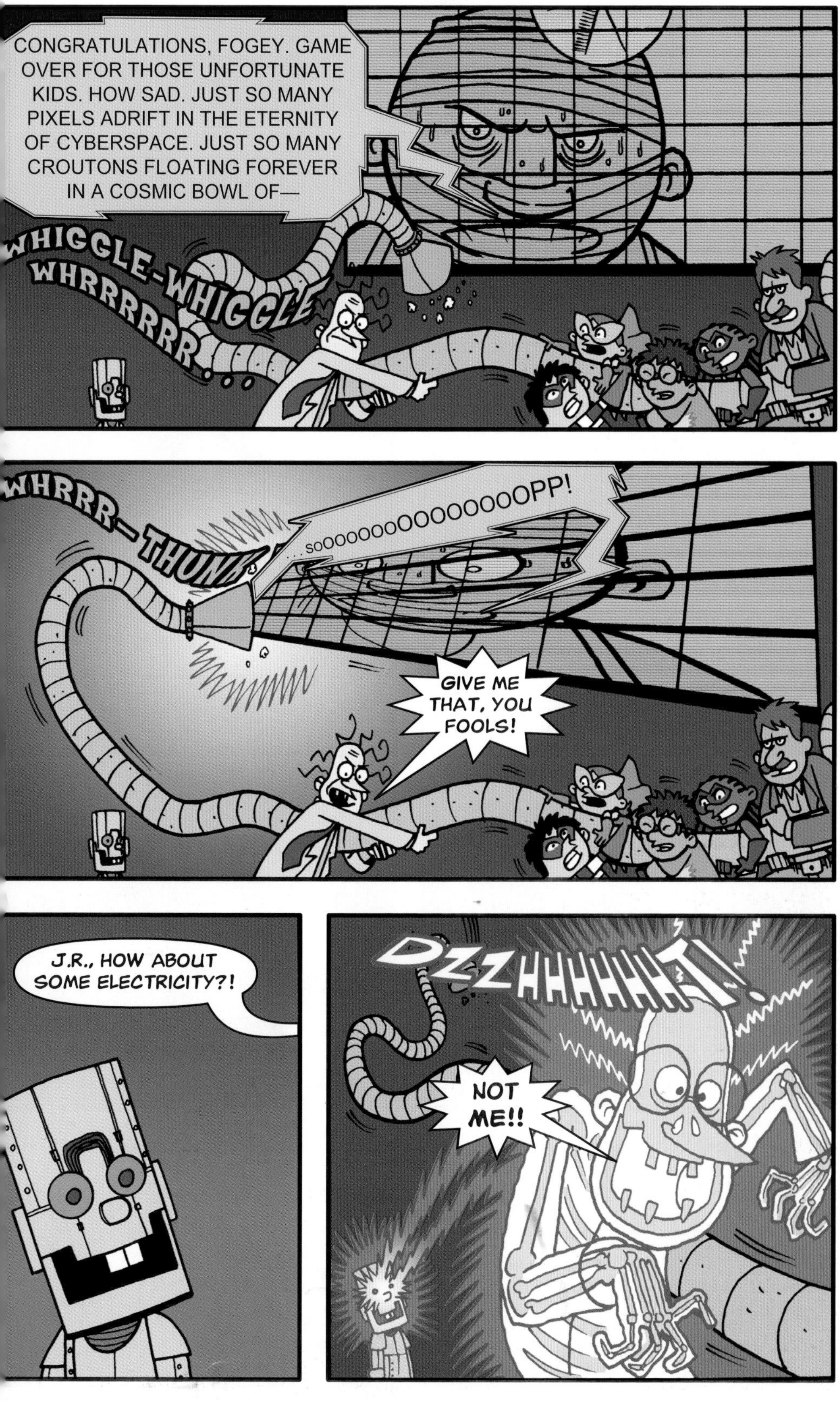

CONGRATULATIONS, FOGEY. GAME OVER FOR THOSE UNFORTUNATE KIDS. HOW SAD. JUST SO MANY PIXELS ADRIFT IN THE ETERNITY OF CYBERSPACE. JUST SO MANY CROUTONS FLOATING FOREVER IN A COSMIC BOWL OF—
WHIGGLE-WHIGGLE
WHRRRRRRR
WHRRRR—THUNK
...SOOOOOOOOOOOOOOOOPP!
GIVE ME THAT, YOU FOOLS!
J.R., HOW ABOUT SOME ELECTRICITY?!
DZZHHHHHT!
NOT ME!!

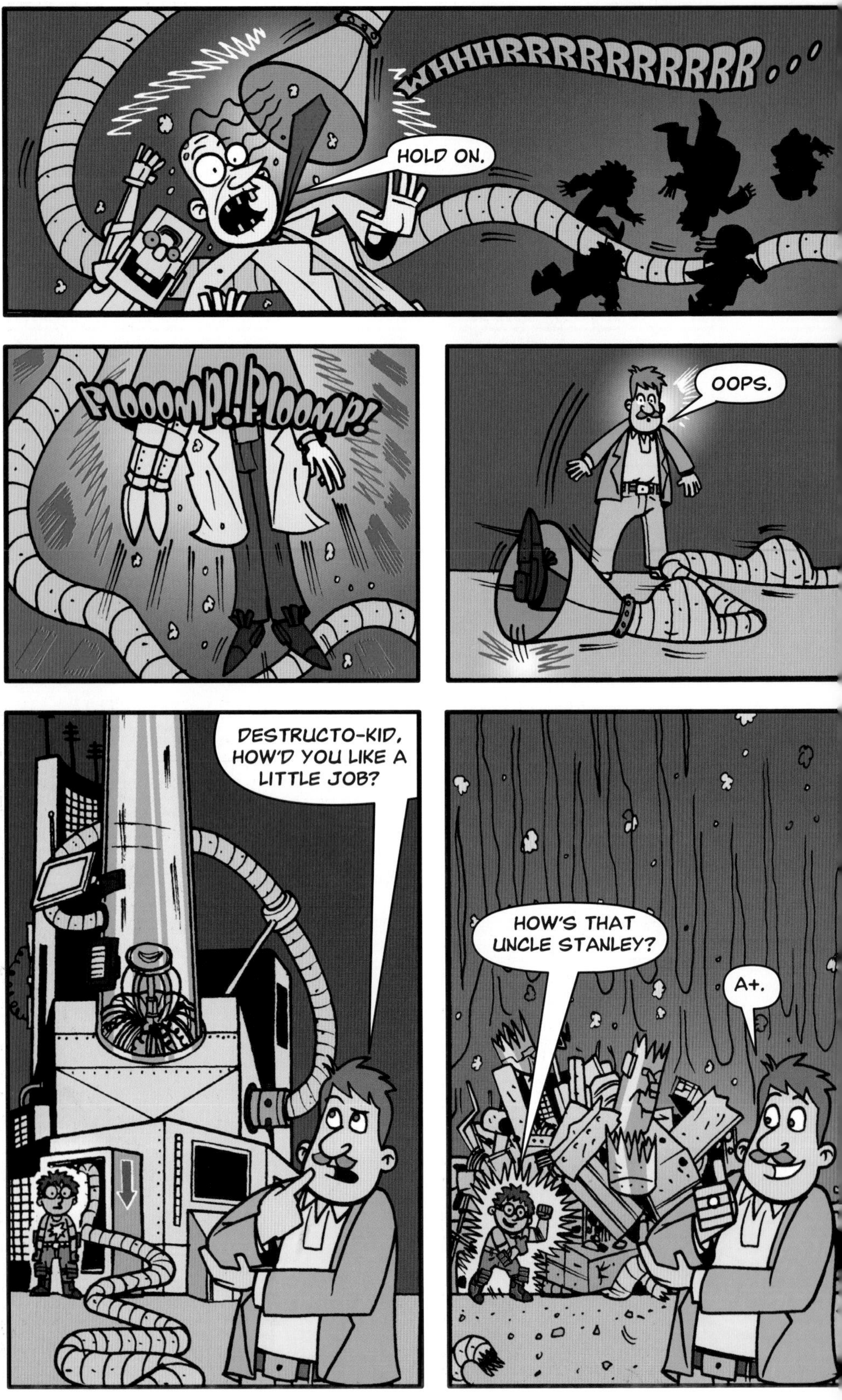
WHHHRRRRRRRRRR...
HOLD ON.
PLOOOMP! PLOOMP!
OOPS.
DESTRUCTO-KID, HOW'D YOU LIKE A LITTLE JOB?
HOW'S THAT UNCLE STANLEY?
A+.

CAN'T LEAVE THIS LYING AROUND.

IT'S OKAY, CHATTERBOX. THIS TIME I'M GOING TO DESTROY IT THE WAY I SHOULD HAVE IN THE FIRST PLACE.

IT'S NOT THAT, UNCLE STANLEY. MY BROTHER— WHAT HAPPENED TO MY BROTHER?

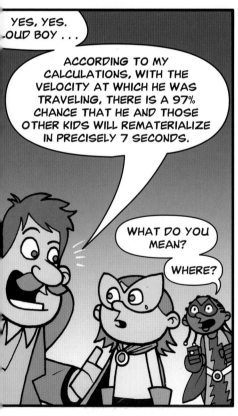

YES, YES. -OUD BOY . . .

ACCORDING TO MY CALCULATIONS, WITH THE VELOCITY AT WHICH HE WAS TRAVELING, THERE IS A 97% CHANCE THAT HE AND THOSE OTHER KIDS WILL REMATERIALIZE IN PRECISELY 7 SECONDS.

WHAT DO YOU MEAN?

WHERE?

COULD BE ANYWHERE IN THE WORLD, WITH SO MANY PORTALS . . .

. . . BUT BASED ON THE FOO'S ANGLE OF ENTRY, I'D SAY THERE'S AN 83% CHANCE THEY ARE ALL HEADED TOWARD . . .

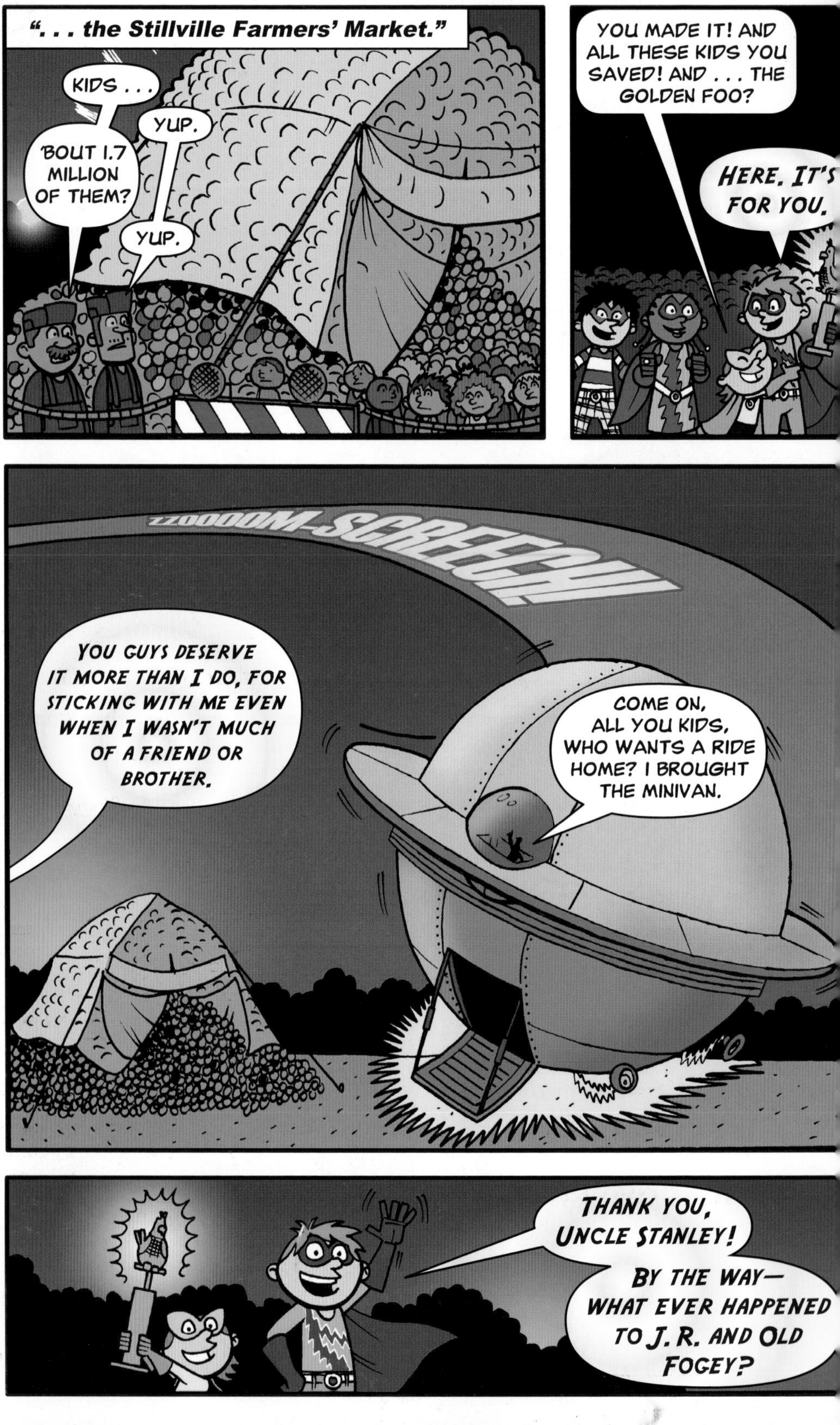
". . . the Stillville Farmers' Market."
KIDS . . .
YUP.
'BOUT 1.7 MILLION OF THEM?
YUP.
YOU MADE IT! AND ALL THESE KIDS YOU SAVED! AND . . . THE GOLDEN FOO?
HERE. IT'S FOR YOU.
ZZOOOOM-SCREECH!
YOU GUYS DESERVE IT MORE THAN I DO, FOR STICKING WITH ME EVEN WHEN I WASN'T MUCH OF A FRIEND OR BROTHER.
COME ON, ALL YOU KIDS, WHO WANTS A RIDE HOME? I BROUGHT THE MINIVAN.
THANK YOU, UNCLE STANLEY!
BY THE WAY— WHAT EVER HAPPENED TO J. R. AND OLD FOGEY?

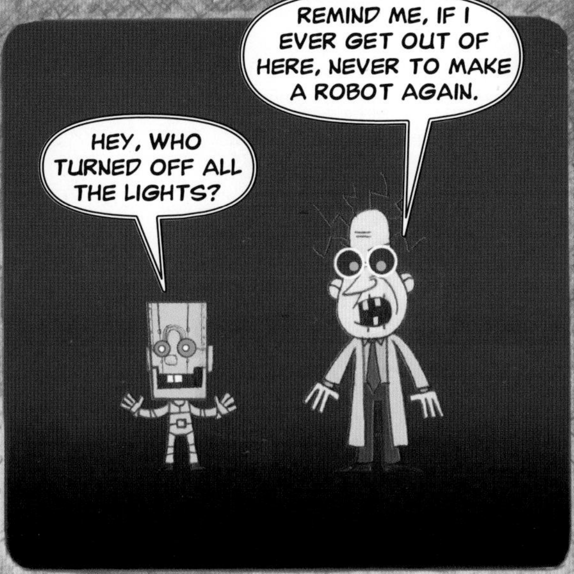
REMIND ME, IF I EVER GET OUT OF HERE, NEVER TO MAKE A ROBOT AGAIN.
HEY, WHO TURNED OFF ALL THE LIGHTS?

And so ends one tale, and maybe even two villains. But where one treachery ends, another must begin—that is the inscrutable law of nature, as sure as there is a secret and sinister society called Kid-Rid. And at the pinnacle of that organization sits one man who has watched all from his far-off chair, far from the noise of pesky kids, far from the hair-raising sight of children playing recklessly; a man who has not stepped foot out of his own front door for 23 years. But perhaps now, he thinks. Perhaps the time has come . . .

—TO BE CONTINUED—

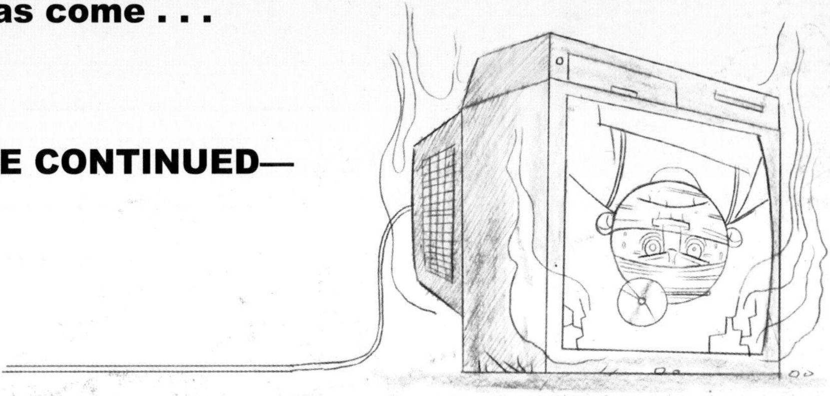

THE ADVENTURES OF DANIEL BOOM AKA LOUD BOY

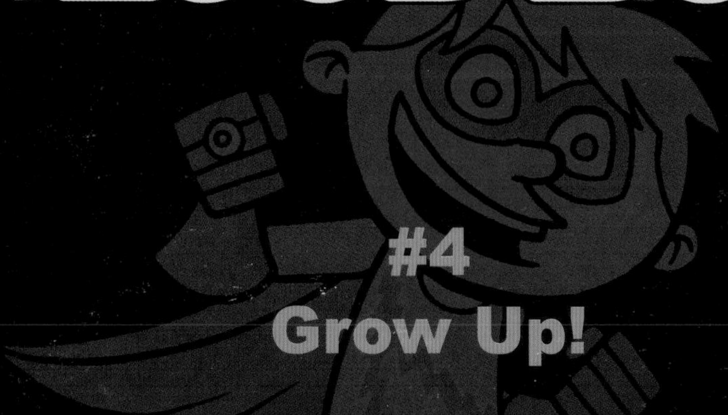

#4
Grow Up!

What in the world has happened to our young heroes? Suddenly they are all acting like little old people!

Why is Loud Boy walking with a cane? Is that Chatterbox with the granny bag and beehive hairdo? Wait a minute, when did Destructo-Kid go crazy for bingo? Is Fidget the new shuffleboard king of the Senior Center? And hold the phone—is that Tantrum Girl over there knitting in a big rocking chair?

Something is seriously wrong here in Stillville . . . especially now that the members of Kid-Rid seem to be full of energy, turning cartwheels in the streets. Is it any coincidence that all this topsy-turvy business started after Doctor Docter came out of hiding? Could this have anything to do with that strange new stethoscope dangling from his neck? There's only one way to find out. Pick up a copy of *Loud Boy #4*. Too scared? Oh . . . GROW UP!